MW00938994

Heart of the Hide

Heart of the Hide

Lou Petrucci

iUniverse, Inc.
New York Lincoln Shanghai

Heart of the Hide

Copyright © 2006 by Lou Petrucci

iUniverse books may be ordered through booksellers or by contacting:

iUniverse
2021 Pine Lake Road, Suite 100
Lincoln, NE 68512
www.iuniverse.com
1-800-Authors (1-800-288-4677)

To Angela Nyberg, one of all-time greatest librarians in the elementary school world. Thanks for every single one of your encouraging words and ideas. Thanks for all the books you told me to read that taught me how to write for children. Thanks for everything. You belong on this page and every other page.

ISBN-13: 978-0-595-38058-9 (pbk)
ISBN-13: 978-0-595-67595-1 (cloth)
ISBN-13: 978-0-595-82428-1 (ebk)
ISBN-10: 0-595-38058-1 (pbk)
ISBN-10: 0-595-67595-6 (cloth)
ISBN-10: 0-595-82428-5 (ebk)

Printed in the United States of America

Dedication

This book is dedicated to my parents, Giuseppe and Antoinette Petrucci, who worked harder than anyone I know to put four kids through college. They gave us strong roots and books along with a clear understanding about the importance of education.

And I can't forget these people as well.

The real Big John.

The real Vincent.

The real Fabrizio.

And the real deal, Gennaro Gambardella Jr.

Luigi and Immacolata Petrucci

Constantine and Irene DeNora

Vincenzo Petrucci

Ralph and Mary Petrucci

Tony Petrucci

Kenneth J. Moscovics, Jr.

Ryan T. Caulfield

Kelley L. Camp

George Charboneau

Todd Francis Caden

Rose Gambardella

The real BP, Robert A. Paduano II

Santiago Suarez

I hope and pray that there is reading in Heaven as well.

Acknowledgements

My most heartfelt thanks to:

Mrs. Deborah L. Blair, the principal who hired me to teach elementary school children and taught me about the true power of the read aloud.

Arthur J. Sapienza, Vincent DiMartino, Al Kozeroski, Tom Hunt, Robert Cuozzo, Pasquale "Babe" Amendola, and Albert Siclari, teachers who always made me a huge part of their classrooms.

My private editors, first there is Kim Tarpinian, who probably reads and talks faster than anyone in America.

Teri Etheridge, who showed me the difference between past and present.

And my main man and long-time friend, Robert Ehalt, a sports writer who truly tells it like it is.

Paul Wilgenkamp, for all the times he brought me lunch, listened to me complain about everything and he never once tried to poison me.

Lana Gluck, Sandra Boulton, Nancy Geikie and Lori Hornik, teachers who believed in me.

The students of my fifth grade class at Fork Lane Elementary School, who taught me how to teach.

Brendan T. Gott, who once said after I wrote a short story, "Wow. That sounds like somebody really wrote that."

To all the students who survived 180 days in Mr. Petrucci's classroom. I thank you for every encouraging word, suggestion, comment and editorial revision all of you gave to me.

Mike Altman, and the rest of my special friends at IUniverse. You should have hung up on me the first time I called.

Aunt Mary and Uncle Ed, for all the times you remembered my birthday and made me feel special.

Nicola "Uncle Nick" Petrucci, for buying me my first baseball glove, for taking time out of your busy days to play catch with me, for cutting my hair when I had it, for being my friend when I needed it most.

Ann Marie Moscovics, the real AM, my best friend who for more than twenty-six years never forgot me. I thank her because no matter how busy her life was she listened, listened, listened and listened again, with love. If it wasn't for her encouragement and support this book would still be wasting away in a rickety old computer.

Contents

Chapter 1
The All-American Way

The final school bell tolled, and minutes later eighteen players filled the top diamond at Painter's Park. Once a week these kids battled for supremacy. They fought for their neighborhoods. They struggled and tussled for pride.

Blood spilled.

Pants ripped open.

Scraped knees ached.

Arguments ensued.

Kids screamed.

Onlookers shouted.

No one called the police.

No one asked the kids to stop.

Neighbors never complained because these kids solved their issues the American way.

They played baseball—the greatest game on Earth.

There were no coaches, umpires or busybody know-nothing-about-baseball parents. Each team brought one baseball and two bats, and they always had fun.

Well, almost always.

Rusty Alves stood at home plate—the most menacing character in the city of West Haven's 200-year history. Two were out, and the bases were juiced.

The kids from Kelsey Avenue led the Morse Park bunch 7—4 in the bottom of the ninth. This Kelsey Avenue crew always played hard, and they had great players. The best in the local Little League came from Kelsey, but this Morse Park gang was a little bigger, stronger, and older. Most of them played on high school junior varsity or middle school clubs.

Nicky Palmieri organized the games for the Kelsey Avenue Crew. Baseball was the ultimate game. Individuals compete in a solitary mode under the umbrella of team. Simply, there can be no greater game.

The Kelsey kids were a little younger than Nicky, but they enjoyed the competition. They knew that playing the older, bigger, more talented children in town made them better.

Throughout the glorious spring afternoon, the sun shone brightly in the cloudless, blue sky. After eight and two-thirds innings, the sun settled beneath the horizon. Nicky and company tasted victory even as Rusty Alves strode to the plate.

For two years, the Kelsey Avenue Crew felt like Charlie Brown. So many times they were inches away from victory only to see it wiped away by a controversial call, a missed base, a horrendous base running error, an amazing catch by Alves or a bad hop in the rocky infield.

In spite of this history, what could possibly happen now? The outfielders were so deep that, if they played this game at Yankee Stadium, they would be standing in the bleachers.

"Let's see how far he can hit it," Gennaro said.

"Throw it down the middle, Nicky," Billy said.

"Where are the outfielders?" Rusty Alves yelled. "I can't even see them."

"That's because you're blind and stupid," Nicky snapped.

"Throw the ball over the plate if you have any guts, Pig Face," Rusty said.

Rusty stood and waited. He wasn't going to swing unless the ball was belt high and smack down the middle. This was sandlot baseball at its finest. The game settled disputes. Umpires were never needed. Kids threw the rules out the window and just played. The games were so good that even the adults who fixed the fields at Painter's Park watched.

"Hurry up and swing the bat, kid," legendary seventy-six-year-old coach Archie Sagnella blurted out. "I'm going to die soon."

"Yeah," Harry Huber added. "I've seen better statues on the top of trophies. What do you want the kid to do—put the ball on a tee for ya? Swing the bat like a man."

"Shut up, old-timer," Rusty retorted. "Why don't you old-timers get back in your trucks and go pick up the garbage at my house like you're supposed to, or are you too dumb to figure out how to get there?"

Fifteen pitches later, Rusty connected with a long, high drive to left center field. This ball was crushed. The runners moved on the swing. Unless Gennaro made another one of his amazing catches, the game was definitely tied.

Gennaro dove and the ball eluded his glove by inches.

The runner from third scored, 7–5.

Gennaro scrambled to his feet.

The runner from second scored, 7–6.

Gennaro rose and threw an absolute laser to the plate.

The runner from first scored, 7–7.

The most amazing throw any of the Kelsey Kids ever saw whizzed toward home plate, and nowhere in sight was Rusty Alves.

Nicky Palmieri covered the plate, so eight-year-old John Sullivan wouldn't suffer the evil wrath of any cheap shots from the Morse Park boys. The ball was on its way to Nicky, and everyone was sure Rusty would stop at third. But he kept going.

"Hold the ball, Nicky. We got 'em this time," Mark Kessler said.

The last brilliant yellow sparkle of sunlight had hit the field more than twenty-five minutes ago. This was definitely the last play of the game. Dusk turned to darkness. Many kids faced dinners colder than blocks of ice, but they didn't care. The Kelsey Avenue Crew knew that a tie against these older, massive players was a cause for celebration—fireworks style. They were one step closer to sending these bums home without a victory.

Rounding third, huffing and puffing with nostrils flaring, Rusty Alves pounded his way toward the plate. Nicky Palmieri knew he was coming.

Nicky remembered the all-time greatest film clip of Pete Rose, when he maliciously ran over a defenseless Ray Fosse in the All-Star game. He braced himself for the worst.

The ball arrived in plenty of time.

One-thousand. No Rusty.

One-thousand one. No Rusty.

One-thousand two. No Rusty.

One-thousand three. No Rusty.

One-thousand four. No Rusty.

One-thousand, oops, here's Rusty.

The collision of titanic proportions shot a dust storm in the air. Rusty Alves running full speed tackled Nicky and sent everything flying. Suddenly, for nine Kelsey Avenue players, life turned into the slowest of slow motion.

Nicky's hat wound up behind the backstop.

Nicky wound up against the backstop.

Seconds, which passed like hours, went by. Finally Nicky's glove bounced off the fence and fell to the ground.

Bedlam arose among the remaining sixteen kids. The Kelsey Avenue Crew was jumping and celebrating the most moral of moral victories while Rusty Alves grabbed the ball from Nicky's glove and rolled it onto the ground. The Morse Park bunch started a bloodcurdling scream of victory.

"We won. We won," Rusty Alves yelled. "Pig face dropped the ball. We win 8–7."

"No way, Rusty, you cheater. You ran over our catcher, and then you pulled the ball out of the glove. You're out, scumbag," Gennaro screamed while he raced in from center field to peel Nicky off the fence.

"You must be kidding, Shrimp," Rusty howled with a rejoicing shriek.

"I touched home plate and he dropped the ball. We win 8–7. You guys will always be losers. You will never beat us."

While the Morse Park bunch jumped all over Rusty and laughed, Nicky lay dazed and confused against the backstop.

"Are you all right, Nicky?" Gennaro asked as the rest of the team helped bring their friend to his feet.

"Sorry, about that pitch," Nicky said. "I tried to keep it low and away, but he wouldn't swing. I guess we have to live with this tie. This is worse than kissing your sister. It's like kissing Rusty's mother's fat butt."

From over the top of the pile, Rusty leaned over to Nicky and said, "Sorry, Elephant Man. You lose again. We win, 8–7."

Nicky suddenly jumped into a rage no one had ever seen before.

"What are you talking about, Rusty? You were out by twenty feet. I held onto the ball long enough. You're out, cheater."

Rusty grabbed Nicky by the face with his pointer finger and thumb. Rusty was a huge kid that nobody messed with in West Haven. He once intimidated a teacher into giving him an A after Rusty promised to keep the kids from egging his house during Halloween.

With Nicky plastered against the backstop, Rusty took his other finger and put it directly into his counterpart's nose.

"I don't like you one bit," Rusty bellowed as his grip on Nicky's face tightened. "I am going to run over you like the little piece of garbage you are and always will be, Pig Face," he added.

"You and the rest of your misfits are never going to beat me and my boys, ever. You are just too ugly. I'm doing you a favor by running you over time and time again. Maybe your parents will smarten up and get you another operation to fix your face, loser."

"Eat me, Rusty," Nicky said.

Good old Rusty's face grew redder and redder. It was almost the same color as his carrottop head and as he raised his right fist to give Nicky the first of many punches. Suddenly, a huge paw came out of the sky and grabbed Rusty's hand.

"Who are you?" Rusty said, shaking, as he turned to see this huge body connected to the paw with the vice grip.

"This is Big John. Big John Wizenski," Nicky smiled.

Chapter 2
The Big Man

People just gawked in astonishment, as parents raced onto the field to find their boys. Anytime controversy swirled its ugly head in West Haven, Big John arrived in the nick of time. He was always the neighbor who rang the Liberty Bell of fairness.

Big John Wizenski.

"You haven't seen the last of me, Elephant Face," Rusty screeched while walking down Kelsey Avenue. "I'll get you tomorrow in school. Jerry's not around to protect you, and this fat old man will be too busy eating."

"Just be quiet and go home, Rusty," Archie Sagnella said. "Big John doesn't have time to deal with a punk like you."

"Leave the little hoodlum alone," Big John interjected. "It's a good thing Jerry's not here. He would knock the little wise cracker into another zip code."

When Big John wasn't around, Jerry Gambardella Jr. provided protection for the neighborhood children. Jerry never let anyone call Nicky names. Many times when he heard secondhand information, he sprinted to the baseball field to help.

"He wouldn't even move his mouth one bit if Jerry were here," Gennaro told Nicky. "He's Mr. Bravery when Jerry's in college. Wait 'til Jerry returns home this summer. Rusty will return to the little worm he is."

The dust finally settled. People often turned to Big John to handle these problems. Big John was "the Man." He could always be counted on as the voice of reason when parents became insane with punitive measures. Big John settled arguments. In his day, he was tougher than Judge Judy without a TV audience.

Big John wasn't an easy guy to figure out, but he was always fair. His life, as he constantly reminded everyone in the neighborhood, "was no Sunday picnic." He grew up in the 1940s when every week friends of his family left only to return months later in pine boxes.

Growing up, Big John's family barely survived. They were always inches away from eviction from their two-room apartment into the streets. Big John said his parents always pushed him to play sports as long as he didn't quit school.

"Let me worry about the money," his mother announced. "When you need a job, I'll let you know. You just go to school, and I'll let you play every sport you want."

To the kids in the neighborhood, Big John was a jolly Polish giant. When you are climbing on stools to be six feet tall Big John was Shaq on this block. At six foot seven and 300-plus pounds, he was the most imposing figure West Haven had ever known.

"What the heck is going on here?" Big John said, watching Rusty as his crew laughed and shouted profanities as they ran down the street.

"We were winning and we had Rusty out at the plate. And then he ran Nicky over when he knew he was out dead to rights," Gennaro shouted. "One day, we're going to get even with that scum bucket."

"Big John, the kid was out by twenty feet, and he ran Nicky over Pete Rose-style," Frank Camp, a park department worker, said. "Then he pulls the ball out of the kid's glove and says he won the game. This punk deserves a good beating."

"Take it easy; take it easy," Big John said. "You've got to play baseball hard and not complain when things don't go your way."

"But Big John, he's a cheater," Nicky said.

"They think they won. We finally tied these jerks. This is not fair."

"Life's not fair, kid, life's not fair."

When Big John spoke, everybody listened. And if you didn't, he spoke louder.

He understood fairness, and he understood life.

Most of the kids on the field were nine to twelve years old, and they didn't know anything about anything. Big John let everyone know it.

"This is just a game, Nicky," he announced. "You guys tied those bums? That's all right. Next time, you make a couple of plays, and you win the game. The gods of baseball are always fair. Don't worry. Trust the gods of baseball."

People in West Haven spelled respect, BIG JOHN.

There was no doubt about it.

In his days at West Haven High School, Big John was widely considered by many as one of the greatest athletes in Connecticut. He played the big three—football, basketball, and baseball. Jerry, even with his tremendous physique and muscular frame at six foot two and 195 pounds, looked up to Big John. Oftentimes the two talked, and Jerry recognized Big John's place in West Haven history.

Jerry always listened and did his best to uphold the legendary status Big John placed upon him. If he heard that people were not treating the Kelsey Avenue boys nicely, he came down to make sure the playing field was fair. Big John had taught him that.

Big John also told him that being a great athlete was not just about the games but also about how you conduct your life off the field, too. It was your life off the field that really counted.

"This kid is the only one who could play with me," Big John bragged. "These other players couldn't tie his shoes."

You see, Big John captained the basketball and baseball teams. Until Jerry, no one else matched or came remotely close to Big John's greatness. The best thing about Big John was that he let everyone and anyone who listened know how good he was. And when people heard him talk about Jerry, it gave the Gambardella kid instant credibility.

"I didn't have the chance to go to college," Big John admitted. "I had to go to work. Sure, I could have played pro baseball, but the scouts told me I would make $100 per month."

"Explain that to a stubborn immigrant from Poland who could barely speak English," he added. "I could make $30 a week at the Armstrong Rubber Company or play in the sand for $25. You don't need New Math to figure that one out.

"But this kid—Jerry Gambardella. He's the one who could make it."

This vote of confidence put Jerry on another level—Big John's level. In West Haven, Big John was king. Everyone knew his life, and respect for him stood in the untouchable stratosphere.

In his youth, Big John made difficult choices. Instead of trying to live the dream of the Big Leagues, he worked at the tire factory and married his high school sweetheart, Immacolata Maria Concetta. Eventually, in the final months of World War II, Uncle Sam sent him to Europe to stop people far more evil than Rusty Alves could ever imagine.

The war and his two-year stint in the Army, however, paled in comparison to his favorite story of courage in Big John's world. "German tanks loaded with Nazis carrying machine guns were much easier to deal with than my parents," Big John recounted when telling of the time when he introduced his parents to the idea of marrying an Italian woman.

"My father didn't talk to me until my wedding day. He tried to convince me that I would wind up making a big mistake. But I knew I made the right choice."

The Kelsey Avenue Crew called his family Big John and Mrs. Big John because few could pronounce "Wizenski." They were the proud parents of three, John Jr. and two daughters, Rose Marie and Diane. None of them left the sanctity of West Haven, either. Big John's grandchildren didn't live on Kelsey Avenue, but they attended local schools.

He understood kids and he loved baseball. Once the Director of the Parks and Recreation Department, Bobby Schotta, told Nicky and the rest of the crew that they couldn't play on the fields after the workers chalked the foul lines for men's softball leagues.

Mr. Schotta complained that Nicky's boys were messing up the foul lines and the softball leagues harassed Mayor Tom Johnson's office. Mean Mr. Schotta wanted to arrest the perpetrators for vandalism.

Well, upon hearing the questionable news, Nicky and Mark Kessler went to work. They decided to contact a dynamic duo that would surely shake the boots of Mr. Schotta.

"Mark, you tell your mother and I'll go tell Big John," Nicky said.

Within twenty minutes, Mr. Schotta didn't know what hit him.

Big John was, of course, big. But the diminutive Mrs. Marie Kessler, at four foot eight and eighty five pounds shook city hall with power greater than Godzilla's.

Chapter 3
The Fair Maiden and a Cause

If West Haven were Hollywood, Mrs. Kessler was more awesome than Jennifer Aniston. She was in her early forties, and she never looked older than twenty-one. Mrs. Kessler was clearly the envy of every woman on the block. She was the closest thing to Teri Hatcher that this town ever saw. Mrs. Kessler expected perfection and didn't settle for anything less.

Her lawn stood out from the rest of the neighborhood because she cut the grass a certain way, one row up and the next across. Her front yard looked like the Candlestick Park in San Francisco. She didn't do it for baseball reasons, however. Mrs. Kessler did it for reasons of her own, which no one dared to argue about. Her three sons were pleased with her landscaping talents, as they didn't have to do any of the work.

The ongoing battle to play baseball on a baseball field raged for years. What irritated the Kelsey Avenue Crew most was that these fat, old, has-been and never-will-be athletes who used the field at night wrecked it. Most of them swung the bat so badly that they couldn't hit water if they fell out of a boat.

Nicky always said he saw better swings on a rusty gate.

Most of the kids laughed at these slo-pitch softball games. They couldn't field. They were too fat to run, and worst of all, they ruined the field. They left beer and soda bottles everywhere, and this burned Archie Sagnella, Mrs. Kessler's father, the most.

In the morning, Mr. Schotta incessantly barked at poor Mr. Sagnella.

"Those fields are a mess," the grumpy Park Director shrieked. "Clean up that mess by the time I get back, or I'll have you cleaning toilets at the beach with a toothbrush."

Mr. Sagnella never talked back or argued. He simply worked. He diligently picked up the bottles, sandwich wrappers, and the other debris the drunken softball players left behind. He was furious, and so was Mrs. Kessler. After all, it was her father that Mr. Schotta never treated fairly.

The only good thing that ever evolved from the drunks using the field was that they became so intoxicated with beer that they forgot their gloves and bats. It was Christmas in July when Nicky's crew found a Rawlings or a Wilson glove. With the finds, it wasn't so bad, except for the fights over the treasure. But Archie— who was Mark, Lou, and Bobby Kessler's grandfather—loved baseball, too. And more importantly, he loved every kid in the neighborhood. Archie took good care of the fields, and he always told the Kelsey Avenue Crew that "as soon as Mr. Schotta leaves, you kids go play."

"Don't worry about that cranky old man," Archie said. "You kids play on the field, but don't tell him I said that. He will fire me on the spot. I need this job."

Mr. Schotta directed the Park Department workers to line the fields at 9 A.M. for 7 P.M. night games. This was totally ridiculous. The boys didn't mess up the foul lines on purpose. The Kelsey Avenue Crew just played. But every time Mr. Schotta drove by the field in his blue Crown Victoria, he stopped at the game and screeched at the kids for playing baseball on a baseball field.

"How many times did I tell you kids that you can't play on this field?" he yelled in a blood-curdling scream. Foam gathered at the sides of his mouth like someone murdered his pet dog.

"You can't play on the field. I've told you kids a thousand times," he said.

"Nine hundred and ninety-eight times, but who's counting?" Gennaro snapped.

"What are you a wise guy?" Mr. Schotta said.

"No, he's not, sir. We just want to play baseball. Where do you want us to play, sir?" Nicky politely asked.

"You kids can use the field down below. The Pit."

Simultaneously, more than ten kids yelled, "Not the Pit!"

And to any budding baseball player in this hood, this field was worse than H E double hockey sticks.

Chapter 4

"The Pit"

"The Pit" was the equivalent of baseball field damnation. It was so bad that not even inebriated, beer-bellied softball players played down there. Abner Doubleday surely rolled over in his grave when he learned that baseball games took place on this field.

The field, located at the bottom of the hill in Painter's Park, was surrounded by a dense wooded area laced with poison ivy, sumac, and bushes with sharp thorns. "The Pit" swallowed baseballs unmercifully. The Kelsey Avenue Crew would rather kiss the ground Rusty Alves walked on than play on the rock-plagued field.

Since decent baseballs weren't in abundant supply, "The Pit" ruined every game. It didn't matter how much the boys loved to play—without baseballs, there was no game. When John Ferrante once hooked a foul ball down the left field line or when Gennaro slammed a homer deep into the woods, the game ended.

Nicky's crew didn't have one of those cool Rawlings buckets filled with used baseballs like most high school or travel teams. Most of the games featured one ball, and usually, that ball was taped, scraped, or beat to a pulp with the stitches practically coming apart.

When Jerry was around, he always tossed the boys a couple of pearls from his bat bag. But with Jerry at college, the boys knew they had to wait until summer for some new balls. Sometimes, the team acquired a decent ball when one of the boys stole one from his team's equipment bag after a game. Other than those rare times, though, one baseball entertained eleven to twelve kids every single time.

And Mr. Schotta tried everything to keep them off the top field.

He yelled at Nicky and his teammates, but that didn't work because their parents could yell better.

He threatened them with the police, but that didn't work, either, because who ever heard of going to jail because you played baseball on a baseball field.

He once told Nicky he planned to fire Archie Sagnella. However, that plan backfired on him quickly because Nicky told Mrs. Kessler. When she heard about the threat, she raced down to the park department office and wagged her finger in a fury.

The spineless Mr. Schotta tried to brush off his comments as a joke. Mrs. Kessler promised Mr. Schotta that, if he ever messed with her father again, she would personally fit the esteemed park director with a neat pair of cement shoes.

Finally, Mr. Schotta bribed the Kelsey Avenue Crew with one dozen Wilson baseballs and promised them another dozen if they stayed away.

It worked for a while. Nicky accepted his offer and ventured to "The Pit." Two hours later, though, the Kelsey Avenue Crew ran out of baseballs. The worst part was spending half the time looking for balls in the woods.

The game didn't even last four innings. "The Pit" was a big waste of time. Baseball was not a game unless you played nine innings.

Nicky was enraged. "We have to teach Mr. Schotta a lesson."

"He always sneaks up on us in his car. He thinks he's so smart."

Nicky and the boys went to work. First, they helped Archie collect the bottles and instead of cashing them at the local A&P, they smashed them in the dark part of the road where Mr. Schotta drove his car.

Then they covered the glass with dirt, sticks, and leaves hoping to give the irascible park director a flat tire. This was their first after-school real-life science lesson. Mr. Schotta drove over the glass, and the boys learned two things.

Radial tires are tough to pop, and picking up glass for Archie was hard work.

*　　　　　　*　　　　　　*

The Kesslers lived across the street from Painter's Park. From their living room window, the boys watched the West Haven High School team play on the main diamond. The field was the pride and joy of the New Haven area, the Mecca of baseball in West Haven.

This piece of real estate was Madison Square Garden, the Forum in Montreal, the parquet floor of Boston Garden, and Wrigley Field neatly rolled into one place.

There was no better field. Even legendary coach Frank Vieira's University of New Haven Chargers, a Division II college baseball powerhouse, played their home games at this baseball palace.

When visitors drove along Kelsey Avenue, they always stopped and admired the gorgeous green grass. The tremendous nostalgic blue scoreboard amid state-of-the-art cement dugouts set this field apart from any diamond in Connecticut, except for Yale Field at Yale University in nearby New Haven of course.

Only special games were played on the field, and the only person who ever took batting practice there was Jerry even though it was not permitted. The high school team didn't even practice on the field. Big John once predicted that they would wind up naming the field after Jerry Gambardella Jr.

Even the Kelsey Avenue Crew's greatest ally, Archie Sagnella, firmly stated that the field was for games and games only. You couldn't even walk across the outfield grass. But Jerry was bigger than any rule, larger than everything.

When it came to athletics, Jerry Gambardella Jr. was the real deal. Everything he touched in sports turned to wins. He defined "athletically inclined." Jerry would be fishing on the pier down the block, and almost every snapper that called Long Island Sound their home jumped on his hook. It was magic. Whenever he went bowling, he selected a house ball. Pins seemed to drop before the ball hit the lanes. Jerry could do no wrong.

So when Jerry wanted to take batting practice at the main diamond, nobody stopped him.

"Hey kids," Jerry said during a break from college. "You boys want to shag some balls for me? My dad is going to throw BP, and I'll get anyone who shows up on the field."

The word hit the streets faster than a Nolan Ryan fastball from sixty feet six inches away. Within seconds, seven or eight kids jumped at the opportunity to play on the main diamond. Jerry took care of everything. Even Mr. Schotta couldn't stop Jerry. The neighborhood kids loved it.

Adjacent and across the main road in Painter's Park were the sandlot fields that the Kelsey Avenue Crew used. These diamonds were legitimate fields at one time, but budget cuts slowly ate them away. The once Kentucky Blue Grass turned into wild West Haven weeds. These fields, though, were the perfect place to learn baseball.

They taught kids how to charge ground balls because every extra bounce spelled trouble. Foul territory was narrow. The street was five feet from the foul line on the third base side while a wooded area crept along the first baseline.

The best part about this field was Mrs. Kessler. She watched every game. She made sure the kids enjoyed baseball. Mrs. Kessler kept the busybody adults away, and she also made sure neighborhood thugs or hoodlums never interrupted games.

Righty hitters fouled balls off into Mrs. Kessler's perfect, green grass, but she didn't care. She really loved baseball, too.

Additionally, the top field made it easy, so she could keep an eye on everything. So, whenever the kids encountered any problems, they went to Big John first. If that didn't provide the needed results, the Kelsey Avenue Crew saved the hammer, Mrs. Kessler, to close any deal within reason.

"Are you telling me that these boys can't play baseball at Painter's Park because of some silly men's softball leagues?" Mrs. Kessler asked, her voice scorching the telephone wires.

"These kids are not causing any trouble, and you tell Mr. Schotta to drive his butt up here and apologize to these kids quickly."

Within seconds after Mrs. Kessler hung up her classic rotary phone, Bobby Schotta's walkie-talkie buzzed in a terrible spot—Big John's Delicatessen.

Chapter 5
Pig Face

For Nicky Palmieri, there was a place where every one of Rusty Alves's mean-spirited comments— Pig Face. Nicky the Lip. Elephant Man—temporarily disappeared.

When Jerry wasn't around, Nicky needed a place for solace. His mom was too busy raising four children. Nicky was the oldest among two baby sisters and a brother. There was no time for small talk. His father, Giuseppe Palmieri, worked two jobs building cabinets.

After twelve hours of loud saws, drills, and hammering, he wasn't in the mood for Nicky's problems. But there was always one thing that Mr. Palmieri did for his son. No matter how hard he worked, Mr. Palmieri found three or four days a week to take Nicky to several different fields to watch baseball games.

They attended any game played on any diamond. A fast-pitch or charity softball game at Quigley Stadium entertained them. A Babe Ruth League or a college game was just as much fun. He often handed Nicky a couple of bucks to buy a hot dog, soda, and a pack of baseball cards at the concession stand.

Mr. Palmieri did it every time.

Sometimes Rusty Alves was there, too, and he always convinced Nicky to play running bases in the area between fields. Nicky wanted to beat Rusty at something besides school. But Rusty was never nice. During these simple run-the-bases games, he constantly waited for Nicky to catch the ball and run him over. Rusty did it to upset Nicky and try to draw tears. But Nicky could always hold back, and he took the pummeling.

"Aren't you going to cry, Pig Face?" Rusty roared after running Nicky over in the middle of the baseline.

"You're out, Rusty," Nicky said. "It's your turn to be the fielder."

Rusty never cared. He worked hard and tried to tag Nicky out and then wait for one throw to run Nicky over and play fielder again.

"Don't you get it, Elephant Man?" Rusty asked. "I'm just playing to run you over like the little twerp you are."

"I can take your stupid cheap shots, Rusty," Nicky screamed. "You're making me a better player." This was Nicky's philosophy because the beatings really started to hurt. He constantly dusted himself and played the game until Rusty quit. Nicky truly felt that he could stand up to Rusty.

When things were going bad, Nicky always remembered Jerry's kind words. Jerry always told him never to quit.

"If you love baseball," Jerry implored. "Don't let Rusty get the best of you. You're better than that."

Nicky considered these countless bruises, bumps, and scrapes a small price to pay for these running bases' victories.

Mr. Palmieri always watched with outward silence. He knew that this made Nicky tougher.

"Who won?" Mr. Palmieri questioned.

"I tagged Rusty out twenty-two times, at least, Dad."

"Anything else happen?"

"Nah, just a little baseball fun."

Deep down inside, Nicky knew that the names hurt more than the beating Rusty handed him. Nicky constantly sought situations where he could win at anything, especially with Rusty.

Then Nicky searched other venues for answers.

St. John Vianney's Church was a nice place, but Father John J. Ladamus was too busy fund-raising. Nicky needed peace and it wasn't his home on Richmond Avenue, but a place a little more than one mile away.

There was a small brick building on the bend of Platt Avenue that served the town of West Haven well, and it probably changed the inevitable course of Nicky Palmieri's life.

Big John's Delicatessen was owned by none other than Big John himself. Big John's popularity was measured by the fact that several businessmen from New York City opened a 7–11 one block away and, six months later, were closed, out of business, and bankrupt. Big John predicted they would be out of town in seven months. He always seemed to have the answers.

Always.

Every small town features a spot where the rumor mill operates. In West Haven, Big John's Delicatessen was the meeting spot for the who's who of politics, sports, religion, and crime. A diverse cast of characters, for sure, frequented Big John's.

They came from various walks of life and wore different clothes. They spoke with different accents. But the best part was that they talked. And if you were smart, you listened.

Big John certainly topped the list, but clearly Richard "Hooker" McMurphy, the city of West Haven's treasurer, made everyone take notice.

Nicknamed "Hooker" for a fabulous hook shot during his West Haven High School basketball days, he wore nifty white and black shoes from the 1960s and a tie with suspenders.

His perfectly groomed haircut never had a hair out of place. McMurphy knew everything about everybody. He strolled into the deli and started telling Big John how the sports program should work. Hooker's aspirations were to be mayor one day, and he knew that Big John could help him. Big John, however, always joked that he wrote checks with his mouth that neither his mind nor his body could cash.

Another set of local cronies featured the laborers at Armstrong Rubber Company. The heavy German, Irish, and Italian accents always came out when they ordered their coffee and treats from Big John. They teased Big John about how Armstrong was starting to make money because he left ten years ago to open his own business.

Then the cardboard dons entered. These were smaller-than-small-time hoodlums who thought they were reincarnated as one of the Corleones from *The*

Godfather movies. They were the town's bookies— professional gamblers who never had any money. They walked around town as though they owned the place.

These hero wannabes thought armed robbery was carrying a pocketknife while reaching into one of those old fashioned metal honor boxes and taking two newspapers. Most of them acted like tough guys around town, with their big bellies and cheap wool suits. They thought extortion was something a dentist did to a tooth.

The most comical of the characters was Tommy Two Fingers, who told people that he lost the last two digits on his right hand in a shootout in Brooklyn. Tommy actually lost two fingers in a fit of anger one night after dropping $200 in a card game. He was so upset that his three queens were beat by four other queens that, when he went to his car to get more money, he closed the door and chopped off two of his fingers. Nobody could figure out if he was mad about losing the cash or that he couldn't understand how seven queens landed in one deck.

It was funny for the Kelsey Avenue Crew to watch these guys complain, especially on Monday. They bet on professional sports events and talked about how close they were to winning. Then they complained how the games were fixed, and Big John laughed all the way to the bank.

And surely among the hustle and bustle, there was Mr. Schotta himself. Big John launched his best insults at the poor parks and recreation director. When Big John wasn't in earshot, Mr. Schotta ran around town trying to tell people what a great pitcher he was. Once a week, Big John asked Nicky for the most tattered baseball. Then when it was really busy at the deli and Mr. Schotta was around, Big John rolled the ball onto the floor and yelled.

"Hey, Bobby, look. It's another one of your great pitches turned into a home run ball that's still rolling around town. You would think gravity would eventually stop some of the shots people hit off you."

Mr. Schotta's face reddened like ripened tomatoes and Harry Huber chimed in.

"You couldn't break a pane of glass with your best fastball, Bobby. Stop telling people how great you are and try to fix some of these baseball fields for the kids."

As soon as that last syllable left Harry's lips, Big John overheard the message on Mr. Schotta's walkie-talkie.

"You giving Nicky and his boys grief about playing baseball on the baseball fields."

"Those kids ruin the lines the field crews put down," Mr. Schotta said, pointing to Nicky.

"Listen to me, Bobby. If you want me to keep ordering your favorite donuts, you better let those kids play on the field, or else I'm going to tell everyone in town about the time you peed your pants in the middle of a game."

"Sh, John, sh. You promised you wouldn't tell anybody," Mr. Schotta said.

"I heard that," Nicky laughed.

"Just let the kids play on the field. Summer's around the corner. Try to be nice for a change."

Big John rescued Nicky again and he loved it. From that day forward, Mr. Schotta never bothered the Kelsey Avenue Crew again.

Never.

Big John in no way bragged about his pull with people in power, and no one ever asked why folks from several walks of life gave him envelopes with lots of money.

"Nicky, are you finished with your work?" Big John asked.

"I'm almost done. I've just got to empty a couple of baskets and sweep the front steps to the store."

Many times Nicky got tangled up in the back-and-forth bantering and forgot to do his work.

"You mean to tell me that you are not done yet."

"No, I forgot to empty the baskets because I got busy cleaning the donut case."

"You know, for a smart kid, you do some stupid things," Big John said. "From now on we are going to call you 'One Cell' because sometimes it seems you only have one brain cell in that head of yours."

That name didn't bother Nicky because he knew he did great in school. He was always in the top of his classes. He possessed the uncanny ability to score one hundred on tests without even studying. English, science, mathematics, and social studies were easy because he learned that listening in class saved him time from studying. So, that meant more time for sports. And if there was more time for sports, there was more time for baseball.

"You have any tests this week?" Big John asked.

"I have a couple," Nicky said.

"You better get out of here soon and go home and study."

"I don't have to study. I pay attention in class."

"Then why don't you pay attention here? How come I have to tell you to do things twice before we finish them the right way?" Big John complained.

"It's too much fun watching you rip the people that come in here," Nicky admitted.

"Get to work. You've got a half-hour left."

Big John paid Nicky two dollars per hour to clean the deli and empty the wastebaskets. The most valuable fringe benefit of the job, though, was when they closed the store and Nicky could talk to Big John.

"You don't mind if I call you 'One Cell,' do ya, Nicky?" Big John's therapy session began.

"Nah, I know I'm doing well in school, but Rusty and a lot of the kids are always calling me names. I really can't stand it. I want to run up to them and start punching them in the face and hurt them, so they can see what it feels like to look like me."

"What are you talking about, Nicky? You look fine. The last operation improved your lip a lot," Big John said.

"The doctors lied to me, Big John. They told me that I would look like the other kids. They told me that this would be the last operation. I don't look like the other kids. I look retarded."

"What did Joe say?"

"My dad told me to listen to the doctors. He believed them, too."

Again, Big John knew everybody, so he knew doctors at Yale-New Haven Hospital. He knew that Nicky's lip needed more surgery. Unlike many people close to Nicky, they thought the truth hurt him more than the operating knives.

"How can I make them stop calling me names, Big John?" Nicky questioned.

"The girls laugh behind my back. The boys use me for their jokes. When is this crap going to end?"

"Nicky, it will end when you end it."

Big John might as well have said those words in Polish, but Nicky played along anyway.

"I understand, Big John. I understand."

The truth was that, as smart as Nicky was in school, he had no clue how to stop the name-calling and the ridicule he experienced every day.

So, when Nicky didn't understand something, he lied. Then when he understood that he lied, he lied again to cover it up.

It wasn't until some time later that Nicky realized the power of words and how, sometimes, you need to read between the lines of life—not the foul lines of baseball.

Chapter 6
A Little Baby

The West Haven neighborhood bustled with growing families. It seemed as if every other week a new baby arrived from the Yale-New Haven Hospital. Giuseppe Palmieri felt an understandable sense of excitement when he raced his wife, Netta, to the emergency room for the birth of his first born.

Mr. Palmieri immigrated to America when he was nineteen years old from the smallest of Italian towns near Naples; Faicchio, Benevento.

He came to the United States with three things—clothes, survival skills, and stubbornness. Nobody knew him ever to be wrong.

On the day of the birth of his first son, the man who could barely speak English learned more words in one afternoon than he had in his previous five years in America.

"Mr. Palmieri, congratulations. You have a son," Dr. Milici said.

"This is good," Mr. Palmieri said. "We name him Nicky after my father."

"Sounds good, Giuseppe. But there is something I have to tell you."

"What? There is something wrong?"

"Everything's fine, Giuseppe."

"Tell me what's wrong? My son has a disease or something," Mr. Palmieri concluded.

"No, no, Signor Palmieri. Your son is fine, physically. There is just one little thing." For some reason, neither Nicky nor anyone else in the neighborhood could figure out why people were afraid of Giuseppe Palmieri. He was an extremely dedicated man to the truth. He didn't enjoy it when people tried to sidestep him or create confusion.

"Your son will need some operations quickly. Today if possible."

Stunned, the man moved from joyous elation to absolute shock. He was awash in disbelief.

Operation?

In fifteen seconds, Mr. Palmieri's worst fears engulfed him like a tidal wave. His boy has one arm. His first born was missing fingers or toes. The perfect son he prayed for was suffering.

"Giuseppe, it is not something we can't fix," Dr. Milici said.

The family doctor asked Mr. Palmieri if he knew a plastic surgeon.

"I don't know what you are talking about," Mr. Palmieri said. "The only doctor I know is you."

"We will need to call a plastic surgeon. An Italian of course."

"Good. Good," Mr. Palmieri said. "What is wrong?"

"Your son has a cleft palate."

"Cleft palate? I don't understand. Is this a bad disease? I want to see my son."

"Giuseppe, I must tell you again that this is something we can fix. When you see your son, it will be shocking at first. But try to remember we can fix this with a couple of surgeries."

"Let me see my son."

Dr. Milici slowly led Mr. Palmieri to a special room. It was extremely quiet.

"Why don't we hear any babies crying?" Mr. Palmieri asked.

"Your son is in intensive care. We need to keep an eye on him."

"Oh, no, this is not good."

"Don't worry, Giuseppe, we can fix this."

This did not ease Mr. Palmieri. He was one of the finest cabinetmakers around. He understood building and repair, but he didn't understand "cleft palate." Mr. Palmieri grew extremely tense because no one could explain to him his son's problem.

"Don't be alarmed, Giuseppe. Your son will be able to function like normal kids. He'll just need a few operations."

"I want to see my son. Where's Netta? Does she know about this?"

"Your wife is resting. We will wake her if you want, but we won't allow her to see the baby until after the operations."

"Is she all right?"

"Yes, Giuseppe, she's fine."

"Let me see my son."

Mr. Palmieri didn't know what to expect. He comprehended few words in English. The West Haven neighborhood was filled with Italian-speaking immigrants, so English was truly a second language. Despite Mr. Palmieri's animated protests, the powers that be at Yale-New Haven Hospital refused to allow Mrs. Palmieri to see her son. The staff sent her home without her baby.

Dr. Milici tried to explain "cleft palate" to the couple, but Mr. Palmieri simply shook his head. Mr. Palmieri took his wife home and returned to the hospital promising not to leave until he could see his son. Hospital staff finally allowed him to enter the intensive care unit with nurses and several members of the security team.

Suddenly, the moment of fear exploded upon Mr. Palmieri.

His son was missing his upper lip. His nose came down to an empty space above his mouth. Mr. Palmieri started to cry.

"Giuseppe, we scheduled a surgery for tonight."

"We will talk to Netta first. Can we talk to her before we do anything? This needs to be explained to me, now."

"Sure, Giuseppe. Sure."

Chapter 7
A Real Matriarch

Strong women always know how to handle the most difficult of situations. This one, however, required a great deal of Netta Palmieri's guile and inner strength. Even with her numerous years of education, Netta couldn't anticipate how Mr. Palmieri would handle the trauma of seeing his newly born son.

A cleft palate was not a disease. It was a birth defect that required several corrective surgeries and a lot of money.

"Netta, Giuseppe is here to talk to you about the operations now," Dr. Milici said.

"Our boy is going to be all right, isn't he?" Mr. Palmieri said.

"Joe, let's have Dr. Milici explain these operations," Netta said.

Netta Altamura Palmieri fluently spoke two languages, Italian and English, so Mr. Palmieri felt more comfortable in the translation process.

Mrs. Palmieri graduated from high school as the valedictorian of Bacon Academy. She never earned a grade less than an A. She was born in America, the youngest of five children to Italian immigrants. Her mother, Irene, taught elementary classes in Italy.

Mrs. Palmieri's father, Constantine, came to America and started working on Staten Island in New York City. He saved his money for four years, and one day he ventured to Colchester, Connecticut, to purchase a 1,000 acre farm because a doctor told him his asthma couldn't handle the dirt and grime of New York City.

Constantine and Irene couldn't stand city life. They loved the fresh air that reminded them of Bari, Italy. Now, this business opportunity came along and they moved the family to the far reaches of Connecticut to raise chickens and sell eggs. The clean air and prospects for a better life thrilled them.

On the farm, Netta learned real life skills, but Irene made her read and read and read. Netta breezed through high school and ventured onto Yale University in New Haven, where she met Giuseppe at an Italian social gathering at the Washington Heights Pietro-Micca Club.

They courted for about seven months, married, and moved to West Haven. This was the way things were done in the old country, and Giuseppe Palmieri wanted the same here. This "cleft palate" thing didn't happen in the old country, so Netta knew that he needed a lot of convincing that things would be fine.

"Dr. Milici says that our son will just need a couple of surgeries and he will be fine," Netta said.

Hospitals didn't sit well with Mr. Palmieri. In Italy, the people he knew who entered hospitals never exited in an upright position. Operations made Mr. Palmieri more nervous than the buildings themselves.

"We can start the surgery in two hours," Dr. Milici said.

"We will fix your son, but I must tell you that numerous surgeries will follow."

"Netta, explain that to me. Why so many surgeries?" Mr. Palmieri asked.

"A cleft palate is a complicated birth defect that will not be fixed with one operation," Netta said.

"Nicky will need many surgeries after this and probably until he is fifteen years old."

"How many operations, Dr. Milici?" Mr. Palmieri asked.

"We don't know for sure. Maybe six or seven by the time he reaches high school."

Dr. Milici was not a plastic surgeon, nor was he good at math, either because Nicky went through six or seven surgeries by the time he was six.

The family doctor didn't know all the answers. He just felt Mr. Palmieri's lack of comfort and wanted to ease his nervousness. Netta knew that there was plenty of work ahead.

"Joe, our son will have to be spoon-fed, and I don't know if our insurance will cover the cost of the surgeries," Netta said.

"Don't worry. I will work two jobs. We will make sure this kid has everything."

Netta knew that he would make sure everything was perfect. Her job was now to make sure that Mr. Palmieri didn't worry because she felt a difficult road ahead.

Chapter 8

Twelve Operations Later

Mrs. Palmieri knew that kids would not be sympathetic to their son's birth defect. She knew that children could be cruel at times, but never did she anticipate someone like Rusty Alves. The cleft palate, so clearly visible, placed an automatic target on her son's head, and she knew that kids would aim directly at it. This was not a disease that no one would see.

Nicky's cleft palate grew more complicated than she expected. Her son suffered a total loss of hearing in the left ear and 20 percent in the right one. The operations on the roof of his mouth closed his ear canals.

Eventually, Nicky needed hearing aids. Mrs. Palmieri also knew that her son required hours of speech therapy and hours of care, but what no one could anticipate were the numerous days of pain her son endured after the operations were over and the stitches were healed.

In this small Connecticut town, back in the day, there were no self-help groups, and what about therapy?

Another joke.

Therapy was a heating pad for your father when he hurt his back. That was therapy.

Physical therapy came in different forms. If kids whined about others picking on them, their dads taught their sons how to fight. These dads understood survival skills—not psychological mumbo jumbo that some were convinced healed wounds.

Mr. Palmieri, the family knew, also needed time for peace, not more buzzing from complaining kids, when the garage door closed at night. Mr. Palmieri worked two jobs. Sometimes he came home at 10 P.M. during the winter months. The sounds of power saws blazing for the past fourteen hours still rang in his head.

He worked to pay for the surgeries and to feed his family. He worked because family, honor, and integrity didn't allow him to accept any handouts. If Nicky were mistakenly awake at 10 P.M., the last thing he thought about was crying to his father about a tough day at school.

Giuseppe Palmieri understood the value of school, not because he went to one but because he didn't have the opportunity to attend one. In Italy, World War II ravaged his small town in the province of Benevento. American bombs knocked down buildings while his father served as a General in the Italian Army in Ethiopia. Nicola Palmieri, Giuseppe's father, was missing in action for eight years. Giuseppe didn't know if his father were dead or alive.

In the meantime, his mother moved Giuseppe and his two brothers from church to church. During WWII, war still respected religion. The churches were off limits and always a safe haven for homeless families. From hearing the stories of going days without food and sleeping on cement floors, none of the four Palmieri children dared complain about the mundane problems of school. No one uttered a sound about a mean lunch monitor or a playground bully. Nicky kept his mouth shut and dealt with his problems.

Therapy.

There was no room for therapy in this West Haven neighborhood.

Mr. Palmieri worked and Mrs. Palmieri raised the kids. She ran the house, and Mr. Palmieri worked to pay for the surgeries that tried to give their son a better life. Twelve surgeries later, the trouble started. No one could see it at the time.

Chapter 9
Learning to Lie

Somewhere Nicky realized from the truth that telling lies was much more fun. They never ended. Nicky made them up and changed the rules as he went along. It was so much easier than dealing with the truth. Somebody once said that the truth hurts. It made sense to a little kid. So, every time there was a problem there was no problem. There was a lie.

"How was school today, Nicky?" Mrs. Palmieri asked.

"Great, mom, I made two new friends."

In fact, two kids helped fix Nicky's Batman metal lunch box so that when he was in line for lunch, they released the latch. To the hilarious delight of twenty-two other sixth graders, a glass thermos hit the ground. His sandwich and snack went flying across the floor, and Nicky wildly punched the first two kids he saw laughing.

These were Nicky's two new friends, and Nicky also got a trip to the principal's office. For Nicky, the truth was only the truth to those who believed him.

"Nicholas, why did you hit those two boys in the classroom?" Mrs. Ida Anderson asked.

"Excuse me. My name is Nicky."

"Don't talk back to me, young man," Mrs. Anderson retorted.

"I'm not talking back. I just want you to know the truth."

"Nobody ever wants to stop Rusty and his friends from picking on me. This has been going on for years, and you people never take my side. It's because I'm Italian and those kids are Irish punks. I know the deal. My uncle Nick told me about your kind."

"I'm not Irish by the way, and what nationality I am is none of your little business."

"Then why do you constantly go into your desk and drink from that flask and a green bottle that says Bushmills?" Nicky cracked.

"You have a fresh mouth, young man. I'm going to call your parents in here to discuss your behavior in school," Mrs. Anderson snapped.

"Well, then why aren't Rusty and Vinnie in the office, too? They were fighting with me."

"Miss Hansen said that they were just standing in line when you started punching them for no reason."

"Those idiots knocked my lunch everywhere, and Miss Hansen says nothing happened," Nicky screamed.

"Watch your voice, young man. You are in bigger trouble now than when you first walked in here."

"Why don't you ask some of the other kids what happened, and maybe you will learn the truth?" Nicky said about one of his least favorite subjects.

"I don't have to do anything of the sort. I know what happened, and you are in trouble again."

Kids were afraid of Mrs. Anderson. She never smiled. She had hairs growing out of unusual places on her face. If Mrs. Anderson shaved a couple of times, she could grow a beard. She was the only woman on earth who had a five o'clock shadow twenty-four hours a day.

Mrs. Anderson never set foot or stumbled into any classroom once during the seven years Nicky attended Stiles Elementary. She seemed so miserable. Somebody once said that misery loves company, but then Nicky wondered why everyone left her alone.

Certainly, this trip to her office meant a phone call home. This was not good.

"They were laughing at me."

"Yes, but is that a reason to hit someone?" Mrs. Anderson asked.

"No, but there is broken glass in my chocolate milk, and this is the fifth time this has happened. All you do is sit there behind your desk and let those punks laugh at me every day."

"Are you finished?" echoed from of pile of disheveled gray and black hairs.

"And one more thing, Mrs. Anderson, how would you like it if there were glass pieces in your scotch bottle?" Nicky added.

"That is not scotch. It's cough medicine," Mrs. Anderson said. "And your mother should wash your mouth out with soap."

"Well, while we are on the subject of soap, Mrs. Anderson, why don't you use some on your face?"

"Mr. Palmieri, you march your disrespectful little behind right out of this office now. I'm going to get your mother on the phone."

Nicky sat on the bench outside the office and waited for the worst. He knew his mother never tolerated this insolence toward any authority, not to mention the principal.

One time Nicky told his mother and father about an incident in which a mean crossing guard spanked Nicky for not following directions. Nicky's mother grabbed the belt and spanked him again.

The truth hurt that time, too.

When Nicky's father came home, there was a repeat performance minus the standing ovation.

The truth hurt again.

While Nicky sat outside the office, bitterness burrowed its way into his mind. Revenge wrestled itself to the forefront.

How could he even the score with Rusty? Nicky didn't want to create any copycat crime. He never liked the sight of blood, so he decided that sports were the answer. He practiced everything so he could beat Rusty at every game.

The truth then hurt even more.

"You are an extremely fortunate young man, Mr. Palmieri," Mrs. Anderson started.

"Your mother is not home, and the Italian secretaries at your father's woodworking shop won't let me talk to him. I will call your house tonight."

"You will spend the rest of the day here until you learn to control your temper, young man. Do you hear me?"

"Yes, Mrs. Anderson."

When other children teased him about his lip, severely deformed from the 12 surgeries needed to correct the cleft palate, Nicky fired into uncontrollable rages. He never thought about the consequences. He just reacted.

He only really felt comfortable when he was surrounded by Gennaro; John Ferrante; his hero, Jerry Gambardella Jr.; and the rest of the Kelsey Avenue Crew. Otherwise, kids in school took turns and hammered Nicky with cheap shots.

"Your face looks like it was run over by a bus."

"I hope the ugly stick somebody beat you with lived for another day."

Those insults bothered Nicky, but the worst was when they called him "The Lip." Other kids laughed behind his back when he was pulled out of class for speech therapy. It even grew worse when an opportunistic hearing aid salesman sold Mr. Palmieri on a ridiculous idea of purchasing two hearing aids.

"Hey, Nicky, you're deaf and ugly," Rusty Alves said.

When a speech therapist at Yale-New Haven Hospital told Mrs. Palmieri that Nicky's speech was delayed because of his near-full deafness in his left ear and the partial deafness in his right, she suggested that hearing aids would help him understand words better and improve his speech. The therapist led Mr. and Mrs. Palmieri to a Beltone hearing aid store, and the salesman sold two hearing aids for Nicky.

Selling Nicky a hearing aid for his left ear was a bigger scam than the one perpetrated on those who bought the island of Manhattan for $24.

The hearing aids just gave kids another target at which to point their ridicule. The biggest problem was that Nicky rarely complained about it to his parents, teachers, or friends. Nicky decided just to fight back.

On the walk home, Nicky knew he needed to explain the broken thermos. He knew the best place to talk to his mother was when she was in the kitchen preparing dinner.

"Mom, I have to talk to you about what happened in school today," Nicky started as he followed up on making the new friends' lie work to his advantage.

"My favorite thermos broke again. It fell out of my lunch box and broke. The glass ruined my chocolate milk."

"This is the fifth time this school year, Nicky. You have to be more careful how you handle your lunchbox," Mrs. Palmieri said.

"I better not tell your father about this one. You know how hard he is working to care for this family. Your father is working two jobs, so we can make ends meet. He's been in a bad mood lately because he hasn't been able to put any money away in the college fund."

"Yes, Ma, I know. I will try to take better care of my stuff," Nicky said.

"Ma, can I ask you something?"

"Sure, Nicky. I can talk while I fry the calamari."

This was one of Nicky's favorite meals. He knew that if he told her about the fight in school, odds stood at 22 to 1 he would be sent to bed without supper.

So, besides playing sports, Nicky turned to what he did best, lie. His great remedy for solving a problem like this one would be to avoid and sidestep truth.

Nicky thought about telling her how the fight started in school as a result of the constant name-calling and other kids' tugging on their lips, but he didn't want to take any chances with calamari on the horizon.

"Ma, how come the doctors keep telling me that this is the last operation and then they schedule another one and another one and another one? When is this going to end?" Nicky said.

"Your cleft palate is new to them. As time moves on, they are coming up with new surgeries every day. The doctors are just trying to fix your lip the best they can," Mrs. Palmieri responded.

"I can't stand these operations. I hate the constant poking around they do to my face. They always have so many doctors in the office. They stand around, nod their heads, and whisper. I really hate the whispering."

"Nicky, the doctors are talking about how well you are progressing," Mrs. Palmieri stated.

"They can't believe how well you are doing in school and sports."

Nicky knew that wasn't the whole truth. Sometimes he overheard Dr. Campari say, "This didn't come out like I thought it would. We will try this new method next."

Nicky hated this the most. He despised being used as an experiment. Even the orthodontist, Dr. Stanley S. Wolfe, tried new methods on his teeth to fix his under bite, another byproduct of the cleft palate. They extracted two perfectly healthy teeth because Dr. Wolfe thought that he could pull the rest of the jaw back.

However, the brilliant doctor seemed to forget one thing: eleven-year-olds still grow. Following the braces and extractions, Nicky's bottom jaw grew faster than the upper jaw over the next six months, and the under bite returned.

It was the upper lip, the one with most of the scars of twelve surgeries that bothered him as well, if not more. Before every operation, Nicky ran to St. John Vianney's and prayed. He asked God for this to be the last operation. Nicky prayed for a smooth, normal lip—not the bumpy one he looked at every day.

One time Nicky fell asleep in the pews and slept there until eleven o'clock at night. Mr. Palmieri felt his son's anguish, but Nicky never spoke to him about it.

Nicky wanted his father to be proud of how brave he was even though every operation scarred him. But Mr. Palmieri was a smart man, and he knew Nicky's patterns.

One day on the eve of the twelfth surgery, Nicky seemed tenser than usual, and Mr. Palmieri knew it. Nicky's father searched throughout the town. He went to the softball fields, the lighted basketball courts, and the bocce courts by the beach. Not even Big John or Jerry knew where Nicky went.

Mr. Palmieri went back to the house and noticed that Nicky's grandmother's rosary was missing. He asked Mrs. Palmieri if she moved the beads. And when she replied no, Mr. Palmieri knew where Nicky had gone.

"What are you doing here so late, Nicky?"

"I'm just praying because I will probably miss church on Sunday," Nicky said.

"Are you praying for anything special?"

"No, Dad. You know how Grandma wants us to go to church every Sunday, and I know I won't be out of the hospital. So I took care of it today."

"That's it?" Mr. Palmieri questioned. "There's nothing else you're praying for?"

"That's it, Dad. I'm not worried about anything else."

It was hard for Nicky to talk to anyone about this lip. This time after the big beef in school—long after the twelfth surgery—Nicky tried to talk to his mother about his deepest fears.

"Ma, you know how in church they say that God takes care of all of us?" Nicky asked.

"Yes, Jesus sacrificed himself for us sinners," Mrs. Palmieri replied.

"Then why did God give me this lip? What is he trying to teach me?"

"Why do you ask, Nicky? Are you having problems in school?"

"Nah, school is great. I told you I made two new friends today."

"But Ma, this lip—is it ever going to look like the rest of the kids'?" Nicky asked.

"The doctors say that the next surgery is simply for cosmetic purposes," Mrs. Palmieri assured him. "They are going to fix your lip like a movie star."

"You mean I'll look like Mel Gibson?"

"No, a real star, like Frank Sinatra," Mrs. Palmieri laughed.

"Frank Sinatra. He's old school, Ma. If I'm going to have more of these surgeries I want to look like Stallone in Rocky."

Mrs. Palmieri swiftly walked across the room and gave Nicky a playful tap to the back of his head.

"I didn't raise you to sound like an imbecile," Mrs. Palmieri began. "What are you going to do after the operation? Run around town, yelling 'Yo, Adrienne. Anybody seen Cuff and Link?'"

Nicky laughed and said, "No, Ma. I know you want me to do well in school, so I don't sound like a moron. But Stallone always has new girl friends. I read about it in the supermarket tabloids."

"Are you starting to worry about girls?" Mrs. Palmieri said, as her voiced raised a few decibels. "Stay away from girls. They are trouble when you're eleven."

"I'm going to be twelve soon, Ma. And if they don't fix my lip," Nicky began, "no girl is ever going to want to go near me."

"Don't worry, Nicky. This next operation is going to make your lip better," Mrs. Palmieri said even though she knew it was far from the truth.

"Plastic surgery is performing miracles these days."

"But, Ma, why did God give me this cleft palate? My brother and sisters are perfect. But me, I have this lip and every time I look in the mirror I hope it will go away and it never does."

"This is about girls, isn't it Nicky?" Mrs. Palmieri questioned.

"No, Ma, it is not about girls. I don't want any more of these surgeries if they are not going to fix what they say they are going to. I can't stand hospitals."

Before the surgeries, Nicky prayed. But after the surgeries, Nicky cried and he never let anyone see or hear him. When he woke after the anesthesia, Nicky ran to the nearest mirror with his eyes closed. He waited, looked, and cried.

The previous five operations were the worst, but number twelve—the last one—brought great promise. As Nicky sat in the waiting room, he waited and then ran to the door of Dr. Campari's plastic surgery office and eavesdropped when his father entered.

"I told Nicky that we are going to smooth his lip with this last operation," Dr. Campari said. "I hope this works."

"How is your son doing with everything?"

"He never complains. He's a good boy," Mr. Palmieri said in his best English.

"How much money I have to pay you for this one?" Mr. Palmieri asked.

"Ten thousand dollars. But since your insurance won't cover this work, I will cut it to five thousand."

"No, no, if that is the price I will pay," Mr. Palmieri said. He was too proud for discounts. He never wanted any favors even though he was the first to offer a helping hand.

"How about this, Joe?" Dr. Campari asked. "Why don't you come over to my house and build the missus some cabinets, and we can call it even?"

"That will be good. I will make the best cabinets. They will last for as long as you live in the house," Mr. Palmieri said.

Nicky listened and hoped that this surgery would be the last. He also knew not to let his father learn the truth. There were many things wrong—the lip and the teasing, the hearing aids and the teasing, no girls and the teasing, the fighting and the teasing. And Rusty Alves. The problems were almost endless, but the solution was simple. Keep your mouth shut around Dad. That worked much better than the truth.

This twelfth operation was the one, Nicky thought. He couldn't wait to go to Dr. Campari's office where they were going to take off the bandages and Nicky could see.

Seconds after the bandages were removed, Nicky raced to the mirror in the bathroom to see the results.

He closed his eyes tightly and prayed once more.

He started to open his right eye first, but closed it quickly for one more prayer. He was ready. He looked. To his delight, the lip was smooth.

The ugly bumps were gone. Tears of joy flowed down his face. It was over Nicky thought.

The teasing and the name-calling gone.

The frightful stares from strangers and little children gone.

People pointing and whispering gone.

The lip was fixed and Nicky was truly happy. Sure, there was some swelling, but the cuts didn't look so bad. The stitches were inside and they disintegrated.

For the first time ever, Nicky thanked God. The lip looked normal. Nicky went to sleep happy.

The doctor gave Mr. Palmieri some pills to reduce the swelling.

Nicky thought it was over.

With each day, the swelling decreased. Nicky looked in the mirror hundreds, thousands of times. Every time Nicky noticed something.

He spotted a little bump

"Okay, no problem. It's a little bump. The operation can't be perfect."

The next day, there were two little bumps.

No problem, Nicky thought. The swelling's almost down.

But then the bumps seemed to grow bigger and bigger.

With each day, Nicky's happiness turned to despair, his hope to hopelessness, his joy to anger, and his dreams to nightmares. Finally, after one week, they visited Dr. Campari.

"This looks good, Nicky."

"I thought it was over, Dr. Campari. I thought this was the last one. But when I went home, the bumps came back. When you took the bandages off, the lip looked perfect. What happened?"

Nicky knew what had happened. Dr. Campari didn't have to answer his question. This lip was Nicky's cross to bear. This lip would never be perfect. He would never look like other kids.

He started talking to himself. "How can I go to school with this lip?" Nicky wondered. "The kids are never going to stop making fun of me. What am I going to do?"

The answers never came, but the questions were endless. Nicky hoped his mother understood and developed some words of wisdom, but Nicky always stopped short before the truth surfaced and pounded him over the head.

"But Ma, I still don't understand why God gave this lip to me. I don't know anyone else with this problem. I never get any answers. The doctors, the priest, you, Dad. I deserve some answers."

"You deserve answers? Are you kidding me? Sure, the cleft palate is a million to one shot," Mrs. Palmieri said. "There are kids with worse problems. Do you want to be paralyzed or have cerebral palsy? Those kids would trade places with you in a heartbeat. Stop feeling sorry for yourself."

Nicky started to cry. His brother and sisters were surprisingly quietly listening to the entire conversation. He feared they would laugh, too, but they didn't. They just listened.

"Why are you crying, Nicky?" Mrs. Palmieri said. "It is about girls, isn't it?"

"Yeah, Ma, it's about girls." Nicky said, wiping the tears from his face with his right shirtsleeve. "I'm just going to have to forget about it for now. The next operation will be the last one."

"That's better, Nicky," Mrs. Palmieri said. "Tomorrow you are going to have a great day at school. Aren't you getting your baseball uniform?"

"Yeah, Ma, Coach Camp is passing out the jerseys. I can't wait," Nicky said.

"What number are you going to ask for?" Mrs. Palmieri said.

"I don't know, Ma."

"How about number five like the great Joe DiMaggio or number one like Billy Martin? Those are two of your favorites."

"I'm going to ask for number twelve," Nicky stated. "It sounds like a good number to me."

Mrs. Palmieri smiled and finished frying the calamari. She knew Nicky had a lot to say.

She knew he was young.

She knew that one day he would surely realize that the truth hopefully sets him and his worst fears and emotions free. It was just that this wasn't the day. She knew it and somehow, someway, Nicky knew it, too.

Chapter 10
A Small Town

West Haven, Connecticut was always a peaceful town. There were no Vietnam War or Desert Storm protests. Hippies were like Bugs Bunny and the Roadrunner to Nicky Palmieri. They were TV characters that people with deep voices talked about on Channel 2 at 7 P.M. Long hair was something that Nicky saw on the floor of his Uncle Nick's barbershop or Mrs. Palmieri's hairdresser's down the street.

Nicky felt that, because of Big John, the world was safe in West Haven. Big John made the world seem simple. Working class people filled the modest houses of this neighborhood. The Armstrong Rubber Company employed almost everybody who could walk and pretend they knew how to chew gum. All the men had jobs, and unemployment was just another long word in the dictionary.

Big John explained these things to Nicky and more.

The West Haven men were skilled laborers—steelworkers, auto mechanics, electricians, plumbers, cabinetmakers, and carpenters. They could create masterful work with the simplest of tools. They helped each other. If something broke, a doorbell rang would ring and the problem would be solved quicker than a late April snowfall.

Nicky and the rest of the Kelsey Avenue Crew admired these men. Most of these men were the Little League coaches, the Biddy Basketball coaches, and the Midget Football coaches.

These hardworking men ran every league, every team, every sports night at the local school gyms. The kids loved them. The gang loved Big John the most, but he was always busy running the deli. So, the guys who were left—they were good coaches and good athletes. Nicky and his crew also saw that they were good liars.

The town was so small that even the kids knew everything that went on—everything.

If somebody's father lost $1,000 playing Texas Hold 'Em, the neighborhood knew by the crack of dawn.

If the cops had to carry Mr. Umbriago home from a late-night vacation sponsored by the Hiram Walker distilling company or Jack Daniels at D.J.'s Pub, the jokes started before the first drop of Maxwell House coffee hit the bottom of the pot.

Then when Nicky and his boys saw Mr. Casanova with a strange lady in red who wasn't Mrs. Casanova, eyebrows lifted and they just laughed.

These were the truths, and these truths were what Nicky learned.

"Hey, Mr. Klink, I heard you dropped one large last night at Lorenzo's house?" Nicky asked.

"Who told you that, wise guy?"

"It's on the streets. They are saying you can't even win at Uno."

"You got the information all wrong, kid. I was down a lot, but I broke even in the end."

Not a great lie, but what else did a sixth grader know.

"Hey, Mr. Umbriago, I heard you had a few cocktails last night," Gennaro inquired.

"I only had two beers. Honest."

Whenever one of these guys used "honest" in a sentence, the Kelsey Avenue Crew would bet every dollar they owned that each word before it was a lie.

The best liar was Mr. Casanova until his wife caught him in one of the most genius moves of all time. Mr. Casanova went to every card game and sports event in West Haven. He always accompanied this woman, who he claimed to work for him as a secretary. The only problem was that no one knew how a West Haven sanitation department employee could afford or need a secretary. What did she keep track of? The number of garbage cans and plastic bags he lifted in one day, or did she count the nickel deposits from cans and bottles he discovered in the rubbish?

One night, Mr. Casanova thought his wife was sleeping upstairs. He decided to call his little honey and used an old fashioned rotary phone in the kitchen. Little did he know Mrs. Casanova was on the other line counting the clicks of the rotary phone. She wrote down the number, called his lady friend the next day, and kicked Mr. Casanova out of the house.

"Hey, Mr. Casanova, where've you been lately? We haven't seen you around. Is everything all right?" John Ferrante prodded.

"I was out of town on business."

"I didn't know that they held garbage men conventions?" John replied.

"Don't be a wise guy, and get the hell out of here."

These were the people the Kelsey Avenue Crew laughed at, but these were the same men that helped them play sports. They didn't care what they did off the field as long as they helped them post those precious W's."

Nicky accepted the lying as a trade-off for sports.

"Whose basketball team are you on?" Big John asked.

"Mr. Klink's."

"Watch your pockets, Nicky. I heard he's going to Lorenzo's tonight."

"I don't care where he goes after the game," Nicky said. "You remember what Mr. Gus Zibelli, president of the Italian-American club, said after the game, "You don't have to go home, but you can't stay here."

Most of all Mr. Klink was so cheap that one time he pulled a five-dollar bill out of his wallet and Lincoln didn't have a beard.

But besides these aforementioned few of West Haven's numerous colorful characters worked two jobs—one to pay the bills and the other to pay for their lies. They left their homes at 6 A. M. and returned about twelve or thirteen hours later.

If the kids feared their fathers, they had a field day. If they were afraid of their moms, they hoped their fathers quit their second jobs soon. And if they were afraid of both of them, they watched where they walked and how they talked. It all made sense to Nicky.

Everybody knew everybody. If any of the Kelsey Avenue Crew created any havoc, the modern day AOL Instant Messenger seemed like the Pony Express delivered a letter from San Francisco. Bad news traveled faster than the speed of light.

While the men toiled in the factories and workplaces of West Haven, women worked the toughest of tough jobs. They turned children into adults.

The women of West Haven also owned tools. They operated spoons, brooms, and belts for many uses. They had quick feet and even quicker hands. For baseball fans, catcher's gear was called the "tools of ignorance." Well, the simple machines the nice ladies used were "tools of tolerance." Simply put, some moms and wives stayed home. They worked the hardest, and everyone knew it. The women didn't need the front cover of *Time* to be honored.

These hardworking folks did not make up the entire populace of West Haven. There were many other people of course. Those with college degrees didn't live on Nicky's block. They lived up the street on Richmond Avenue with the three digit house numbers. They were insurance men, bankers, lawyers, and politicians. They wore neat suits with thin blue ties and polished black and brown shoes. Their starched white shirts had neat, crisp collars. One of them was Rusty Alves's father—the most miserable of them all.

They never talked to anybody. They always carried the same game face. They wore the same frowns and disdain for the day ahead. They left for work at 8 A.M. and arrived home at 4 P.M. These men's Monday-through-Friday mannerisms were more accurate than their fancy Rolex watches. Their habits would surely be used for fun at a later time.

What bothered Nicky the most about these men with their high-priced education and smarts was that they knew the torture he endured from the other kids—but only Big John and Jerry Gambardella Jr. had the guts to do anything about it.

Chapter 11
Our Idol

Kids—now that certainly was a different story altogether.

Every neighborhood featured a Rusty Alves, the know-it-all dumb jock who won everything. Luckily for Nicky, Rusty's parents divorced several years ago, and he didn't live nearby on Wednesdays and alternate weekends. When he wasn't living in the ritzy Richmond Avenue section with his miserable father, he lived by the beach with his mom, near Morse Park, home base for the West Haven Little League.

On Nicky's block, there were so many kids better then Rusty. There were children with more style and grace. This neighborhood protected each other, and it started with Jerry Gambardella Jr.

Because of Jerry and Big John, the kids in Nicky's neighborhood played the big three sports at Painter's Park during winter, spring, summer, or fall. Nicky and the rest of the Kelsey Avenue Crew played anything, anytime. These Painter's Park kids respected and loved Nicky.

Rusty was more than just afraid of Jerry. He respected Jerry. He and his cronies never called Nicky names with Jerry around. Jerry always protected the kids on this block. He was bigger than Don Corleone with a baseball bat, but he never hurt anyone. Jerry convinced people to change their minds without making them an offer they couldn't refuse.

Whenever Jerry heard someone call Nicky "Lip" or "Elephant Man," he never grew angry. He spoke to them in a calm and miraculous way. He informed them that it wasn't right and necessary, whether Nicky was around or not. Jerry always stopped the name-calling—always.

Gennaro was Nicky's best friend. What Big John was to Nicky, Jerry Gambardella Jr. was to Gennaro. Jerry taught Gennaro to stick up for his friends. Gennaro fought anyone who ever said a bad word about Nicky. It didn't matter who it was. Gennaro started upright punching and jabbing, and few times would he not go down swinging.

When Gennaro was about eight years old, he met Jerry. Jerry was the modern-day Big John. Jerry worked at Painter's Park in summer camp, and he taught Gennaro and Nicky how to be a good friend. Jerry was a better person than he was an athlete even though he captained the three main sports teams—the big ones, too, football, basketball and baseball.

Jerry wore number twenty-two, double deuce. He was everyone's hero. In football, he was the quarterback, the punter, and the kicker. In basketball, he played two-guard, shot threes, rebounded, and laughed because no one could stop him. And then there was baseball

This was Jerry's favorite. He was a monstrous kid with broad shoulders. He was an Adonis, a Greek god. Jerry practiced every day.

He hit in the batting cages with his father, who was also a great baseball player and West Haven High legend. His father, Jerry Gambardella Sr. hit 11 homers and drove in 43 runs in one 22-game high school season. His team won the last state title for West Haven. In Connecticut scholastic baseball, Jerry Sr.'s records were comparable to Joe DiMaggio's 56-game hitting streak.

Jerry's father taught Jerry Jr. to help others since he came from good stock. What made Jerry truly great was that he was always willing to share with Nicky and the rest of the little kids, but it was Nicky and Gennaro that he took the most interest in. Jerry helped both of them with their hitting. His patience marveled adults. For hours, he hit fungoes, threw pitches, and played catch with the two boys. The best part was that every minute they played sports Jerry taught Gennaro to stick up for people. Jerry talked to Gennaro about friendship and spirit, and Gennaro listened to every word.

Along with Big John, Jerry epitomized what a role model stood for and the most awesome aspect of this was that he didn't have a business to run so he was always around until one sad day news arrived that crushed the entire town.

Jerry was so proficient at sports he could have enrolled at any college he wanted.

Florida State recruited Jerry for baseball.

Duke University offered Jerry a chance to play quarterback on the football team.

Every college scout, after they were finished drooling over his athletic talent, loved Jerry, but he grew attached to Hofstra University in Hempstead on Long Island and off to New York he went.

Jerry picked Hofstra because Hempstead was similar to West Haven, a microcosm Nicky said. They had Jim's Deli, which was like Big John's, and everybody in town knew everyone else—a perfect place, West Haven II.

Jerry decided to play baseball of course, and he started almost every other game during his freshman season. He batted .300 with a couple of homers and experienced the growing pains of Division I college baseball.

During the summer, Jerry worked out every day. He was determined to enjoy a great sophomore season. Like every kid who ever swung a bat or played catch, Jerry dreamed of playing in the Major Leagues, and he clearly possessed the skills and desire to do it.

One time Jerry took batting practice on the heralded Painter's Park main diamond. There were more than twenty-five guys playing basketball on the adjacent courts. As always, Jerry went on a batting practice roll. He started slamming majestic shots over the fence.

One by one, baseballs bounced off houses on Kelsey Avenue more than 375 feet away, and oddly enough—no one knew whether it was luck or divine intervention—but Jerry never broke a window. He smashed a shot off an awning, a brick facade, or aluminum siding here and there. He never broke a window, though. It was truly magic, Jerry Gambardella-style.

Suddenly, the basketball game stopped. The players turned toward the field and watched Jerry hit. Each pitch was absolutely crushed. There were no ground balls, no line drives, no pop ups, and—certainly—no misses. The field was a launching pad for white cowhide spheres that, after Jerry hit them, turned into little gray dots against the deep blue sky.

"Holy, cow, is this guy in the Big Leagues?" one basketball player said.

"Those balls are hit out of sight," contributed another.

Every hoopster stood and watched in amazement as Jerry dotted every house while Nicky and Gennaro darted in and out of oncoming cars and ran around Kelsey Avenue chasing every ball down.

Starting from the right field line and moving all the way to center field, Jerry hit every house, every lawn, and every driveway with one of his titanic swings. Never in the seventy-five-plus year history of baseball at Painter's Park—which probably included more than 10,000 games—did basketball players stop to watch a game, an at-bat, or even one pitch. Never mind a solo batting practice session.

This was the effort in which Jerry practiced to prepare for the baseball season. He worked and worked until he could work no more. Jerry took thousands and tens of thousands of swings. He fielded thousands and tens of thousands of fly balls and grounders.

Jerry wanted to make sure that, when he returned to Hofstra, he would dominate the next season.

Jerry started off on a hot streak and only improved with every game. In one Colonial Athletic Association playoff game against the University of Delaware, he crushed a dramatic grand slam walk-off homer that hit the top floor of the Hofstra University Recreation Center 420 feet away.

He was playing his best baseball. Nicky and Gennaro heard every story. They were never surprised by Jerry's success. They expected it. The whole town lived vicariously through Jerry. Every kid in the Kelsey Avenue Crew wanted to be just like him.

The homers.

The three-pointers.

The long spiraling touchdown bombs he threw.

The pretty girls who called his house or acted goofy every time he walked by.

Along with Big John, Jerry epitomized what a role model should be, and the best aspect of this was that he didn't have a business to run. He was always around until one sad day the news arrived that crushed the entire town.

It was one day after the Great Chocolate Milk Conflict that sent Nicky to the principal's office.

The phone rang at Big John's. It was 6:22 P.M.

Everyone in the store stopped.

The word eerie sells the scene shorter than any attention deficit disorder could.

"Hello, Big John's Deli," Big John answered.

After about a minute, Big John, always boisterous and loud, whispered.

"You have got to be kidding me?"

"This happened playing football? That kid is in the best shape of any athlete I have ever seen, Coach Dotolo."

Slowly, Big John put the phone down, but he didn't hang up. It was unbelievable. Nicky didn't know what was going on, but it wasn't good.

You could hear the voice on the other side, yelling "Big John, Big John, are you there?"

After ten seconds, Big John put the phone back to his ear.

"This is terrible. This is the worst thing to ever happen to this town."

Nicky had never experienced anything totally tragic before. He thought about the worst.

"Jerry blew his arm out. No problem—we have Tommy John surgery," Nicky thought.

"Jerry ripped his knee. No problem—arthroscopic surgery can fix those things every time," Nicky wondered.

When Big John finished the phone call, Nicky waited with baited breath.

"What happened, Big John?" Nicky asked.

"Is everything all right with Jerry?"

The look on Big John's face meant trouble. This was not a blown knee or a torn tendon. This was serious.

"I'm sorry, folks. Everyone is going to have to go. I have to close the store. We have a big problem," Big John said as he ordered Nicky to get in his car.

This confused Nicky the most. Big John was giving up customers and money? Nicky didn't know what to think.

"Big John, what's going on?"

"Help me close the store, and I'll tell you in the car."

Nicky thought the car would never start. Life was now in slow motion.

"Nicky, sometimes adults don't have the answers to everything," Big John started.

"You guys love Jerry, don't you?"

"Sure, Big John. Jerry's the best."

"He always plays with us, no matter what. He umpires our games for nothing. He practices with us. When kids or adults call me names, he sticks up for me," Nicky said.

"If something bad happened to Jerry, Big John, you have to tell me."

"You are going to have a big job ahead of you," Big John reported.

"If it is about Jerry, I will do whatever I have to do," Nicky said still waiting for his task.

"You are going to have to tell Gennaro," Big John replied.

"What? Tell Gennaro what?"

"Sometimes, Nicky, God teaches us strange lessons," Big John started.

"The good people are put on this earth for reasons that are bigger than life. Jerry is one of those people who are gifted."

"Big John, tell me. What happened to Jerry?"

"Nicky, Jerry had a heart attack."

"Oh, no, that can't be, not Jerry?" Nicky said as sheer panic shot through his voice.

"He's in a good hospital. Right, Big John? Can we go to the hospital to see him?"

"Nicky, Jerry suffered a bad heart attack. The hospital couldn't save him. He died on the football field."

"On the football field?" Nicky asked.

"The baseball team was working out, and they were playing touch football. And Jerry had a heart attack and died on the field. Paramedics couldn't save him."

Nicky started to cry uncontrollably.

Fear roared through his mind while the big question lingered.

"Who is going to tell Gennaro?"

Chapter 12
Dodging the Truth

This was Nicky's first real experience with death. There were always hints of people going to a "better place," but there was a gray area in this black-and-white world that kept Nicky far, far away from this particular tragedy. Sometimes Nicky didn't see certain people for a while, and the answer always was that they moved to a "better place." Nicky still had four living grandparents along with plenty of uncles and aunts. He really didn't know what to do about the blackest of bleak subjects

For these reasons, Nicky never walked past a funeral home. He steadfastly refused. He always crossed the street. He avoided certain parts of reality whenever he could. But now the enormous task Big John placed before him made him think.

Jerry's family was going to be crushed.

Gennaro was never going to be the same.

The kids were going to pick on Nicky again, and no one was going to stick up for him.

"You have to tell Gennaro," Big John said.

"You're his friend."

Nicky knew this task was difficult, but not impossible. This was truth facing him in the kisser. Certainly, Nicky couldn't lie to Gennaro, but he knew he didn't want to be the one to tell him about Jerry.

Big John knew this was a great lesson for Nicky. These growing pains would help him face the truth. Big John always understood how Nicky lied about everything when it came close to painful experiences.

"Hey, Nicky, I heard you got suspended from school for fighting and arguing with the principal," Big John commented, referring to the Great Chocolate Milk Conflict.

"It was just a little misunderstanding," Nicky lied.

"No, I heard this is the one that your father plans to kick your little behind and knock you out of commission for a few weeks," Big John replied.

"Why don't you tell me what happened? Were the kids calling you names again?" Big John finished and patiently waited for Nicky's response.

"The kids were fine. It's just that the principal yelled at me for slamming my thermos on the ground while we were getting in line for lunch," Nicky said, distorting the beginning of the painful truth.

"Why did your thermos hit the ground?" Big John asked, anxiously anticipating the next piece of the upcoming tall tale.

"I was mad that I only scored a ninety-eight on the reading test," Nicky responded, stretching the elasticity of truth a little further.

"You know how my mother wants me to do well in school, especially reading."

"Yeah, I know, Nicky. I wish I read as much as you did. But I heard you punched some of the kids in the class."

"That's not true. I was so upset about my thermos that I pushed them away when they tried to help me."

"Oh," Big John said, as he smiled. Nicky buried his head while rolling down the passenger side car window.

"I was worried the kids were still calling you names and harassing you."

"Nah, even Rusty is starting to be nice to me. I'm making lots of new friends since I can hear what people say better with my hearing aids."

"By the way, where are those hearing aids your father paid $500 apiece for?" Big John inquired.

"They're home. I wanted to rest the batteries so they would last longer in school," Nicky said, knowing full well the hearing devices were tucked away in his classroom desk in a dusty Ticonderoga pencil box.

There it was in a nutshell for Nicky. A simple story turned into seven lies. Little did Nicky know that Big John went to high school with Mrs. Anderson, and the second phone call she placed that afternoon wasn't to order a turkey sandwich on rye toast.

"Okay, now, listen to me. You won't need your hearing aids for this," Big John said.

"You are going to go tell Gennaro about Jerry."

"I can't do it. Jerry was his best pal."

"You have to do it," Big John implored. "This is what friends do for each other. You have to help him understand that this is God's will."

God's will?

"Is it God's will that I have this lip all mangled like this and then Jerry dies?" Nicky asked, changing the subject quickly.

"What did me and Jerry do to deserve this?"

Big John's brow furrowed and Nicky could tell he wasn't going to tell a joke.

"Who taught you to be so selfish?" Big John stated.

"This kid who would stick up for you died and all you're worried about is your lip. You've got to be kidding me."

Nicky started to cry again. For the third consecutive day, tears engulfed his face. He didn't understand this bad streak.

The game.

The endless name-calling.

And now, this great idol and protector was gone for good.

"I'm going to drop you off at Gennaro's house, and you tell him about Jerry. That's it—no excuses." Big John sternly implored.

"He would want to hear it from you. You are the oldest kid in the neighborhood."

"Okay, I guess I better do it. But maybe I should walk from here. I need time to think about what I'm going to say."

So, off Nicky went, but he knew he lied again. He knew he could never break the news to Gennaro. As he walked, he used the time to think of another lie. Nicky never liked lying to Big John or Gennaro, so he developed a scheme to go around the truth on this one.

"Hello, Mrs. Casserta, is Gennaro home?"

"Why, Nicky, isn't it awfully late to be out at night? Don't you have school tomorrow?"

Here started the great 56-lie streak.

"Yes, school," Nicky uttered his first lie.

"I won't take too long." The second fib slid out easily. Whenever Nicky talked it always took too long.

"I have a big science fair project I have to finish, Mrs. Casserta." The third lie grew from the others.

"I just have to tell Gennaro one thing about Jerry."

Four lies in ten seconds. Nicky was like butter. He was on a roll.

"Okay, Nicky, come on in."

There was Gennaro happier than happy could be, playing video games on the TV with a giant glass of Foxon Park cola to his left and his best friend entering on the right.

"Yo! What's up Nicky P.? It's almost eight o'clock. How did you get out of the house?"

"Well, I haven't gone home yet from work at Big John's. We just closed the store." Lie number five.

"I have to tell you something about Jerry," Nicky said.

"What did Jerry do? Hit another homer off the Rec Center?" Gennaro asked.

"Yeah, that's it," Nicky said, racking up number six.

"Let me tell you the story. Hofstra had a big game today against Dan Gallagher's Fordham University Rams, and we should have been there. Jerry did great. In the first at-bat, he doubled in two runs."

Nicky's streak continued, rolling off three quick ones to take the total number to nine.

Gennaro and Nicky knew more than most college players about college baseball. They researched the teams Jerry played. They wrote letters to the schools requesting media guides and other facts from every sports information office they could reach.

They knew about New York Tech's hard-hitting outfield and coach Bob Hirschfield's greatest victory, a 3–2 upset win in April over defending NCAA Division I champion, Rice University.

Gennaro and Nicky knew St. John's University's starting rotation, the set-up men, and the closer. They called Jerry to tell him about the Red Storm's highly regarded reliever, Mike Rozema, who pitched in three games the past weekend at Pittsburgh. Jerry probably wouldn't face him in Tuesday's night game in Queens.

The boys were publicity agents, advance scouts, and Jerry's biggest fans neatly rolled into two elementary school bodies.

"The second time up, he dragged a bunt down the first baseline for another hit," Nicky said, hitting double digits at ten lies and counting.

"But, Nicky, I saw Mr. Gambardella at the park," Gennaro said. "He never misses one of Jerry's games."

"Oh, they just put this game on the schedule," Nicky said. "It's a makeup from one of last week's rainouts. Jerry probably didn't tell him because of the short notice."

"So, anyway, Jerry flied out deep to center in his third at-bat, and then Hofstra was losing 7–4 in the bottom of the seventh and Jerry crushed a grand slam." Unfortunately, Nicky's lies were the only grand slam of the day as he approached 56 in the next few minutes.

"Really, that's great. I know Jerry's going to make it to the Big Leagues and give us autographs, baseball cards, and tickets."

This made Nicky's job that much more demanding. Gennaro beamed with pride. Gennaro's face gushed with so many happy emotions about any success Jerry achieved.

"Gennaro, there's just one thing. Jerry might have injured himself during the game," Nicky said.

"What happened? It's probably his left knee. The one he hurt in that football game his senior year against Montville when he ran over Bill Romano twice," Gennaro said.

Nicky hesitated. The truth rallied to reach his lips. With the lie streak accomplished and in the bag, Nicky dug down deep for an ounce of courage that outmuscled the pain.

"You're right, Gennaro. It's the knee again. He may be out for remainder of the season."

As a tiny morsel of truth escaped Nicky's lips, the streak ended, but he couldn't start a string of reality.

"Jerry's okay, though. He's resting. He is in a better place."

"I'm going to call him on his phone," Gennaro said. "He gave me his number."

"You probably better not," Nicky said. "He's definitely sleeping."

"How do you know, Nicky."

"I was at Big John's. How else do you find out about this stuff?"

"Nicky?" Mrs. Casserta interrupted. "I think Big John's car is outside. Is he giving you a ride home?"

"Oh, I guess. Yes, he is," Nicky said. "Thank you again, Mrs. Casserta, for letting me hang out for a little while with Gennaro on a school night."

"It's all right. Now, make sure you tell your mother and father I said, 'Hello.'"

"Sure will, Mrs. Casserta, I sure will."

"Wow," Nicky thought. That was harder than Nicky ever expected, but the next great challenge awaited in the brown Chevrolet station wagon just fifteen feet away.

"I knew you would still be here," Big John started.

"Did you tell Gennaro about Jerry? How did he take it?"

"He took it better than I thought he would," Nicky replied.

"I'm glad you told him. I don't think Gennaro should find out about it in that stupid *New Haven Journal*. They don't care about local sports anymore."

"Yeah, it was hard, but I told him," Nicky said.

"Good, it's about time you started to learn about dealing with reality."

"Nicky, do you think your father's home yet?" the big man added.

"I don't know. What's today? Friday? If it's past eight, he should be home. If not, he'll be there soon. You can bet your life on it, Big John," Nicky said.

"Good, but I'd rather bet yours. I've got to talk to your father about making you go to the wake and the funeral."

This was a prime example of how pain treated Nicky. Just when he thought the healing process started further bouts of future misery ensued. To Nicky, Jerry's death was like another surgery.

The healing was much more excruciating than the cuts.

Chapter 13
Life after Death

Despite Nicky's curiosity with death, he anticipated the inevitable unbearable pain. He never thrived during moments of separation and change. Every time Nicky's grandfather, Nicola Palmieri, departed America to return to Italy, he cried the length of the entire ride to Idlewild Airport.

But Jerry wasn't returning. He couldn't come back. His ticket to Heaven was one-way. Only airlines printed roundtrip tickets to the sky.

Nicky contemplated this and much more. He started to think about other kids in his life. He remembered his friend Vincent with the purple lips. When Nicky was eight years old, he used to visit his grandfather's house.

Vincent was the next-door neighbor, Mr. Mezzanotte's grandson. Everyone told him that, since Vincent was inflicted with a terrible heart defect, Nicky could not run around. This would hurt Vincent.

For years, Vincent and Nicky played. They played board games. They played Italian card games, scobe and briscola. They shared Italian pastries. They were good friends.

Then one day Nicky saw Vincent's father's Cadillac, and he raced to the door to ask if Vincent could come out and play. Suddenly, Grandpa Palmieri, who was one of the better soccer players in the Italian army, hurdled bushes faster than Carl Lewis and sprinted to the door to stop Nicky.

"Nicola, come over here," Grandpa Palmieri said. "Vincent is not here. He went to Italy for an operation. He will be back soon."

Every time Nicky visited, he would look for the brown Cadillac and politely ask if Vincent had come back. The answer was always the same.

"The doctors are still trying to help Vincenzo," Mr. Palmieri said. "He is in a better place to fix his heart."

Nicky's parents always tried to help their son. Mrs. Palmieri couldn't always find words to help Nicky. She thought that, if Nicky saw other kids with greater problems, it would make her son realize that his lip wasn't so bad.

To help Nicky understand other children's setbacks, Mr. Palmieri took Nicky to see Fabrizio once a week on Mondays. This young boy suffered from severe cerebral palsy.

Fabrizio couldn't play any sports, and he couldn't walk. He couldn't speak too well, either. Fabrizio spent his short ten-year life in a wheelchair. Suddenly one day, the visits stopped along with his existence in Nicky's life.

"How come we're not going to see Fabrizio this week?" Nicky asked.

"Fabrizio went back to Italy with his mother and father," Mr. Palmieri said. "He is in a better place."

"Like Vincent, Dad," Nicky inquired.

"Yes, just like Vincent."

"I want to go to Italy someday and see Vincent and Fabrizio again."

"We will go to Italy one day, and you will see everybody," Mr. Palmieri promised. Italy, Nicky remembered from the way his father and grandfather spoke of it, must be Heaven.

This background knowledge prepared Nicky for the worst.

He knew Jerry wasn't going to Italy. This was good.

But Nicky didn't know where Jerry was going.

All he knew was that he wasn't around anymore, and this was worse than a cleft palate.

Nicky knew or believed that the operation would come where every nagging problem would disappear—the bumps, the scars, the humiliation, the fear, the name-calling, and Rusty Alves. But memories of pain were different from the loss of people.

They never left Nicky. He remembered everything—every snicker, every funny look from little first graders, every whisper, every finger pointing, every laugh.

With Jerry's death, Nicky started to realize that, in some strange way, life resembled reality. Life wasn't all about the dreams.

Dreams had always been abundant in Nicky's life. Making the Big Leagues was a dream. Having a normal lip and face was a dream. Walking around town without people turning their heads was yet another dream, and listening to the sweet sounds of a stereo could only be imagined. The cleft plate even made eating corn on the cob or biting into a green apple dreams, too.

Bringing Jerry back was another—and definitely impossible—dream.

"Big John, how did a nineteen-year-old superstar athlete like Jerry have a heart attack?" Nicky asked.

"All the doctors will say is that Jerry had an enlarged heart," Big John answered.

"These doctors are funny, Big John. They go to school for ten and fifteen years, and I know just as much as they do. And I'm in sixth grade," Nicky added.

"How's that, Nicky?" Big John replied.

"Well, they said Jerry has an enlarged heart. Heck, I knew that Jerry had a big heart the whole time. He's the best.

"These doctors are full of it," Nicky added.

"Never mind. You just better go to the wake, Nicky,"

"I'm going right after school."

Nicky truly didn't know what to do. He couldn't bear the thought of seeing Jerry this way, especially in front of people and, even worse, strangers.

Nicky saw his mother writing a card, so he decided to go to DiNapola's Card Shop. Nicky looked for the biggest card, but he decided against it. He didn't know what to write.

On the walk to DiNapola's Funeral Home, Nicky thought about what to say.

"How are you Mr. and Mrs. Gambardella?" That was more embarrassing than smart, Nicky contemplated. The more he thought about what to say, fear dug itself deeper into Nicky's mind until finally he approached the room and walked away.

He walked faster and faster. Up Circle Street and down to Ocean Avenue. When he finally reached Richmond Avenue, it was a flat-out sprint home to change and go to work at Big John's.

"Did you go see Jerry?" Big John asked.

"Sure."

"How was it?"

"Sad."

"Were any other kids there?'

"No."

The lies were so much easier for Nicky. He figured one or two hours in confession at St. John Vianney's cleared the whole mess up, and he could start over. This was Catholicism's greatest attribute. One could screw up the entire week, say a few prayers, and start over again.

Religion was like a bad baseball game—a couple errors or strikeouts are simply forgotten by the time the next game started. Catholicism was the perfect religion for Nicky Palmieri.

Nicky, however, started to feel terrible when Big John explained things to him as though he knew Nicky never went in the building.

"You know, One Cell, people have wakes so you can honor the dead and show your respect.

"You don't have to talk to people. You just go in kneel at the casket, say a prayer, and move on. Whisper 'Hello' to a few people, and get out of there. Any idiot can do that."

This made Nicky think hard and long. Tomorrow was Jerry's funeral. No way could he deal with that.

He thought about it for hours.

"I've got to honor Jerry. I've got to do something."

He stared at the ceiling in his room until finally a light clicked at about 2:22 A.M.

Nicky scrambled out of bed, put on his favorite jeans, and packed his baseball uniform along with other items in a bag. He crawled out his bedroom window and raced to DiNapola's.

Out of breath and sweating profusely, Nicky grabbed his father's favorite screwdriver out of the bag. He quickly whittled away at the wood on a back door until he could pry the lock open.

Nicky maneuvered through the dark, dank building. Finally, he found Jerry's open casket. Nicky reeled off every prayer he ever knew. When he was finished, he emptied his bag.

For good luck, he took his uniform and brushed it gently on Jerry's hand. Then he grabbed a baseball, his favorite glove—a genuine Rawlings "Heart of the Hide"—and his cleanest New York Yankees' hat signed by Mickey Mantle.

He quickly found strategic spots for these things inside the casket. Nicky rattled off a few more prayers and raced home in the darkest of mornings.

This was better than a card. Nicky remembered from school that in ancient Egypt the pharaohs took their money, food, drinks, pets, and other worldly possessions with them to the afterlife.

Jerry was certainly more important than King Tut or Hatshepsut. It made perfect sense to equip his friend for the afterlife. People like Jerry were much more vital to life than the history of a 5,000-year-old Egyptian king who made his mark by killing and stealing money from his own people. Jerry gave Nicky everything he wanted. Giving Jerry his glove for baseball in Heaven was the least he could do.

Arriving home at any unusual time, Nicky received the usual welcoming committee of one, Mr. Palmieri. This day was no different, and he didn't look too happy.

"Where were you, sonny boy?"

"I went to DiNapola's to say good-bye to Jerry."

"Aren't you coming with me to the funeral?" Mr. Palmieri said.

"No, Dad, I don't think I can take it."

"You are going to go to school?'

Nicky knew the names and teasing were much easier to deal with than this mess, but maybe Rusty Alves would lay off for one day at least.

Then again, maybe not.

"We are going to learn more about ancient Egypt," Nicky said.

"Did you know that the rich people took their money with them to an afterlife?"

"That's good. Now that I know I won't have to leave you any of my money, you can get your little behind back into bed where you belong," Mr. Palmieri chuckled.

The morning walk to school wasn't easy. Nicky strolled past Jerry's house on 101 Kelsey Avenue. Gennaro didn't speak one word until they arrived at school.

"Nicky, I don't feel like going to school today."

"Where are we going to go?" Nicky said.

"If the truant officer spots us, we'll be in big trouble."

"Don't worry about that drunk," Gennaro said as the duo made a 180-degree turn and a mad dash toward home.

"I've got an idea to honor Jerry."

Chapter 14

Hearts Galore

Gennaro was stronger than Nicky. He learned about the tragedy on the WTNH–TV Channel 8 morning news. Gennaro forgave Nicky's lies because he knew he wouldn't be able to do it, either.

Since he started hanging around with Jerry, Gennaro ate, slept, and breathed loyalty. He attended every minute of the wake, and he never left. He sat in the front row and didn't even cry one tear.

Gennaro was tougher than anyone would have ever guessed. He believed in Jesus, and with that he always said that Jerry's time blessed everyone who knew him. For Gennaro, honoring Jerry was simple.

But strangely enough, he couldn't attend the funeral. That was way too much. His parents went with the Palmieris, so no one was home.

Nicky and Gennaro went to work on their plan. They were going to honor Jerry at the friendly confines of Painter's Park.

The place was any kid's sports sanctuary. It was a vast, expansive playground with five baseball diamonds. It featured pristine tennis courts, water fountains, two basketball courts, swing sets, and restrooms. It was a place of freedom, and it was all the Kelsey Avenue Crew had. It was everything.

In the early 1900s, William Painter donated the land to the city of West Haven. The kids didn't know—nor did they care—what his role was in West Haven. They were just overjoyed that he lived on Kelsey Avenue, which paralleled Richmond Avenue, and that he donated the land to the city for recreation use.

The park was empty this sad day. Even mean old Mr. Schotta gave the work crews the day off to attend the funeral. In fact, almost everyone in West Haven was at the funeral.

Two busloads from Hofstra University drove into West Haven. Many people from various walks of life arrived. Even parents of the Hofstra players drove ninety miles to honor Jerry. There must have been more than 2,000 people at St. John Vianney's Church. Every store in West Haven closed for the day. Mayor Johnson even shut down city hall.

"Come on we have got to hurry to get this stuff ready," Gennaro said about his plan. The boys went to their major work. They cut, pasted, cut, and pasted again for two hours.

"Hurry, Nicky, you slow poke. We haven't got much time," Gennaro said. "This has to be ready before the funeral procession moves down Kelsey Avenue."

"I'm almost done. This is the last one."

"Okay, great. Let's go."

The boys raced to the park and grabbed piles of dirt from the top field, placed it in the wheelbarrow and went to work.

Finally, seconds before the first car climbed the hill at Kelsey Avenue, Gennaro's tribute was complete. The procession slowed to a crawl as it passed the top field at Painter's Park. Heads turned toward Gennaro and Nicky's creation. Some of the cars stopped and people stood to view the work.

Everyone was amazed at the scene. There were red hearts everywhere. They were decorated with a baseball in the middle and a "22" on each one. They were taped to people's houses and decorated lawns.

Gennaro sprinkled dirt from where Jerry played first base on the hearts. The ones on the grass needed more, so the gentle ocean breeze from Long Island Sound wouldn't blow them away.

Big John and Mr. Palmieri, who served as pallbearers, knew exactly what was going on as their car drove past the field.

"Those hearts represent the home runs Jerry hit at that field," Big John tearfully said.

"Look, Joe," Big John said to Mr. Palmieri. "They are only between the right field line and the Kessler's house. This is unbelievable. I wonder who did this."

Nicky and Gennaro tried to duck before they were spotted, but it was too late. Shaking fingers meant to get back to school and after grabbing a couple of sandwiches, they signed in late, knowing they had done an excellent job.

Chapter 15
The Aftermath

One thing about Nicky and the rest of the Kelsey Avenue Crew was that they were amazingly resilient. The day after the funeral, the boys slipped into their routines without missing a beat.

It wasn't disrespectful.

It was simply life.

Nicky and the boys knew more ways to honor their hero and continued to do so.

On this one block between Kelsey and Richmond Avenues, there were more than twenty kids—enough to make two baseball teams, two football squads, and four basketball teams.

Nicky and Gennaro orchestrated the entire crew to write "22" on everything they owned. You did this if you wanted to be part of this team because Painter's Park was the place to be.

As soon as the last whisper of pencil lead touched the homework papers, the Kelsey Avenue Crew went off to the park. No one ever wanted to be left out.

"Be home in time for dinner," the curfew limit echoed, as the kids left their houses for the daily parade to Painter's Park. Since Nicky lived the farthest away, he and his brother, Ralph, always led the charge accompanied by a stolen shopping cart from the local supermarket parking lot. Kids heard the metal cart rattle as the wheels rolled along the sidewalk cracks. One house at a time, kids emptied onto the streets.

First there was John Antonio, or John A. This was not a negative nickname, but an identifier of necessity. Since there were so many Italian families, Giovanni in Italy and John in America were the favorite names of the day. The kids used the first letter of the last names to identify themselves among the bevy of Johns. There was John Ferrante or John F., John Garamone or John G., John Sullivan or John S., and John Keegan or John K.

This puzzled Nicky somewhat.

"Hey, Dad, how come most the kids around here have the same names as their father's and I don't?"

"Let me tell you something, sonny boy," Giuseppe Palmieri said. "When your mother yells, 'Giuseppe, it's time for bed, the last person I want to see in there is you."

Nicky wouldn't really comprehend the joke until he was twenty-two, but understanding his father's wit and wisdom clearly required greater intelligence than any sixth grader could muster.

Obviously, the first name followed by the surname initial became a sign that you were okay and "in" with the "in" crowd. Nicky always saw to it that everyone wasn't left out.

Johnny K. was the next player to rumble onto the streets.

John F., who lived on Painter Avenue, raced from a backyard.

Johnny G. and his brother, Bill G., gravitated to the sweet sound of cracking wooden bats against the metal cage.

Gennaro bolted from his home, joining the Kelsey Avenue Crew as the cart strolled to the field while gloves and bats poured into the wire basket.

The kids took turns pushing the cart. When it finally reached the field, the Kesslers— Mark, Bobby, and Lou—emerged. Others appeared, popping out of the woods into their field of dreams. These woods brought friendships that lasted a lifetime.

"What are we going to do today?" became the stupid question of the moment.

"Let's see we have eighteen players," Nicky started. "Let's throw the gloves in the middle, and Gennaro you separate them into two piles. Those will be the teams."

One pile had nine and another had eight.

"Who didn't throw their glove in?" Gennaro inquired.

"Not me."

"Mine's in," John G. said.

"Where's your Heart of the Hide, Nicky?" Mark K. asked, referring to Nicky's prize possession that Big John gave him for winning Battle of the Books at school.

"Oh, I must have forgotten it at home," Nicky said. "I'll just borrow Gennaro's today."

Gennaro and everyone else knew something was up.

Nicky's never went anywhere without his glove. That Rawlings mitt cost more than $200. It was the best money could buy. This was the glove worn by many players in the Big Leagues. Mickey Mantle used a Heart of the Hide, as did Reggie Jackson, Ozzie Smith, Lou Piniella, Jim "Catfish" Hunter, Goose Gossage, and George Brett.

Nicky's two all-time favorite Italian players, Rico Petrocelli and Rocky Colavito, also used the Heart of the Hide glove.

Nicky owned a piece of a baseball world that he wished and hoped to be a part of, along with many millions of American boys. A Heart of the Hide was the top of the line glove, and it was made in America, not overseas.

The mitt was Nicky's pride and joy. When Big John gave him the glove two years earlier, Nicky spent two days showing everyone around town his prized possession. Even his godfather, Uncle Nick marveled at the glove's distinguished features.

The glove had a special "T" model web, and Nicky let everyone take turns using the glove. The inside was softer than a pillow. No matter how hard someone threw the ball, you never felt the sting. It was made of genuine cowhide leather, and it was the best there was. And it wasn't on the field.

Gennaro, forever fearless, popped the big question.

"Nicky, what's going on?" he asked incredulously.

"That glove is always with you. There is no way you lost it."

"I just can't find it," Nicky lied.

"Tell the truth, Nicky. Did your dad take it away because of the Great Chocolate Milk Conflict?"

"No, I just misplaced it in my room."

"I'm sure you will find it. That glove is the best."

But Nicky knew the glove was in a better place. It was with Jerry, and there was a game going on in Heaven. Nicky lived comfortably with that thought, but not with the thought of explaining the missing Heart of the Hide to his father or Big John.

The game was ready to start, and Nicky stopped everyone.

"We need to have a moment of silence for Jerry. They do this on television a lot of the times before the Big League games."

Nicky remembered a rain-delay tape on television when New York Yankee great Thurman Munson died in a plane crash. He always watched the Yankees' games, and Munson was one of Nicky's favorites because of the way he played. Munson's birthday was also June 7, the same as Nicky's.

"Then we are going to have the first pitch with every player on the field except at first base and center field where Jerry played."

The Kelsey Avenue Crew bowed their heads while the moment of silence lasted two minutes. Wiping tears from his eyes, Archie Sagnella, Frank Camp, and the rest of the park department crew couldn't believe what they were witnessing.

Surely, no matter where he was, Jerry Gambardella Jr. did.

He was in a better place.

Chapter 16
Rules We All Must Live By

For the first time, Nicky didn't care whether he won or lost this game. This latest real-life experience taught him invaluable lessons. Nicky started learning to enjoy the sunshine of life.

Playing the game meant more than the outcome even though he lived by one of New York Yankees' great Billy Martin credos—"If nobody cared about winning they wouldn't keep score."

The boys played the game they loved so much anyway. They played hard, but their first ride on the emotional roller coaster calmed everyone. The first nine innings served the boys as a tune-up for the next encounter with the Crusty Rusty Alves' All-Stars.

When Rusty lived with his mother, he didn't look too well. He wore filthy clothes, clearly stained with remnants of yesterday's meals. Thus, Gennaro aptly dubbed the evil foe, "Crusty Rusty."

"He's a slob," Gennaro reported.

"A homeless person could survive for a week on the stuff off his shirt," he laughed.

"He probably hasn't changed his tighty whities in two weeks. His clothes are real crusty."

This was one of many shots the Kelsey Avenue Crew hurled against their villain, but they never dared utter these words to his scrunched-up freckled face. This was one of the unwritten rules the Kelsey Avenue Crew lived by. There were other simple rules, but you always knew where to draw the line.

More rules for sure.

Some labeled them rules of engagement. They called them rules for survival. These were real-life Darwinisms.

They weren't into sundials because what do you do on cloudy days? After a couple of spoons and brooms snapped on the kids' rumps when they were late for dinner, they attached themselves toward the sure bet.

The White Collars were the guys in West Haven who only got their hands dirty when they touched the mailbox on a rainy day. They sported perfectly manicured nails to match their perfect haircuts. They could afford landscapers and maids. They were the clean-cut All-Americans of the town, but best of all, they were meticulous.

They featured the same mannerisms and behaviors—everyday. When it was time for dinner, you'd watch for Mr. Farrell's silver Mercedes to roll past Painter's Park at the same time everyday.

Five minutes after six.

Everyday.

Just like clockwork. It never failed.

Never.

The Blue Collars, however, lived by different rules. If any of the Kelsey Avenue Crew weren't home in time for dinner, they didn't eat. After a long day at school and a couple hours at the baseball field, even the meals kids despised the most tasted like Big Macs from McDonald's. These children learned to respect others and appreciate this great life. They made sure they were home on time, or else the punishments were severe.

The rules were easy. Everyone had a job. One person was in charge of silverware and glasses. One person was on the plates and napkins. And everyone was in charge of cleanup detail.

The punitive responses were a little more difficult.

"Nicholas, why isn't the table ready for your father?" Mrs. Palmieri asked.

"The game ran a little late, Ma. We are practicing for the big game with Rusty."

"I don't care about this dumb feud you have with this kid," Mrs. Palmieri snapped. "You have responsibilities here, or else there will be no baseball game for the rest of your life.

"By the way, where is your glove? You never go anywhere without it. I haven't seen it for a few days."

"Gennaro is borrowing it. He likes that mitt a whole lot," Nicky lied with a tinge of truth.

This glove issue was surely going to be a problem.

"Maybe I should tell Mom the truth and see if she can help me out," Nicky quietly contemplated. As soon as he completed that thought, Nicky heard the creaking sound of the garage door. This meant that Mr. Palmieri was home. The odds of winning a Powerball lottery jackpot were far greater than Mr. Palmieri's understanding of this situation with the glove would be, considering its value was twelve to fourteen hours of work. As unreasonable as the punishment appeared for dinnertime tardiness, Nicky knew that another story was necessary to explain the glove.

Nicky went to his great bag of tricks. He waved a wand and pulled out his change-the-subject routine.

"Ma, what's for dinner? It really smells great."

"Never mind, just get to work and set the table. I hear your father coming up the stairs."

Nicky rarely crossed the line to find out if his parents upheld their word. Every game for Nicky meant the world. To miss one game was like serving a life sentence. This threat kept Nicky punctual every time.

This glove issue needed to be handled later. Now, for those other times in which Nicky knew his father worked overtime, more of the White Collars never let him or any of the other kids down.

For the 7 P.M. dinner bell, Mr. Schmidt came through with flying colors. Mr. Swan worked the 6:30 shift, and Mr. Pastore rang the 6 P.M. silent bell. There were no traffic jams or rush hours in West Haven. The great rush was the mad dash home where kids dreamed they were Jackie Robinson stealing home plate. They sometimes envisioned themselves wearing a St. Louis Cardinals or Oakland A's uniform so they could be Lou Brock or Ricky Henderson on his way to second.

It was rush minute.

Sometimes there were ten to fifteen kids sprinting down the street to beat their fathers home or face the wrath of a wooden broom or genuine leather belt. Track stars these kids were not. Survival experts—they surely were.

In this neighborhood, dinner was a daily early-evening meeting of the entire family. There were no excuses. They had to be there on time, or they didn't eat. There was no "I'm not hungry, now. I'll eat later." These kids ate the prepared meal and didn't complain. No one knew if it was the Italian way, the Irish way, the Polish way, or the German way.

But it was mom and dad's way. It was that simple.

That's what those future Big Leaguers concerned themselves with if they wished to eat. And for Nicky and some of his crowd, understanding these table manners helped them stay healthy, happy, and walking.

Those were unwritten, nonnegotiable rules. They didn't have a say when they were written, nor were they consulted when amendments were made by the house.

Kids certainly could exercise their first amendment right to free speech. That's when moms or dads started exercising their arms or legs to chase them down and teach them about a process that heard no appeals.

This was law and order at its finest.

This was West Haven, Connecticut.

Chapter 17
Baseball is Heaven

Mr. Palmieri taught Nicky many valuable lessons, but the best one included the benefits of hard work. Even when school was in session for those 180 days, Nicky worked two jobs.

In the morning, he and his brother, Ralph, delivered papers, *The New Haven Journal*. They shared the forty-five-customer route handed down from Lou Kessler. Nicky worked Kelsey and Painter Avenues while Ralph handled the Richmond Avenue portion so his older brother avoided unnecessary contact with Rusty Alves.

The brothers started at approximately 6 A.M. and were finished in less than forty-five minutes. Nicky hated the coldness of the morning air. He sprinted on his side of the route to improve his speed for baseball. Ralph also possessed great speed and did likewise. They raced each other to see who would finish first.

Upon the insistence of Big John, Nicky's second job started after dinner on school days. He worked for one to two hours a day cleaning around the deli. Nicky swept the floors, sidewalks, and driveways. He emptied garbage pails and, once in a while, helped peel potatoes for Big John's legendary German potato salad. Big John paid him two dollars per hour, and Nicky saved every dollar, neatly rolling and storing it in an old-time Tootsie Roll container.

His time at Big John's was never a job. It was therapy and a mental health break, craftily jammed into one- or two-hour sessions. The best part was that Big John, even though he never went to college, owned every necessary skill that applied to all the degrees.

A master's degree in social work couldn't match Big John's real-life experiences. Big John had information about law and knew how the courts were too lenient. He ran the city and the world with an iron fist. The code of Hammurabi was no match. An eye for an eye was soft punishment for Big John.

Big John also specialized in marriage counseling.

"You said 'I do' now go home and be a good husband," Big John offered whenever some tired old loser registered a complaint against family life.

For religious guidance, too, Big John's Deli was the place. Big John knew how to solve the problems of the Catholic Church from Boston to Boise.

"Bring back the nuns with the sticks," he said time and again. "A couple of solid whacks on the hands and the rump, and then watch these kids today. They'll learn to stop lying. And maybe when they become adults, they'll respect and trust the good Lord, too."

Nicky knew this was the time. Maybe this was the time to talk to Big John about the missing glove. Nicky knew he had to give it his best shot.

"Hey, Big John, is there really baseball in Heaven?" Nicky asked, as he inched closer to the truth of a possible difficult subject matter.

"Sure, there damn well better be because at my age, you never know when I'm scheduled to pitch," Big John laughed.

"Seriously, Big John. I put some stuff in Jerry's casket the night before the funeral like the ancient Egyptians.

"I hope he can use the stuff I left him," Nicky said perilously touching the fine line between truth and a buried Rawlings mitt.

"What did you do, Nicky?"

"I gave Jerry my Yankees' hat, my entire collection of Yankees' cards, and a couple of game balls from the Little League season. I figured he could use them in Heaven."

"When did you do that?"

"I snuck out of the house early in the morning and broke into DiNapola's," Nicky answered.

"The security alarms didn't go off?"

"No, I had Gennaro fib a little to Mr. DiNapola when he stayed to help him shut down the funeral parlor.

"Gennaro didn't activate the alarm, and I was able to break the lock on the back door. Nobody knew I was there until now."

"You are lucky you didn't get caught. Your father would have killed you this time for sure," Big John commented.

"I didn't get caught by the police, but Dad was waiting for me when I got home."

"Did he get mad?" Big John asked.

"No, I told him I went to see Jerry, and he didn't even bat an eye. It was unbelievable."

"That's because you told him the truth, One Cell. One day you will figure it out."

"Where's the glove I gave you? Let's go outside and play catch."

The impromptu meeting with truth quickly ended.

"I left it home," Nicky fibbed.

"You left the glove home?" Big John said with great curiosity.

"I heard you guys had a game today, and you were the only one without a glove. Is that true?"

This truth thing was starting to bother Nicky.

"Every time I try to leave this truth business, it keeps pulling me back in," Nicky whispered to himself in *Godfather* mode.

"I borrowed Gennaro's today," Nicky blurted.

"Well, let's have a catch. I have an extra glove in the car."

Big John was always prepared. Amazingly, he always had the answers to everything. But Nicky knew in his heart of hearts that he had to tell Big John about putting the mitt in the casket.

"Big John, can I tell you something?"

"Sure, Nicky, go ahead."

"What do you think Heaven is like?"

"Heaven, Nicky," Big John began, "should be filled with hundreds of baseball diamonds with green grass. Everybody should have brand new uniforms, wooden Louisville Slugger bats, and mitts like the one I gave you," Big John added, waiting to see Nicky's reaction.

"YYYYeah, tha—, tha—, tha—, tha—, that would be gr—, gr—, gr—, great, Big John," Nicky stammered.

"The games will go on all day," Big John continued. "But you have to take turns working on the field, cutting the grass, and putting the lines down. People will paint the wooden dugouts and fix the fences."

"The games will be pure and simple. Everyone who crosses the pearly gates can play and have fun—not like these overpaid jerks with high-powered, money-grubbing agents we watch on TV today."

"Yeah," Nicky added. "There's no domes or artificial turf. Green grass and new baseballs, pearls, the real white shiny ones they only use on game days. They probably have the façade of the old Yankee Stadium on every field. That sounds fun to me, but I don't want to go there yet."

"That's right, One Cell," Big John said, figuring out where the missing glove rested. "You have a lot of things to do. One day, you have to give back to this great game. You can't keep taking. You always have to give back."

"What do you mean by 'give back?'"

"What I mean is that you must try to help others enjoy baseball, too," Big John answered.

"If you really love this game," the big man added. "You have to dedicate some of your time coaching and teaching kids. This is what keeps the dream alive."

"What's the dream, Big John?"

"The dream, Nicky, is a part of baseball that keeps all of us young. First, the dream starts with making it to the Big Leagues. But then the day comes when you realize maybe baseball should be just a game and not a profession."

"How do you find that out, Big John?" Nicky asked.

"Well, even if you're Mickey Mantle or Joe DiMaggio, the day comes when someone tells you that you're not good enough anymore. Everybody gets cut eventually. It's just a matter of how long this part of the dream lasts and where you are when it ends."

Big John took another swig of his coffee and prophesized a little more.

"The dream is what keeps people watching games. The dream allows us to watch a kid's game or one at Yankee Stadium and hope that we can win the game with a big hit or a big play. The dream is that even through coaching or watching that we will see someone or help a player reach the Big Leagues," Big John continued.

"The dream is that one day we can reach out and touch the Big Leagues whether we are in it or someone we helped makes it."

"You remember what Jerry did, don't you?"

"Sure, Big John," Nicky said. "He played with us every chance he had. He was the best."

"Do you remember Jerry's attitude toward baseball?" Big John asked.

"Sure, Jerry dedicated everything to baseball. He worked harder than anyone else I ever knew."

"He would always take time to work with us on our throwing, hitting, or anything else we would ask," Nicky continued as tears slowly trickled down his face. "Jerry would even stop what he was doing to play with us."

"That's the dream, Nicky. Everything Jerry did is a small part of that dream," Big John said.

"You miss Jerry, Nicky?"

"Like you wouldn't believe, Big John," Nicky admitted stepping near the painful truth one more time. "I just pray nobody else close to me dies. I don't think I could...."

"You have to handle it, Nicky," Big John interrupted. "This is how life works. We're not going be around all the time to protect you from reality. Remember, there has to be baseball in Heaven. God wouldn't have it any other way."

And Nicky truly believed that this was something in a dream that would happen besides a fixed cleft palate.

Chapter 18

Broken Glass and More Lies

After playing catch with Big John for twenty minutes, Nicky thought about many things on the mile walk home. He knew that someday either Big John or his father needed to know about the glove. Luckily, with his birthday around the corner, that day wasn't today.

Inside Nicky's house there was one guy who ruled over everyone and could certainly scare Judge Judy.

Sometimes, Mr. Palmieri talked about some mischief Nicky, his brother, and sisters were involved in. Then, somehow, someway, Big John used his irascible, booming voice to soothe matters.

Whenever Giuseppe Palmieri walked across the street to visit, Nicky opened the windows no matter how cold it was to hear Big John's reaction. He could hear him a mile away, and never did he wish to miss a syllable.

One of Nicky's major problems was in his own backyard. He and his crew failed to realize that baseballs don't bounce too well off glass windows. It was something he probably should have figured out by his teenage years, but what kid thinks that he is going to throw one away or, even worse, foul a pitch into a small kitchen window.

Since Mr. Palmieri was an outstanding cabinetmaker and magician with wood, he also served as the most resourceful person anyone knew. He turned scrap wood into additions on people's houses. Whenever he manufactured cabinets for a neighbor or a friend, he amazed people at how little wood he wasted.

He even built cabinets for fun. He taught Nicky about how a passion for work was really not work at all. You just enjoy creating, and then you hope that people appreciate your work. Mr. Palmieri even built the cabinets for the concession stand at Bailey Field, where most of the Kelsey Avenue Crew played in the organized football and baseball leagues.

Nicky realized that his father, who never played one inning of baseball, gave back to the great game in his own way. Nicky knew that maybe his father understood about the glove, but he never quite pulled the trigger of truth.

Mr. Palmieri decided to make his contribution one day when Nicky had a game. Mr. Palmieri was hanging out at the concession stand and talking to Big John when he noticed that the cabinets were dilapidated. Mr. Palmieri always looked at the work.

"This must have been made by a shoemaker. I could do it better," Mr. Palmieri said.

Those comments about the shoemaker were his magic words. Then Big John shot back, "Then why don't you show us how much better you can make cabinets, big shot?"

"Come down next week, and I'll show you some real cabinets."

So, with the challenge issued in full view, Mr. Palmieri went to work.

The next day his reliable 1976 powder blue Dodge Station wagon arrived at his customary Richmond Avenue resting spot filled to the brim with wood. Neighbors saw Nicky and his brother unloading the wood, former trees from some far-away California forest, knowing hard work was around the corner and that they couldn't escape. Whenever Mr. Palmieri put his mind to a project, the whole neighborhood knew chores were in store.

Kids always make the best gofers.

"Go for the wood."

"Go for the screwdrivers."

"Go for the broom and clean up the mess."

All during this exercise Nicky and his brother heard words of wisdom echo like no others.

"Study in school so you don't have to work like this your whole life."

"Read those books in your room," Mr. Palmieri always said.

The directions were simple. However, when you are close to twelve, playtime always became the better option.

These cabinets were going to be perfect because Mr. Palmieri never settled for anything less. He refused to take money for the work or the supplies. He loved his craft and enjoyed showing people what he could create. Mr. Palmieri loved giving and giving back.

For seven consecutive nights, Mr. Palmieri worked on the new furniture and cabinetry for the Bailey Field concession stand. He worked until 11 P.M. because these cabinets would be in the building by the time he promised.

And they were.

"Hey, Joe, look at these new cabinets," Big John commented. "Who made these, some carpenter?"

"I'm a cabinet maker, wise guy. I have skills. Who do you think made these? Look at these cabinets. This is no job by a shoemaker, heh?"

The cabinets and countertops shone in the old brick building. People couldn't help but comment on the craftsmanship and the precision of Mr. Palmieri's timing and work.

"I told you I could do it in a week. This is good work, eh? Big John?"

"Yeah, yeah," Big John snapped back. "How about some of these cabinets for my house?"

With that Mr. Palmieri started chasing Big John around the building, laughing the whole way. He never asked anything from the Babe Ruth or Midget Football Leagues that used the concession stand. Mr. Palmieri always visited and inspected the concession stand to make sure people took care of the cabinets. They had to be cleaned daily or else he went crazy.

When he visited the cabinets once and spotted a speck of dirt, he cleaned the cabinets himself and complained each step of the way. Then he did it week after week.

Clean and complain.

Complain and clean.

It was the Italian way.

It was always fun to watch and listen to the side comments until Nicky and his brother— and anyone else within earshot—were recruited to help with cleanup after the game. The cabinets represented so much of Mr. Palmieri's identity. He took great pride in his work and made sure nothing failed.

When it came to food, Mr. and Mrs. Palmieri stocked the basement with enough supplies to last two snowed-in winters. Mr. Palmieri, like most of the other Italians in the neighborhood, always had a backup for everything.

If the kitchen freezer went down, there was another one in the basement.

If a door hinge bent or broke, a new one was in the cabinet downstairs.

And of course, everyone knew Mr. Palmieri didn't leave anything to chance.

With baseball players in the house and the neighborhood, glass windows always made the list.

One glorious afternoon with fewer than two weeks remaining in the school year, a foul ball kissed the kitchen window good-bye. Before the first piece of glass hit the grass, pure panic set itself in Nicky's mind.

"Oh, no. I'm going to be punished for the entire summer," Nicky thought.

Mission Impossible number one: Clean up the mess.

"No hardball in the backyard," Mr. Palmieri yelled before he left for work.

"Don't worry, Dad. We're not stupid," Nicky said.

When it came to school, Nicky was a borderline genius. When it came to lying, Nicky was better. He was hall-of-fame material.

Mission Impossible number two: Distract Mrs. Palmieri to initiate Operation Replace Window.

"Mrs. Palmieri," Gennaro said. "Do you have any Band-Aids for some cuts on my legs?"

"Sure, Gennaro," Mrs. Palmieri said. "Come into the kitchen, and I will clean you up and make you leg just like new."

Mission Impossible number three: Find the spare window; clean and replace.

Mission Impossible number four: Make sure all evidence self-destructs.

Mission Impossible number five: Replace glass in frame before Mr. Palmieri arrives home in twenty-two minutes.

Since the Kelsey Avenue Crew were still kids without a car, the only miracle they knew happened on television at a place called Thirty-Fourth Street in New York City. This situation called for a savior, someone who could assist in the most improbable of impossible missions, Big John. Luckily for Nicky this catastrophe occurred on a Thursday—Big John's day off. He worked six days a week and closed the store on Thursday. Why Thursday? Nicky never knew, but this day sure came in handy.

"Nicky, look. Isn't that a donut box from Big John's?" John Ferrante said.

"Yeah, so, how is that going to fix the window?"

"Big John's is closed today, moron," John informed Nicky. "Those are the Wednesday donuts."

With summer recess around the corner, Nicky didn't realize what day it was. The days simply melted into each other. School was the only way this fun bunch had any clue as to what day it was because they counted to five in anticipation for two days off.

Rituals made life interesting in West Haven. Since Big John's family survived tough times equal to the Great Depression, wasting food was worse than striking out with the bases loaded in the bottom of the ninth. On Wednesday nights, Big John brought the remaining bakery products home and gave them to friendly neighbors. Nicky's house featured four sugar-loving kids with sweet teeth that helped enrich the local dentists.

For the Palmieris, every Wednesday was more than just Prince spaghetti day. It was Christmas and Easter neatly organized in a huge Better Eatin' Donuts box. At 8:22 P.M. there was a knock at the door, and Nicky didn't need the CIA or the FBI to figure out who it was.

While four kids scrambled en route to the front door, people in other parts of West Haven heard Mr. Palmieri yell, "You better be knocking on the door with your feet."

Big John always hollered back, "If I hit this door with my fist, I'd knock your whole house down."

The door opened and Big John's arms were carrying tremendous donut boxes.

Glazed, chocolate-covered, jelly, cream, and plain donuts. There were poppy-seed and cheese-filled pastries, too. Every Wednesday at 8:23 P.M. the entire neighborhood enjoyed a bedtime snack.

Just like clockwork.

The next morning with a couple of glasses of milk, breakfast was served. If Nicky went to church and they asked him to describe Heaven, baseball and the Wednesday-night donuts made the top headlines.

Realizing that Big John was home, the kids sprinted and poured glass into empty donut boxes. They knew who to turn to for the next best thing to divine intervention.

"Hey, nice job on the window, guys," Big John said after two minutes of laughter.

"Wild pitch or foul ball?" he added.

"Foul ball," Nicky said.

"Oh, well, we better take care of this before Joe gets home."

"Did you replace the broken window?" Big John said.

"Sure, that's done, but now we have to bury the broken glass and fix this window."

They threw the glass in Big John's garbage pail and they piled into his old, beat-up, brown Chevrolet station wagon.

"Let's go see my friend at the glass shop," Big John said.

"We don't have any money or time," Nicky replied.

"Don't worry. You can work it off at the store on Friday, Saturday and Sunday."

And that's what started the greatest and worst summer of Nicky Palmieri's life.

Chapter 19
The Rites of Summer

In this West Haven neighborhood, summer can't wait until school ends on June 22. It started on opening day of the local baseball season. This was bigger than Christmas or any national holiday. The anticipation between seasons was longer than twenty-five shopping days and the hope that a jolly, fat man in a red suit with a white beard brought you a new bat or a glove.

For the Kelsey Avenue Crew, the wait was a torturous nine months from season to season. And while Christmas lasts for forty-eight to seventy-two hours and depends on the toys beneath the tree, baseball stays forever. The boys looked forward to every event of the twenty-game season, playoffs, and all-star games.

The organized games were fun because they kept standings, and the kids enjoyed the polyester uniforms. But the real games were played at Painter's Park.

If the summer lasted seventy-three non-school days, the schedule was 146 games. One game in the morning before people enjoyed their first coffee break, and game two of the double header started at 12:05 P.M. after a lunchtime respite.

They played games by breaking the Crew into teams and any other group of kids who showed up at Painter's Park on any given day. But it was the Crusty Rusty All-Stars that they looked forward to the most.

Since Rusty's custody between parents rotated from week to week, Nicky and his crew couldn't plan on him showing up every day. But on Saturdays, Rusty went to his mother's house, so there would always be a game.

Nicky planned his whole life around Rusty's games. He wanted to beat him at all costs. When the thought of Big John's plan of a weekend-long list of laborious duties came to Nicky's mind, a greater pain and misery encircled him. Rainouts Nicky could deal with. They rate way below the grimacing thought of sitting in a dentist's chair and hearing the buzz of a drill.

Missing a game because of an unnecessary punishment—well, that was even worse. Because of Nicky's poor shot, his employment responsibilities jumped to full-time.

"Tomorrow's your birthday, Nicky," Big John said. "Do you have any big plans?"

"Nah, we are just going to practice because we are playing Rusty on Saturday."

"You better schedule the game after you're done working."

"What time do you think I'll be done?" Nicky asked.

"Start your paper route early and be in by six. You'll be out by 2 P.M."

"Eight hours?" Nicky cried.

"Hey, you are great at math, too," Big John replied.

"Do you want this window fixed or what?"

"Eight hours is the least I can do, Big John. Thanks again," Nicky conceded, knowing that Saturday's version of doom was much easier than the pending wrath from Mr. Palmieri.

"Did you find your glove yet?" Big John asked.

"No, I can't believe I misplaced it. I think Rusty stole it from my house."

"You think Rusty stole the glove? How could he possibly do that? Don't you sleep with that mitt under your pillow?"

Nicky felt another lie pushing its way to the top. This was Nicky's biggest dilemma, stopping the fib from escalating higher than the Sears Tower in Chicago.

"He probably snuck into my house during the day when my mom goes shopping," Nicky embellished, still fighting the truth about his favorite glove.

"You know what a big jerk Rusty is," Nicky said.

"Yeah, you think he's a thief and a liar, right?" Big John responded.

"Sure, he lies all the time." ·

Finally, salvation came when they arrived at a glass shop down the street from Big John's.

"Let's get this window fixed before your father gets home. Okay, One Cell?" Big John said.

"Great. You saved my life again," Nicky said.

"Don't mention it, Nicky. Just try to hit the ball forward next time." ·

"I will, Big John. I will. Thanks again."

Nicky knew he escaped another jam, but he started to realize that this battle with truth was starting to bother him more than the wrath of Rusty and his friends, Mr. Palmieri's mood, and the cleft palate combined.

Chapter 20

The Birthday Boy

Big John's Deli served everything a neighborhood needed in a jiffy. If a customer wanted some cold cuts and wished to avoid painfully long lines at the A & P Supermarket, they visited Big John.

A can of dog food, a desperate need for a quick soda or chocolate milk, donuts for the house or office, a loaf of bread for dinner or lunch, a quart or a half gallon of milk, hot dogs, hamburgers, the accompanying buns—all were to be secured at Big John's.

Nicky loved this place. Nobody called him names, and he didn't have to lie too much. His missing glove, though, throttled his mind every day.

One day, Nicky decided he had to tell somebody about his mitt. Nicky knew Big John had the answers. Big John knew everybody by his or her first name. You didn't walk into his store and not receive the friendliest of greetings. He'd ask about your family and your job. He always seemed to know everything. He earnestly cared about everyone who was kind enough to do business in his store.

Nicky trusted Big John. The funny thing was people in West Haven ventured to Big John's to save time. They wanted to avoid the hustle and bustle of Stop and Shop or A & P, but they never could get out quickly.

Big John was always busy. Nicky didn't know when he could talk about this glove situation. Big John spoke to everybody. The more Big John made everyone feel welcome, the more uncomfortable Nicky began to feel about making him mad.

People went to Big John's because of him—not for the food, the prices, or the convenience. Big John simply made everyone feel good, special, and comfortable—especially Nicky Palmieri.

Big John knew that Nicky's family didn't have much money. He knew how expensive it was to run a house and pay for four kids. Big John also knew the high-priced doctors that Mr. Palmieri hired for Nicky. He always appreciated Nicky's hard work at the store. The one thing that Big John loved more than life itself was putting smiles on people's faces. Big John loved giving and, when it was fun, he gave even more.

Big John sponsored every team Nicky played on, no matter what the price. If Nicky needed new sneakers, Big John found a way to slip them under Mr. Palmieri's mountainous pride. Big John always had a friend in every business.

"Don't worry, Joe," he told Mr. Palmieri. "The Irish guy who sells the Converse All-Stars to the colleges threw me a free pair for your son."

"Okay, okay. You know I no accept no handouts," Mr. Palmieri said in his improving broken English. "You sure these shoes don't cost you any money. If they do, you tell me the price and I give you the money."

"No way, Joe. These are on the house," Big John replied.

Not easily convinced but always appreciative, Mr. Palmieri allowed Nicky to accept Big John's gifts—even two years ago when the $200 Rawlings Heart of the Hide baseball mitt landed under the Christmas tree after Nicky won the Battle of the Books. That was probably Nicky's greatest day.

For hours and hours, Nicky sat in his living room and smelled the sweet aromatic leather from the new glove. Friends visited just to take a whiff of the legendary glove and check out a real Heart of the Hide. This glove was the same kind professional players used.

"Look at this glove, Ralph," Nicky exclaimed to his brother. "Only the real good players in West Haven would have one. Rawlings gloves were the only ones the real players on television would use, and now I have one. This is Christmas."

A genuine Heart of the Hide was the Cadillac of baseball mitts. Everyone wanted one, but few could afford it. Even Crusty Rusty didn't have a mitt as good as Nicky's.

Every one of the Kelsey Avenue Crew used Nicky's glove. Nicky always shared his baseball equipment because baseball was the one thing, other than his family and Big John, he truly believed treated him fairly.

But Nicky knew his pride-and-joy baseball glove was in a better place now. Also, with the summer season around the corner, he couldn't dare ask anyone for a new one.

"Hey, Nicky, your birthday is coming up tomorrow," Big John began in another of Nicky's favorite pre-work talks.

"What do you want for your birthday?"

"I don't know, Big John, I haven't really thought about it much," Nicky fibbed.

"How's the glove I gave you holding up?" Big John started, as he bustled around the kitchen, boiling the potatoes for his famous German potato salad.

"You know the pros change gloves every year, except the players who are really superstitious."

"You mean like Wade Boggs and Sparky Lyle?" Nicky said.

"Those two have been using the same glove since they broke into the Big Leagues."

"I remember when one of the fans stole Sparky's mitt out of the Yankees' bullpen, and they put out a huge reward for the glove," Big John added.

"Sparky almost wouldn't pitch without that glove," he concluded.

"Yeah, I know the feeling," Nicky responded.

"By the way, did you ever find your glove?" Big John asked.

"No, I can't believe I still can't find it. I think Rusty stole it from my bag in the school closet?"

Nicky lied, but in some strange way he could feel that Big John knew about the exact whereabouts of the glove.

"Big John, you know I put some stuff in Jerry's casket when I went to the funeral home," Nicky said as the truth trickled to his throat.

"I put some baseball cards, a couple of game balls, a hat signed by the Mick, and some other stuff," he added as the truth struggled to escape.

"Yeah, I remember we talked about this a couple of days ago. Did you put anything else in there?" Big John said, stirring the pot in more ways than one.

Nicky didn't know what to do. Ten seconds went by, and Nicky said nothing.

"Hey, One Cell, did you hear me? Did you put anything else in there?"

"Nah, I figured a lot of the stuff I brought would be enough to take to baseball Heaven. I just hope no one else goes soon."

"I hope you are right, Nicky. I know you boys miss Jerry, and now you better focus and get to work. Here, you keep on eye on these boiling potatoes. I have some phone calls to make."

Big John worked the phones better than an insurance salesman during a company contest. He could recall phone numbers from memory better than anyone.

He called Nicky's mother first.

"Netta, what are you going to do for the kid's birthday?" Big John asked.

"We are just going to have a few people over from the neighborhood. But Joe said that if you bring anything, he is going to kick you out of the house."

"Tell Joe his soccer days are over. And anyway, he's not tall enough to reach my fat behind in the first place."

"Oh, boy. You better not let Joe hear that. He'll probably build a stool just so he could kick you in the behind to tell everybody he did what everybody in this town hoped they could do," Netta laughed.

"I've got a little surprise for my boy," Big John replied.

"You are too nice to Nicky," Netta said. "I know he really appreciates everything you do for him. The kids at school are really getting to him, and I think he likes this new girl who moved in up the road."

"How do you know that?"

"He's starting to actually stand in the bathtub when he takes a shower now," Netta joked.

"For the longest time, Nicky thought hygiene was waving hello to Gene Carmazzi next door.".

Nicky heard Big John's bellowing laughter all the way outside.

Mrs. Palmieri always displayed a great sense of humor. It was her way to help Nicky deflect bitter feelings and distract him from bits of reality.

"John, this girl is a real cutie," Netta added. "She's Italian, too, so that will keep Joe happy as well."

"You sound like the kid is going to get married soon," Big John said.

"I don't think we have to worry about that. It is his first real crush since Marcia Brady," Netta said.

"In the last few days, Nicky is talking about the operations and the things that bother him," she continued. "This girl started talking to him near the baseball field, and he hasn't stopped talking about her since."

"Is she coming to the party?" Big John asked.

"I went over to her house, and I invited her and her mother over and they said they would come," Netta stated.

"It will be funny to see how Nicky is going to react. The only girls ever to attend one of his birthdays were family members. She's got to be a baseball player, too. I can't see Nicky talking about shopping at the mall or the latest matinee idol."

"Wow. That surprise is certainly going to be better than mine."

"What's in your bag of tricks, John?"

"Oh, nothing I can't put my hands on," Big John said with the gleam of a cat that swallowed the last mouse on earth.

"Come over at about seven o'clock. Joe promises to be here on time."

"Sounds like a great party. I can't wait."

Chapter 21
B-Day and D-Day

Nicky Palmieri loved routines.

Baseball is a game laced with routines and rituals.
Step up to the plate.
Spit in your hands.
Squeeze the bat.
Dig your spikes into the holes in the batter's box.
Check the defense.
Find the outfielders.
Look for the holes in the infield.
Tap the bat against the corners of home plate.
Eye the pitcher and go to work.

This was a hitting ritual.

Nicky also had fielding and pitching routines as well. He worked on them constantly. He watched the New York Yankees do it every night on television.

He loved hearing the stories from his father and Big John about the great broadcasts on WPIX, Channel 11 with Frank Messer, Bill White, and the Scooter, Phil Rizzuto.

Routines, routines, routines.

And even though it was Nicky's twelfth celebration of his birth, it didn't surprise anyone that June 7 started like any other day.

The 6 A.M. wake-up shove from Mrs. Palmieri to start the newspaper route.

Two Stella Doro cookies. Margherite Combination of course. The vanilla one first followed by the chocolate one.

A cup of his mother's famous Italian version of milk and coffee, "latte e' cafe" and off to the races with his brother to see who could finish the route first.

"Happy Birthday, Nicky," Ralph said. "Do you want me to do your half of the paper route for you today?"

"Get out of here. Are you crazy or something?" Nicky replied. "You've been listening to too much Jimi Hendrix or Credence Clearwater Revival. I plan on beating your butt today, and you don't have to count my trip to the Marriotti's house."

"Is that where the new girl that moved in lives?" Ralph said.

"Yeah, wise guy. I just added them to the route two weeks ago."

"Ma, Nicky's got a new girlfriend," Ralph laughed. "I didn't know he was over the fact that Marcia Brady is dating the quarterback from Riverside High."

"Shut up, Ralph, I just want to make the paper route as big as we can so we can make some more money."

Since *The New Haven Journal* was the morning paper in West Haven, it was only printed Monday through Friday. *The New Haven Register*, the evening paper, took care of Saturday and Sunday mornings. This helped increase Nicky and his brother's availability for baseball on the weekends.

"Besides, the season is right around the corner and who has time for girls," Nicky said.

"You'll make time, lover boy," Ralph retorted as he sprinted out the back door to start his route.

"I'll kick your butt when I get home, wise guy."

"Take it easy, Nicky," Mrs. Palmieri said. "He's just teasing you, and don't start any trouble on your birthday. I'm going to make your favorite Italian-style cream puffs."

"Thanks, Ma. I love those cream puffs with the filling you make. It's going to be a great birthday. Who's coming over?"

"You know, Nicky, the regular crowd," Mrs. Palmieri took her turn at skipping over the jump rope of truth.

Nicky's parties were usually small family affairs. Mr. Palmieri's brother, Nick, always came over. Uncle Nick was Nicky's favorite and his extra special, real-life, godfather.

"Ma, Uncle Nick's coming over, right?" Nicky asked.

"As soon as he closes the shop. You know Fridays are busy for your uncle. He said he would be here by seven o'clock."

"Great," Nicky said. "Uncle Nick never lets us down. We'll eat and then we can watch the Yankees pound on the Tigers at eight o'clock at Tiger Stadium."

Nick Palmieri, Mr. Palmieri's younger brother, bought Nicky and Ralph their first baseball mitts on Nicky's fifth birthday. They were Joe DiMaggio models. But the best part was that Uncle Nick just didn't drop the gloves in a box or a bag. He always made time to play catch with Nicky.

Uncle Nick owned and operated Andy's Barber Shop in West Haven. He bought the business at twenty-one after saving most of his hard-earned money working at competing barbershops in Hamden, New Haven, and any place that would hire an Italian barber.

Andy's Barber Shop was the busiest in West Haven. It was widely due to Uncle Nick's personality. He was nice to everyone and Nicky was amazed at how many people stopped by to say hello. Some didn't even come for a haircut. The locals stopped, cracked a few bad jokes, and hung around for a bit before leaving.

Mr. Palmieri brought the boys down for their monthly haircuts, and they spoke in Italian for hours. But Nicky knew they were talking about his doctors. Sometimes Uncle Nick gave Nicky money to sweep the hair clippings off the floor in the shop to move him out of earshot. Since Uncle Nick dealt with people from various backgrounds and personalities, he knew doctors as well, and he always asked lots of questions. He always did everything possible to make his godson's life better.

Uncle Nick Palmieri closed the barbershop on Wednesday and Sunday. In the great spirit of Italian tradition, Sunday dinner at noon was a weekly event with the entire immediate family. For many years, Mr. Palmieri drove the family over to Grandfather Palmieri's house, where Uncle Nick lived. Since they returned to Italy when Nicky was six, however, Richmond Avenue was the new place for Sunday afternoons.

Nicky loved Sunday when Uncle Nick visited. People understood that dinner was served at noon on the dot because Nicky's father wouldn't have it any other way. One time, Mr. Palmieri's in-laws were invited, and they were ten minutes late. This did not sit well with Mr. Palmieri's routines. Mr. Palmieri demanded to eat at noon and he always did.

"Giuseppe, you can't wait for us to eat?" Mrs. Palmieri's mother, Irene Altamura, said staring at Mr. Palmieri's smiling face and empty macaroni dish.

"When you eat at my house, we eat at twelve o'clock, not ten after when you decide to get here," Mr. Palmieri laughed.

Uncle Nick simply shook his head and laughed as well because everyone knew that when Mr. Palmieri said something he meant it. Since dinner always started on time, Uncle Nick made a special effort, when the weather was nice, to reach the Richmond Avenue house early to play catch with Nicky. For years, Nicky waited patiently on the front steps of the house for Uncle Nick's arrival at 11 A.M..

Uncle Nick knew how to talk to Nicky. They always discussed everything from baseball to family members to school. Nicky loved those times, and now his favorite uncle was coming to his twelfth birthday party.

"Ma, who else is coming?" Nicky asked.

"Oh, stop worrying about who's coming to the house. We are going to eat as soon as Uncle Nick arrives," Mrs. Palmieri explained.

"Dad is going to wait until seven o'clock to eat?" Nicky said.

"Are you going crazy, Nicky? Your father will eat at 4:48 and not a minute later. Go start your papers, and let me worry about the eating arrangements."

Nicky left in a whirlwind because now he had to make up some time and catch his nine-year-old brother to win the paper race. Nicky hated losing anything— games, contests, challenges, debates, pencils, pens, and especially baseball equipment. The people who really knew Nicky definitely suspected something afoul when he couldn't locate his favorite glove.

So many times, Nicky struggled with his thoughts.

Why did he have to put the glove in the casket in the first place?

Why can't he tell people the truth about where it was?

Thousands of questions raced through his mind. Similar to most of his mistakes and what he labeled "mistruths," Nicky ignored them until he was struck by Cupid's arrow—and it wasn't even remotely close to Valentine's Day.

"Hi, Nicky," said a sweet voice that seemed to come from nowhere as Nicky placed the morning's paper in the front door mail slot.

"Nicky, up here. Up here to the left," the voice exclaimed.

Nicky squinted and shielded the bright morning's sun that hinted summer was around the corner. He located the voice.

"Hey, you scared me. I didn't know where that voice was coming from," Nicky said. "I thought I was the only idiot up at six in the morning."

"You're not an idiot, Nicky," the melodic voice continued as Nicky battled the sun with his newspaper bag as if he were catching the winning out of a game with Crusty Rusty.

"Do you have a little time before you have to go home?" the voice asked.

"Sure, what's up?"

Since most girls only laughed and giggled amongst themselves whenever they talked to Nicky, this was a frightening but interesting experience.

"I was wondering if you would like to play catch with me."

Even though this was a girl, when it came to sports—especially baseball—Nicky was never at a loss for words.

"You play baseball?" Nicky replied.

"Sure. What? Do you think girls can't like baseball just because you don't see them on TV?"

"I could, but I don't have my glove," Nicky replied through the curiosity that raced through his mind about when the lip insults would come.

"I'll let you borrow my dad's old glove. I'm trying to break in my new one. It's a Heart of the Hide."

Nicky's heart almost stopped while it took him a couple of seconds to pick his jaw off the ground.

This conversation passed the one-minute mark, setting a record for the longest interaction with a female other than a family member.

"You have a Heart of the Hide from Rawlings?"

"Sure, why is there any other kind?" the voice said. "Why do you ask so many questions by the way? Do you think that it is impossible for a girl to have a nice glove?"

"Nnnn, no," Nicky stammered. "It's just that I've only known one person around here to have one and that's me."

"You have one, too?"

"Yeah."

"It's the greatest glove you can get," the voice said. "You must be a pretty good player. I'm coming down."

Nicky stood in the middle of the long sidewalk stunned as he waited for the chance to match the face to the voice.

"Hi, Nicky. My name is Ann," said the voice of a girl with the most amazing hazel eyes he had ever seen. "We met one day walking home from the baseball field. Don't you remember?"

"Yeah, I remember. We talked about why you didn't have to go school because you moved from Florida."

"So, you do remember."

"Of, course, I do. I never forget a prett…, ah, I mean, powerful conversation about baseball."

Ann tossed the glove to Nicky, and he examined it like the doctors that look at his cleft palate.

"This glove belongs to your dad?" Nicky said in great amazement.

"He used to play in the minor leagues for the New York Yankees in Fort Lauderdale and West Haven."

"Is he home? Can I talk to him?"

"Stop asking questions and just catch the ball," Ann instructed.

Within four throws Nicky noticed that Ann was not only a lovely sight but a talented player as well. Her throws were crisp and chest-high. She moved gracefully to catch Nicky's return throws, and this made Nicky forget about beating his brother home.

"Are there any teams that need players?" Ann asked.

"Our team is always looking for players," a smitten Nicky Palmieri said.

"Can you get me on the team?"

"I'm positive you could join our team. We play almost every day up at the park when school ends," Nicky said. "Just come down tomorrow at about two o'clock and I'll introduce you to the rest of the guys.

"We have a game every Saturday now that the weather is better," Nicky quickly said as his nervousness moved his words into warp speed. "Once the rest of the boys see you throw, they will welcome you on our team in a heartbeat."

After a few more long throws, Ann stung Nicky's hand with a laser, as her mother called Ann inside.

"I've got to go help mom prepare breakfast for my brother," Ann said excusing herself. "Thanks for having a catch with me. See ya, soon."

"Thanks," Nicky said. "That was fun. Make sure you come to the field tomorrow. We're going to play Crusty Rusty."

"Great. I can't wait to start playing baseball again," Ann said, smiling as she and her mother stood in the doorway and waved good-bye.

Amazed by this recent interaction with a person of the opposite sex, Nicky started walking home instead of his usual sprint. He thought about the last ten minutes and smiled. It was the first time he could remember having fun with a girl without worrying about his lip.

Ann made Nicky feel comfortable without trying. Nicky beamed the entire way home until he remembered that his brother beat him.

"I finally beat you, Nicky. I won. I won. I finally won," Ralph said, jumping on the top step of the Palmieri house like Rocky Balboa at the Philadelphia Public Library.

"You won, fair and square," Nicky said, surprising even himself with a good lie. "You must be getting faster. I'm going to beat you on Monday."

Mrs. Palmieri watched from the living room window, hung up the telephone, and smiled. She knew that Marcia, Marcia, Marcia finally left Nicky's life.

Chapter 22

Clouds on a Sun Shiny Day

The walk to school took on greater meaning this day. There were only ten more wake-ups for school. Uncle Nick was coming over for Nicky's birthday party, and another big game with Crusty Rusty loomed the next day. And finally, a girl had spoken to Nicky for more than five seconds without cursing or laughing at him. Ann even owned two Heart of Hide baseball gloves, and she knew how to use them.

As the Kelsey Avenue Crew grew strength on the daily walk to school, one by one the kids jumped down the stoops from their homes and wished Nicky a happy birthday Kelsey Avenue-style—twelve friendly taps in the head from each person in the gang.

Nicky loved this day. These were his true friends. He knew that most of them were going to the party. These kids never picked on Nicky or ever mentioned the cleft palate.

In a strange way, they understood Nicky's birth defect better than the doctors did. They never lied to Nicky, and they never wasted his time. They always protected Nicky, and the best part was that Nicky didn't have to wait for an hour or two in a stuffy office with two-month-old magazines to see them.

"I can't wait for the party tonight," Gennaro said. "I'm going to eat ten of your mother's cream puffs."

"Yeah, me, too," cried John Ferrante.

"Take it easy," Nicky blurted. "Save some for me."

Suddenly, the laughter stopped as they approached the steps to Stiles Elementary School.

"Hey, I didn't get an invitation to this party," said a voice from a dark cloud.

Unlike Nicky's morning experience, this was a voice that was far too familiar.

"I'm talking to you, Elephant Face."

"Shut your pie hole, Rusty," Gennaro said.

"We didn't invite you to the party because you would have to change your underwear for the second time this week," Nicky piped in.

"I'm going to rip your wise guy heart right out of you one day," Rusty said, pulling his lip out and mocking Nicky.

"Why don't you go back to the trailer park and hang out with the rest of your low-class friends?" John Ferrante yelled.

The crowd of kids multiplied quickly and chanted "Fight, fight" until another familiar voice echoed from the top steps.

"Break up this mess, and you boys better get to class in a hurry."

"Nicholas Palmieri," a voice from behind another white, bearded cloud bellowed.

"I want to see you in my office right now."

"But Mrs. Anderson, I have a spelling test first thing this morning."

"Don't worry, Mr. Palmieri. I want to have a word with you."

Slowly, Nicky trudged up the steps and made the familiar right turn into the principal's office. The Great Chocolate Milk Conflict was not yet behind him.

"I haven't been able to contact your mother the last couple of days," Mrs. Anderson began.

"I've been pretty busy with end-of-the-year paperwork," she added.

"Yeah, I know. Gennaro and I saw you and Miss Hansen stumble out of Randall's Bar and Grill last night," Nicky said.

"Excuse me, young man. I was having a relaxing pastrami sandwich for dinner, but that's none of your business."

"Besides, I spoke with your teacher, and I've decided to give you a three-day in-school suspension starting today."

"What? But those punks started the whole thing. When are they going to get in trouble for the stuff they start?"

"Never mind them, young man. You will spend the next three school days in this office. Miss Hansen already sent your work down," Mrs. Anderson said.

"There's your desk. Now sit down and get to work."

"This is such bull...."

"Watch your mouth, Nicholas."

"My name is Nicky."

With that latest episode of Nicky's insolence, Mrs. Anderson grabbed Nicky by the left ear and took him to a desk outside the office loaded with piles of papers and books.

"You can have your lunch at twelve noon," Mrs. Anderson squeaked. "You will ask me whether you can go to the bathroom, and you will not leave this desk until this work is completed."

"But it's my birthday. I want to be in class," Nicky cried.

"Your poor behavior forces me to take the privilege of being with your class away.

"Also, I'm instructing you to write an apology letter to Rusty before you set one foot in that classroom again," Principal Anderson continued.

"Okay, I'll do that, but who is going to read it to him. I plan on using words with two syllables."

"This fresh mouth of yours must be attended to immediately, Nicholas. If I were you, I would keep my mouth shut and get to work."

In Miss Hansen's class, birthdays were special days. She normally bought each kid a chocolate chip cookie from the snack cart and the birthday boy or girl got to help grade papers and tests. Nicky looked forward to this day from the beginning of the year, but now Rusty and the bearded villain—the evil Mrs. Anderson—took this day away from him.

Nicky feared most that this just gave Rusty more ammunition to take pot shots at him. Besides, sitting at a desk in the hallway outside the principal's office was a lonely and cloudy way to spend one's birthday that started with the brightest of bright sunshine.

While Nicky fumed, he finished his spelling test and worked on math. The morning went by pretty quickly. He figured that Rusty or some of his wise guy friends planned to come by the office to rile Nicky, but so far they were leaving him alone.

Noontime arrived and Nicky took it upon himself to open his lunchbox and enjoy his favorite sandwich. His mom packed him a thick collection of Italian cold cuts on his favorite semolina bread.

Nicky loved his birthday. It reminded him of the numerous fun times he enjoyed with his father, Uncle Nick, and Grandpa Palmieri. Whenever they visited Grandpa Palmieri's house, they played Italian card games, scobe, and briscola. The highlight always was when Grandpa Palmieri sneaked Nicky around to a little cabinet and put a little anisette in Nicky's espresso. Nicky always modeled his behavior after his grandfather. Grandpa Palmieri always laughed and enjoyed life.

He didn't even need a car. He had so many friends that they always took him around town. Nicky admired the way nothing ever bothered him. He never even worried about money. Grandpa Palmieri loved to eat, drink beer and wine, watch baseball games, and laugh gregariously.

He taught Nicky everything about Italian traditions without books or worksheets. Nicky learned to relish the imported Italian sandwich delicacies—the fresh prosciutto di Parma, sweet supressatta, mortadella that melted like butter in your mouth, and fresh mozzarella. All this neatly fit into a huge chunk of Italian break lightly soaked with balsamic vinegar.

This would be a great birthday, but this time alone helped Nicky reflect on missing his grandfather who emigrated back to Italy as soon as the operations started. Grandpa Palmieri always knew how to turn tense situations into hysterical laughter. Nicky was sure that the guns and violence of World War II in the Italian army taught Grandpa Palmieri how to teach his namesake to handle the thieving, lying doctors and mean, conniving school children. Nicky surely benefited from a hearty Grandpa Palmieri chuckle.

This dark, ominous cloud always loomed over Nicky's head. He knew his birthday would still be so much fun, but he missed Grandpa Palmieri's touch. With these thoughts running circles in Nicky's mind, he added another one to the mix. Nicky loved his heritage, and he couldn't understand why Mrs. Anderson continually punished the Italian kids.

He couldn't figure it out. Nicky's mother told him that his responsibility was to worry about himself and avoid fights in school. So many times Rusty's friends pulled mean pranks on Nicky, and they never, ever got caught. He always hoped that one day someone would catch them.

But with ten school days remaining, hope turned into the idea that one of Rusty's divorced parents moved to another part of town. This dream couldn't come soon enough, but only after the Kelsey Avenue Crew beat Rusty's team just once.

Lunch finished without incident. Nicky quickly went back to work, hoping to finish this set of assignments before the dismissal bell. The clock-watching started at about two. It was the world's most unbelievable phenomenon. Time moved so slowly for Nicky that whenever he watched those old-style schoolhouse clocks tick, the hands seemed to take hours to move one click.

Nicky started thinking about the big game the following day against Crusty Rusty and his group. He loved the mental part of baseball because Joe DiMaggio once said that the game doesn't start with the first pitch. The game started when you wake up in the morning and you run the game through your mind until you go to sleep at night. Baseball was a thinking game where you always had to be one step ahead of your opposition. Nicky often wondered why he couldn't apply this theory to Rusty's mean-spirited comments as well.

"Hey, take a look at Elephant Face," Rusty shouted down the hallway as the dark cloud reappeared. "Great way to spend your birthday, loser. After we beat your team's brains in tomorrow, you'll wish you stayed here over the weekend."

"Shut up, freckle face," a familiar voice from the morning interjected. "I've watched you play, and you're not that good."

"Look who we have here," Rusty chuckled. "Little Miss Priss, or shall we call you, Ms. Tuffy Wuffy? And what's a girl going to do against my club? Are you going to join this loser's team and lose to us tomorrow, too?"

"Why don't you go back to your class and learn to spell CAT for the first time without somebody giving you the C and the A," Ann said. "I'm going to play on Nicky's team and wipe that stupid smile off your freckle face."

Mrs. Anderson quickly barged from the office.

"What's all this racket out here, Nicholas?"

"My name is Nicky."

"I'm growing tired of that fresh mouth. Do you want me to add another day to this punishment?"

"No, ma'am."

As Ann's mother, Mrs. Marriotti, entered the school, Ann said to Mrs. Anderson, "It wasn't Nicky's fault. These kids were bothering him."

"You know Nicky?" Mrs. Anderson said.

"Yeah, I met him a couple of weeks ago, and we played catch this morning."

"Really. Didn't your mother teach you not to hang around with the riffraff of this town?"

"Take it easy, Ida," Mrs. Marriotti said. "Nicky invited Annie to play on the team tomorrow. She needs to make friends in this town. We hope to stay here for a while."

"That was certainly surprisingly nice coming from this fresh-mouthed little rascal," Mrs. Anderson noted. "Come on into my office, and we'll talk about enrolling your son for next September."

"Can I stay out here, Mom, and talk to Nicky?"

"I'm sorry, Annie. I want you to come into Mrs. Anderson's office and let Nicky finish that work on his desk."

While Ann walked into the office, Nicky managed to catch her eye and mouth some special words without the sound, "Thank you so much." Ann gave Nicky a quick wave as Mrs. Anderson closed the door behind them.

This latest ray of hope warmed Nicky in a way he never felt before. He couldn't wait until the game. He knew that somehow God sent Ann down to help the Kelsey Avenue Crew beat Crusty Rusty.

Maybe, Nicky thought, that after Ann, God could send down a doctor to fix his lip. For now, though, he thought about tomorrow's game.

Surely, this was going to be a great game, dark clouds and all.

Chapter 23
Defense from Afar

Ann and her mother sat in Mrs. Anderson's office for quite a while. Nicky heard laughter emanating from the room, but he failed to figure out what they were discussing.

In a surreal way, as far as Nicky was concerned, it didn't really matter what they were talking about. Nicky was sure that after Ann stood up to Crusty Rusty they weren't laughing at him.

Finally, the dismissal bell rang, and Mrs. Anderson emerged from the office.

"Let's see the work, Nicholas."

"My name is Nic–...."

Nicky stopped mid-word because he feared Principal Anderson would keep him after school.

"Were you saying something, Nicholas?"

"No, ma'am,"

"I'm almost sure you were starting to say, 'My name is Nicky.'

"Weren't you?"

"No, ma'am. It's a little after three o'clock, and I'm learning my lesson. I promise not to talk back to you ever again," Nicky said this using his best pre-Christmas, suck-up-to-an-adult routine.

"Well, Nicholas. That's nice to hear. I hope you can keep your word."

"I sure will, Mrs. Anderson," Nicky said, crossing each and every one of his ten fingers.

"May I be excused to walk home with the rest of my friends?"

"It looks as though you completed your assignments," Mrs. Anderson said, peering at Nicky over her wire-rimmed, cat-shaped glasses.

"I did a lot of thinking, too, while I was out here, Mrs. Anderson," as Nicky's bid for an early release continued.

"I know that we only have nine days left of school, and I will try my best not to have another fight with those Iri—. I mean, those nice kids in my class."

"Okay, Nicholas. But you will spend the next two days here.

"I hope you have a happy birthday."

"Thank you, Mrs. Anderson. May I ask you one small favor?"

"Yes, Nicholas."

"Can I have a drink of water from the cooler?" Nicky asked.

"Sure, is there anything wrong?"

"No. It's just that my tongue hurts from biting it."

"See you on Monday, Nicholas."

Even Mrs. Anderson cracked a little smile on that one as she shook her head while Nicky raced out the front door and down the steps, hoping he could catch Gennaro and the rest of the Kelsey Avenue Crew.

"How did the suspension go?" Gennaro asked. "The whole school was talking about it at recess."

"It wasn't too bad," Nicky said.

"Rusty came by to bother me a little, but the new girl, Ann, showed up out of nowhere and told him off."

"Really? What was she doing in school?" John Ferrante inquired.

"She and her mother had some business with Mrs. Anderson," Nicky explained.

"It was the first time I ever heard Mrs. Anderson laugh."

The boys couldn't believe it either. Many people in West Haven snapped photographs with her at school functions during her twenty-five-plus years as a teacher and principal. A smile or a glimpse of happiness on Mrs. Anderson's face, it was commonly understood, had never been seen by anyone.

"Nicky, are we going to be short some players for tomorrow?"

"No, we should have plenty, and I invited Ann to play with us."

"Is that the new girl that moved into the Lacy house?" Gennaro asked. "Can she play?"

"She's pretty good, Gennaro," Nicky explained. "I played catch with her this morning. She's got a strong arm."

"But that doesn't mean she can hit, Nicky."

"Let me tell you something," Nicky added. "She must be pretty good because she's from Florida and her father played for the New York Yankees in the minor leagues."

"What?"

"Her father played in the minors?" Gennaro exclaimed.

"Do you want to hear something better than that?"

"She owns two Heart of the Hide gloves," Nicky said.

"Are you kidding me? I don't know any girl who would even know what a Heart of the Hide is, never mind own two of them," Gennaro screeched.

"She's excited about playing, and now that Rusty said some mean things to her, too, she's happy to help us beat his butt."

"Speaking of gloves, Nicky," Gennaro added. "Have you found your glove yet?"

"No, I haven't, but it must be around the house somewhere. I'm going to need the glove tomorrow," Nicky said as Gennaro climbed the steps to his house.

"I'll see you in a little while. What time does the party start?"

"Come over early before the others arrive at about seven, Gennaro. We'll play catch in the backyard. Bring another glove in case I still can't find mine."

"Sounds like a plan, Nicky. See you then."

The neighborhood's tight proximity allowed for the small group of friends to scatter into their houses as Nicky walked home, thinking about ending the string of lies that followed his Heaven-bound Heart of the Hide.

"Smells, good, Ma," Nicky started as he walked into the only dwelling he had ever known. "Where did the ravioli come from?"

"Your father stopped at Tony's Ravioli in New Haven and bought your favorites," Mrs. Palmieri said. "He promised to be home at the regular time, so we will eat soon."

"We have to save a plate for Uncle Nick," Nicky demanded ever so gently, not to upset his mother. "He'll be here before seven. I'm sure even though the shop is busy on Fridays."

"How was school today, Nicky?" Mrs. Palmieri asked. "I heard you spoke to Mrs. Anderson again."

"How did you hear about that already?" Nicky asked, holding great fear of his mom discovering more tidbits regarding his behavior following the Great Chocolate Milk Conflict.

"Do you think that all I do is hang around the house all day?" Mrs. Palmieri queried. "I have friends, too, you know. And this is a small town and people know every move you make."

"Oh, oh," Nicky thought as he looked around the kitchen for clues that secured the spot for cream puffs that still highlighted the dessert menu.

"Don't worry, Nicky. I made the cream puffs. Look in the refrigerator, but don't touch anything."

"Now, go in your room and read some of *The Hardy Boys* books your grandmother bought you until your father gets home," Mrs. Palmieri insisted as she constantly impressed upon her children to read at least one hour every day.

Nicky moved to his room, grabbed a book, but stared at the pages, thinking about his glove. This glove business was getting to him.

Nicky knew he lied way too much. He could not figure out why or how it started. The untruths became habitual, but suddenly it started to bother him. As he sat alone, he wondered why he couldn't tell people the truth. Nicky wondered how this Heart of the Hide glove situation mushroomed into a soon-to-be big mess any day now.

If he ever made an error in a real game with Mom and Dad watching, the questions would surely pour faster than water from Niagara Falls. He truly felt bad about lying to his parents and Big John all the time, but he could never figure out how to stop it.

With summer around the corner, Nicky feared a punishment worse than eight hours of chores per day at the house or Big John's. His father still lived by "old country" standards of child-rearing. Child abuse, hah. Back in the day, child abuse led to the child getting arrested for making life miserable for the parents.

Parents layed out the rules and without any discussion or negotiations, they were followed. Parents were the police, the lawyers, the jury, and the judges. They dispensed the law, and their law was forged with the Gospel and the Holy Bible. Everyone recognized their power.

It didn't matter which parent spoke to any of the Kelsey Avenue Crew, they knew they enjoyed free reign with their behavior. The laws were the same throughout the neighborhood. If anyone's mouth was fresh with Mrs. Ferrante, she enjoyed the privilege of knocking teeth down a kid's throat. No questions asked.

Then, if these kids arrived home and complained about why two front teeth were missing or loose, they faced greater consequences. Children were expected to behave a certain way inside the home and to be better in public. Parents ran the homes with an iron fist, a ladle, a belt, or a back hand. No one dared raise any objections or overrule any pending decisions by the highest court in the land.

All these thoughts raced through Nicky's mind. He knew that somehow he had to tell the truth or buy another Heart of the Hide. Explaining how more than $200 was missing from his savings would create another string of fibs. Then, breaking the glove in would take weeks, and Nicky couldn't risk making an error in fear of losing a game.

After pondering these options, Nicky knew that the only thing left was finding a way to tell the truth.

One problem remained, though—where to look for it.

Chapter 24

Playing Catch

The Richmond Avenue telephone rang, and Nicky in a wild attempt to answer the phone knocked over his sister, Mary, along with a Barbie doll-house.

"Hello, Uncle Nick. Is that you? You're coming over early?" Nicky bellowed.

"Nicky, it's not your Uncle Nick," a melodic voice on the other side gently whispered.

"Oh, Hi. Ann," Nicky replied. "I'm sorry. I thought it was going to be my Uncle Nick. Hey, how did you get my number anyway?"

"You're the paperboy, aren't you? You gave it to us when we signed up for the newspaper," Ann said.

"Oh, yeah, I forgot. I always look forward to my Uncle Nick coming over to play catch."

"What are you doing now?" Ann asked. "Do you think I could come over and play catch?"

"Sure, Ann. Let me ask my mom and I'm sure it will be fine."

Mrs. Palmieri overheard the entire conversation, and before Nicky could turn around to ask her, she nodded her head with a smile.

"My Mom says it's okay. Come over as soon as you can," Nicky excitedly said.

"Do you want me to bring both my gloves?"

"Yeah, that would be great. I still can't find mine."

"See, you in a little while."

"Great. See you soon, Ann."

While Ralph started teasing Nicky about his female friend, Nicky sprinted to the bathroom to wash critical areas around his face and neck where dirt or other unknown debris was known to find its way around active young boys.

"Ma, do you think Ann could stay for dinner and the birthday party?"

"Maybe, Nicky. Just maybe," Mrs. Palmieri replied, already one step ahead of her nervous son and knowing she invited Ann and her mother yesterday.

"Great, Ma. Do you know Mrs. Marriotti?"

"You don't know who I know," Mrs. Palmieri said. "Now make sure you clean your face and behind your ears real good, so this girl doesn't realize what a slob you really are."

Within ten minutes, Ann arrived and they played catch in the backyard.

One of the best parts of baseball in Nicky's eyes was playing catch and talking. Whether it was with Uncle Nick, Big John, Jerry, or his father, there was always something soothing about talking between the sounds of the baseball popping in leather gloves.

"Hey, Ann, I really want to thank you so much for sticking up for me with Rusty," Nicky started.

"He's been picking on me every since we met. Not too many people have the guts to stand up to that jerk. I can't wait for the game tomorrow, so you can help us finally beat him and the punks he calls friends."

"What is your favorite position?" Nicky asked.

"I can play anywhere you want me to so long as we can beat him and finally shut him up," Ann responded.

"I'll even catch or play first base. I just enjoy playing baseball," she added.

"Great. I can't wait to play tomorrow. I know we are going to finally beat him," Nicky said.

"Your team has never beaten Rusty's team?" Ann asked.

"Never. We come close, but we just never get that clutch two-out hit, or they manage to make an amazing play on us in the late innings," Nicky reported.

"But Ann, one day we are going to win. I know he always has older kids on his team. But our team is getting better every game, and I know we are going to beat him at least two or three times before this summer is over."

"How many times has Rusty's team beaten you?"

"Do you want an estimate or the exact number?"

"Do you know the exact number, Nicky?"

"You bet I do. I remember every loss like every op—...."

Before Nicky started talking about his operations, the painful experience of looking in the mirror and hoping the lip appeared the way he dreamed of quickly entered his brain. But Ann had such a soft, soothing touch about her. In the back of Nicky's mind, he could trust her. But way in front, fear dominated his next syllable.

Nicky felt no one understood. No one possibly knew the feeling of helplessness when post surgical bandages were removed and the mirror entered the picture and told the truth while simultaneously crushing another dream.

This was true defeat for Nicky.

And now losses gave Nicky the same empty feeling in his stomach. He wanted to win every game. A baseball game was far different from the cleft palate. With baseball he felt in control of his destiny. If Nicky misplayed a ground ball, he took 200 the next day. When a fly ball alluded Nicky's outstretched glove, he had somebody hit him fly balls until he couldn't see straight.

If he didn't come up a clutch hit, he stood in the back yard until the wee hours of the night to practice his swing. When Nicky reared back and threw his best pitch only to feel negative results, he threw baseballs against the brick wall of his house until his arm hurt or his father couldn't take the sound of the pounding any longer. Playing baseball gave Nicky a good feeling because he knew there was nothing that his determination to improve couldn't fix.

But his lip had far different dynamics. People mocked him, laughed at him, and teased him. These events Nicky couldn't control. Baseball games were much easier to deal with because there would always be the next at-bat, the next inning, the next play, and the next game. Baseball was so much better than football.

On the gridiron, you had to wait an entire week to offset a bad game or a loss. Basketball featured the same seven-day mourning period, but baseball season had game after game after game. You didn't need the football pads and helmets. You didn't need a gym or fancy uniforms.

Baseball was simple. It was the real deal—kids vs. kids, pitcher vs. batter, one on one in the concept of team play. Baseball gave Nicky hope when doctors' promises brought him despair. And now as he almost spilled his guts to his new friend, Nicky stopped suddenly before the fine line of truth.

"What are you saying, Nicky?" Ann inquired. "Losses are like what?"

"You know, Ann. I just remember every loss," Nicky answered.

"We must have lost to Rusty forty-four times in the last two years. In the beginning, his team would crush us by ten runs every time," Nicky admitted. "They would laugh the entire time, and about twenty games ago we started to cut the final score down to half. Now, the games are nail-biters to the end, and we are wiping the smiles off their silly faces. They're sweating a little."

"Do you think we will be able to beat them tomorrow?" Ann questioned.

"We will just need to make some key plays; and if we somehow get some two-out hits, we'll win. I can feel it," Nicky proudly responded.

"Plus, we're going to have our secret weapon."

"What's that, Nicky?"

"It's you, Ann. They won't think you can play. They will surely be surprised."

"You have never seen me hit," Ann said. "How do you know how good I am at the plate?"

"Anybody who throws the ball as well as you do must have played a lot of baseball," Nicky noted. "I'm sure you can hit any pitch they throw at you."

"Don't put so much pressure on me," Ann kidded. "It's only my first game."

"If it truly is, I know it won't be your last."

With this conversation aside, Nicky breathed a sigh of relief while escaping the truth about the operations and, more importantly, the inner fears of how the outside world perceived him.

"Enough talk," Ann exclaimed. "Let's throw."

Similar to their morning game of catch, Ann continued to demonstrate exceptional skills. Her throws were crisp, chest-high, and extremely accurate. They threw for twenty minutes while Nicky and Ann smelled the sweet aroma of Mrs. Palmieri's tomato sauce.

"When's your party start?" Ann began.

"Soon, I hope," Nicky said. "I'm hungry."

"Hey, Ann, why don't you stay and eat with us? I'm sure my mom won't mind."

"I wish I could Nicky, but my mom expects me to come home soon."

"Do you think you could come to my birthday party?" Nicky ventured.

"I don't know, Nicky. I think my mom has something planned."

"Oh, that's too bad. I wish you could come back, and I want you to meet some of the players on the team before tomorrow."

"That would be great Nicky, but my mom taught me to honor our word, and I think we promised someone we would go over to their house tonight."

"That's cool, Ann," Nicky sadly replied. "But listen, I'll see you tomorrow. That game will start around 2 P.M. If you want to take some swings before the game, get to the park an hour early."

"Sure, Nicky, that's great. I can't wait to play."

"See ya, tomorrow, Ann. Thanks for coming over."

"See ya soon, Nicky."

Sooner than Nicky knew.

Chapter 25

Surprise, Surprise

Nicky watched Ann's cute little wiggle bounce down the street. As soon as she was out of sight, another great vision appeared.

A sky-blue, two-door Dodge Dart raced along Kelsey Avenue and made the immediate right turn onto Richmond.

"Uncle Nick, Uncle Nick, you're here," Nicky yelled.

"Ralph, come on outside. Uncle Nick's here." One by one, the Palmieri family moved to the front door to greet Nicky's godfather. Mr. Palmieri cracked a few jokes in Italian about Uncle Nick's hair and instructed Mrs. Palmieri to start the ravioli.

"Nicky, go get your glove, and we'll play catch," Uncle Nick said.

"Yeah, sure I'll be right out. My arm is pretty loose already because my new friend, Ann, came over and threw for about twenty minutes."

Uncle Nick made eye contact with Mrs. Palmieri, and they smiled that smile that kids always see but never know what it means until they become adults—a subliminal look impossible to understand until one turns twenty-one or some adult fills kids in on what it means. Nicky raced into his room and retrieved the Joe DiMaggio glove that Uncle Nick gave him seven years ago.

"See, Uncle Nick, I love this mitt," Nicky said. "Today's a great day to have a catch with the first glove you bought me."

"That's nice, but where's that sweet Heart of the Hide Big John gave you a while ago."

"I don't know where it is, Uncle Nick," Nicky sinned. "We have a big game tomorrow against Crusty Rusty, and I hope to locate it before the game."

Uncle Nick made more of that annoying adult eye contact with Mr. Palmieri and Nicky felt a bit uneasy.

They start tossing the ball around, and nervous Nicky airmailed his first throw over Uncle Nick's head into Mr. Jimmy Constantino's graveyard for baseballs.

"Kiss that ball good-bye," Uncle Nick said in reference to the neighbor who hated flying baseballs in his sacred vegetable garden. "He must have some collection."

"He could open up his own sporting goods store with all the balls Nicky tosses in that yard," Big John howled from the kitchen window.

"Hey, Big John, you closed the store early to come to my party," Nicky said.

"No way, One Cell," Big John countered. "Your biggest fan, Harry Huber, volunteered to work a couple of hours and close the store." Big John leaned out the window and flipped Nicky another baseball. Nicky resumed his game of catch.

"Thanks, Big John," Nicky said. "I'll try to throw this one to Uncle Nick once in a while."

"Now this will be a big switch," Big John cracked. "You throwing the ball to a target is something I want to see."

The game of catch continued as Big John led the parade of guests for the 7 P.M. dinner bell. Birthday parties at the Palmieri house were big events, but they were always superseded by Christmas, New Year's, and Saint's day celebrations.

Calling Mr. Palmieri "old school" was as great an understatement as saying that Yogi Berra was a good catcher. Mr. Palmieri lived and breathed Italian traditions. Everybody already knew that Sunday dinners were mandatory. When Mr. Palmieri sat down to eat, everyone ate. If one didn't like the fare, one didn't eat.

"This is not a restaurant," Mr. Palmieri bellowed whenever a cry for "I don't like escarole and beans" echoed from one of the four children. "You'll eat what's on this table and that's it."

The best part was that Mr. Palmieri always fought American traditions with stories about the grand style of Italy. When there were birthday parties he reminisced about how each of his children knew when the Saint's Days were for every relative. Mr. Palmieri reminded everyone of the great parades for St. Joseph's day. He constantly reflected about the wonderful food and amazing celebrations.

With this in mind, Mrs. Palmieri knew how to make birthdays special as well. Out of the closet came the china gifts from Mr. and Mrs. Palmieri's wedding day. The inserts to the kitchen table were neatly in place covered with the finest linen tablecloths. The metal folding table, which added twelve places, was brought up from the cellar and made an appearance in the kitchen.

Foxon Park soda bottles glistened on the table in the great flavors—black cherry, orange, grape, cola, and Nicky's favorite, Gassosa—the much tastier Italian version of Sprite. The sight of soda meant celebration.

The trays of antipasto were neatly in place, and now it was time to eat. For Nicky, Tony's Ravioli was a present in itself. Nicky loved the ricotta and the fresh pasta taste from the squares. When his mother wasn't looking, Nicky sometimes ate them raw while the raviolis were laid out on the wax paper, thawing before entering the boiling water. Nicky loved ravioli so much that when he was little he asked his mother if the boiling water hurt the raviolis as it did the lobsters he saw at local seafood restaurants.

Everybody arrived and to Nicky's surprise he heard the melodic voice again. Three times really was a charm.

"Hello, Mrs. Palmieri, thank you for inviting us to the party," Ann said as she and her mom strolled into the kitchen.

"Hey, look, Mary," Ralph began. "Nicky's girlfriend is here. Isn't this cute?"

"Shut up, Ralph," Nicky said. "Don't act like an imbecile every day."

"Nicky, please watch your fresh little mouth," Mrs. Palmieri interjected in a classic Mrs. Anderson imitation. "We have guests here."

Mr. and Mrs. Palmieri welcomed Ann and her mom.

"Ma, I didn't know you knew Ann's mother," Nicky said.

"If I told you once, I have told you a thousand times—you never know who I know," Mrs. Palmieri stated.

Mrs. Marriotti and Mrs. Palmieri shared another one of those treasured adult laughs while Nicky shrugged his shoulders, looked at Uncle Nick, and sneaked another raw ravioli into his mouth. Without batting an eyelash, Mrs. Palmieri threatened her son again with bodily harm if he did not keep his hands off the uncooked dinner.

John Ferrante, Mark, Lou, and Bob Kessler arrived. Gennaro waltzed in a couple of seconds later, earning the usual Mr. Palmieri stare-down, and dinner began.

The clanging of forks, knives, spoons, and the passing of plates lasted about two minutes before the first question Nicky fretted hit the floor.

"How was school, today, Nicky?" Mr. Palmieri asked.

"Great, Dad," blurted Nicky.

"Did Miss Hansen do anything special for your birthday?"

"Yeah, Dad, she bought me a chocolate chip cookie from the cart, and I even got a chocolate milk too," Nicky said as Ann quickly turned her head.

"So, how many papers did you grade today?" Mr. Palmieri inquired. "I know you were looking forward to being the teacher's helper on your birthday."

"Too many, Dad. I lost count," Nicky answered while Ann didn't move a muscle but stared at her plate.

"It is nice that Miss Hansen makes kids' birthdays special," Mr. Palmieri continued as this time Big John looked at Nicky with an icy stare.

People continued to eat while Nicky breathed more easily when Gennaro changed the subject.

"These ravioli are great, Mrs. Palmieri," Gennaro said. "They must be from Tony's in New Haven."

"Good work, Gennaro. You've been here too many times on Nicky's birthday. He will want to eat these ravioli when he's fifty."

"If I know Nicky, he'll want Tony's Ravioli in his casket," Gennaro said. "It will be just like the ancient Egyptians, won't it, Nicky?"

Nicky started to choke as Big John rose from his chair and patted him on the back.

"Don't worry, Gennaro, Nicky's got a long way to go before he can start worrying about what people will put in caskets," Big John laughed. "Are you all right, Nicky?"

"I'm fine, Big John," Nicky said. "Some sauce went down the wrong pipe."

West Haven was such a small town people knew Nicky's fate before the day even started. While Nicky's uneasiness increased with time, he started to eat faster.

"Pass the meatballs, please." Nicky loved his mother's sauce and the meats that simmered in the pot since the day before. As the bowl with the sausages, meatballs, veal, pork, and bracciole moved across the table, the subject matter changed quickly.

Mr. Palmieri and Big John started discussing the St. John Vianney's church restoration fund-raising efforts. Mr. Palmieri, again in his old school mentality, did not comprehend why the church was always asking people for money after Saturday and Sunday mass.

In Italy, there were churches at every corner. In Mr. Palmieri's small town, he counted twelve churches. He could name the priests and their pets as well. In America, things were surely different, and Big John let him know it every single day.

The friendly banter continued through the remainder of dinner until the congregation moved to the living room for, as always, New York Yankees' baseball. Unless Nicky was in school or played in a game, he and Mr. Palmieri never missed a game on television. Sometimes Nicky pulled out his Wilson baseball score book and kept the score of his favorite players.

Nicky loved the numbers of baseball—the batting averages, the ERAs, the slugging percentages, and the records of yesteryear.

"Hey, Big John, Bernie Williams got a twenty-one-game hitting streak," Nicky started. "I don't care what anybody says, no one will break DiMaggio's fifty-six-game streak."

Then Big John, Gennaro, Mark K. and John Ferrante started talking about how after Cleveland Indians' third baseman Ken Keltner made two amazing plays in game fifty-seven, DiMaggio hit safely in the next seventeen contests.

"Don't forget about the play Lou Boudreau made at shortstop on the one-hopper behind second base," Big John added. "It just shows you how many breaks you have to get to hit in fifty-six games. In every baseball game, there's a turning point between the winners and the losers."

Nicky loved this baseball talk the most. He learned from every conversation, every word Phil Rizzuto or Bill White threw on the air. He remembered watching Uncle Nick's old VHS videos of NBC's Tony Kubek and Joe Garagiola on the *Game of the Week*. Those guys were great announcers, too, but Nicky loved the Yankees and everything about them. Since Mel Allen was a former Yankees' announcer, *This Week in Baseball* was another one of his favorite tapes with highlights and commentary of the old-school players.

Ann joined the conversation, and the boys were amazed at how much she knew about baseball—never mind the Yankees. For Nicky and company, this was their first experience with a peer of the opposite sex who knew just as much about baseball as they did. Sure, there were mothers who knew baseball like Mrs. Kessler and Mrs. Palmieri, but few sixth graders—boys or girls—knew one-tenth of what they knew.

"Hey, what about the Mets?" Ralph P. chimed in. "They are doing much better than the Yankees. Bud Harrelson is having a great year, and so is Tom Seaver."

In the Palmieri house, battles raged in sports between the brothers. Nicky loved the Yankees. Ralph loved the Mets.

In football, Nicky loved the New York Giants, and Ralph loved the Dallas Cowboys.

In basketball, Ralph loved the New York Knicks, and Nicky chose the Boston Celtics.

In hockey, Ralph loved the New York Rangers while Nicky, of course, loved the Boston Bruins.

Then the debating stopped when the call came for the Italian coffee and birthday cake. But Nicky wasn't interested. He wanted those Italian cream puffs. There's always something extraordinary about a mother's specialty. Mrs. Palmieri best culinary skills surfaced during birthdays and holidays. Nicky's list of favored sweets was long but amazingly simple— cream puffs, Italian cheese cake, grilled cheese sandwiches in tin foil cooked under the iron, Saturday-afternoon grilled pastrami sandwiches, Tony's Ravioli, Hunt's chocolate pudding, meatballs, and homemade cavatelli.

And lastly, Mrs. Palmieri made the best tomato sandwiches. She used the tomatoes from the vegetable garden sprinkled homemade Italian bread with oil and vinegar. She crushed the tomatoes and rubbed them on the bread and left the skins in the sandwich.

This vision ran through Nicky's mind as he always knew that, as his birthday arrived, summer was around the corner. That meant baseball every day and no school to boot.

"Ann, don't eat anything else until you have one of the cream puffs first," Gennaro said. "Those are the best."

Mrs. Palmieri filled the table with the finest Italian pastries. Uncle Nick always came through with the cannolis and chocolate cakes from Egidio's Pastry Shop. Big John brought trays of goodies from his store.

In the Palmieri house, they never wasted time with the traditional happy birthday song. The desserts were far more fun than bad singing you could hear at cheesy chain restaurants.

"Nicky, you want some espresso?" Mr. Palmieri asked.

"Sure, Dad. I'm going to have some in honor of Grandpa," Nicky said.

"Okay, but no anisette. Your grandfather taught you some bad habits."

"But those are happy habits, Joe," Uncle Nick interjected.

"I have to raise this kid and teach him that booze is not the thing twelve-year-olds should be involved with," said Mr. Palmieri, whose only dealing with liquor was a White Russian at a yearly wedding.

On the other hand, Grandpa Palmieri loved his Ballantine Beer, wine, and anisette. He never abused the stuff, and he enjoyed life to the fullest.

Uncle Nick shared the same flavors in life. So, when Mr. Palmieri wasn't looking, he slipped a little anisette into Nicky's cup and gave Gennaro a little bit, too.

"Your Uncle Nick is the best," Gennaro said. "What kind of present do you think you'll get from him?"

"I don't know," Nicky stated. "But whatever it is I know it will have something we can use in the game tomorrow."

Within twenty-two minutes, dessert ended amid buzzing conversation and oohs and ahs over the cream puffs.

"Those cream puffs were the best," Ann said to Nicky. "Does your mom make those often?"

"Only twice or three times a year," Nicky answered. "She saves the best for special occasions."

"Thanks for inviting me and my family, Nicky," Ann said. "Most boys never invite me over because they think I'm a tomboy."

Nervously, Nicky realized he wished he had invited Ann, but he smiled warmly because his mom surely set up the whole thing.

"Anybody who thinks that you are a tomboy doesn't know what they are talking about," Nicky started. "I know that I have only known you for a little while, but I can tell that you are a nice person. People should try to get to know people first before they pass judgment on them."

Mrs. Palmieri and Mrs. Marriotti overheard the conversation and smiled.

"Everyone, let's move to the living room. Shut the TV off and let Nicky open his presents," Mrs. Palmieri said.

Nicky rifled through the cards first, shaking them vigorously as money and checks fell out.

Uncle Nick handed him a long rectangular-shaped present neatly wrapped in gold paper.

"It's those new aluminum bats, right, Uncle Nick"

"I saw Vinnie Bonnizoli use one in the games last week," Nicky commented. "The ball flies off those metal bats."

"No way, Nicky," Uncle Nick insisted, "is my nephew using an aluminum bat. Just open the present and see what it is."

The wrapping paper flew from the box while Ann and the rest of the Kelsey Avenue Crew eagerly anticipated the package's contents.

"Wow, thanks, Uncle Nick," Nicky exclaimed. "It's a Roy Hilton White model. This is the best bat I've ever seen."

Nicky proudly showed his thirty-two-inch white ash smoke tempered wooden Louisville Slugger bat to everyone.

Next to Thurman Munson, Roy Hilton White was one of Nicky's favorite old-time Yankees. He wore number six and played great outfield. His switch-hitting batting stance was one many kids in the neighborhood imitated. White didn't hit the homers that Mickey Mantle did, but he always came up with unbelievable clutch hits.

"Nicky, let me see the bat," Ann said. "I can't wait to use it tomorrow to beat the pants off Crusty Rusty."

"Me, too," Gennaro added. "We haven't had a new bat to use for a while."

Nicky opened the rectangular boxes with the customary new clothes, and then Big John entered the room.

"Here you go, Nicky," Big John said. "Mr. DiNapola and me got you this present. I know you'll like it."

Nicky halted his gift-opening frenzy and froze.

Questions raced through his mind.

Why did Mr. DiNapola team up with Big John for his birthday present?

Did they know something that Nicky thought was a secret?

Did they combine together for a free funeral and the traditional post-burial party?

Nicky continued his Academy Award acting, issuing comments on how thrilled he was with the new socks and shorts until a little Big John push led to a Mr. Palmieri shove.

Chapter 26
The Truth Hurts

"Let's go, Nicky. Let's see what Big John and Mr. DiNapola gave you," Mr. Palmieri said. "This should be interesting." The adults gave their simple, quiet stares that communicated more than 10,000 words in one single look.

Seconds later, conversation stopped and silence filled the living room. Practically everybody in West Haven knew that Big John had given Nicky his treasured Heart of the Hide. This box was big enough for a catcher's head gear for the team or one of those cool New York Yankees' batting helmets without the ear flaps. Nobody, except Nicky, expected to uncover a glove in this box.

Everyone waited since they knew how much Big John stocked Nicky's baseball closet with bats, balls, and other necessities.

"I'll open this later. Let's go in the kitchen everyone and have some more cream puffs," Nicky stammered.

"We'll eat later if we're hungry," Big John said. "Come on, Nicky. Open the box."

"I'll be embarrassed, Big John. You always buy me the best gifts. No matter if it's my birthday, Easter, or Christmas. You bring me presents I never deserve."

"Open this one, Nicky," Big John insisted. "I know you will be surprised."

"Mr. DiNapola helped with this gift, too, Big John?" Nicky asked.

"Yeah, he helped me pick it out," Big John stated. "He wants me to call him as soon you open it to see the look on your face."

"I'll open it later," Nicky said.

"Now, Nicholas, don't be rude," Mrs. Palmieri interceded. "An extremely special guest brought you a nice gift. Now you better open it, or the party's over. And you will go to your room."

"Nicholas."

This word became a prickly thorn in Nicky's side this week. People used this word when they meant serious business. Mrs. Palmieri, who could be forceful even at her small height, employed this moniker before critical doctors' appointments and major disciplinary actions forthcoming.

Nicky's mother taught him that power doesn't necessarily require a big body. The diminutive Mrs. Palmieri at 4-foot-11 and 92 pounds carried a lot of weight in West Haven and even more at 11 Richmond Avenue.

Nicky knew that she was bigger than Bowie Kuhn, the Commissioner of Baseball.

She wielded more power than Father Ladamus at St. John Vianney.

When Mrs. Palmieri used "Nicholas," things better happen and quickly or there will be problems.

Nicky shook the box a little, sniffed the outer edges, and realized exactly what it was. He thought it was a new glove to replace the missing Heart of the Hide. But now, another series of even more difficult and intriguing questions entered his mind.

Did Big John purchase a new Heart of the Hide?

But with that, why was Mr. DiNapola involved in this glove?

Does he have some discount connections with D and N Sporting Goods?

Maybe Mr. DiNapola knew someone in the Rawlings front office, and he bought a demo model. Maybe Mr. DiNapola knew someone in the Major Leagues, and they gave Nicky a glove because he lost his. Or maybe Mr. DiNapola, like most other adults, knew more than Nicky realized.

Now, Nicky's crew started.

"Come on, Nicky. Let's see what you got," as Gennaro led the charge.

"Open it, Nicky," Ann chimed in. "Maybe we could use it for the game tomorrow."

"Don't worry kids," Big John said. "He'll be happy to use this for the game tomorrow."

The urgent cheers for Nicky to open the last of his gifts increased with an incredible crescendo with a most recognizable voice leading the charge.

"Nicola," Mr. Palmieri started what was surely soon to produce a set of stern Italian instructions.

"Okay, okay, Dad, I'll open it," Nicky said, hoping to avoid a harsh lecture in front of Ann and his friends. "I'll open it now. All these great presents make me shy." Mr. and Mrs. Palmieri joined together in the usual rolling of the eyes while Nicky gently peeled the wrapping paper away from the gift. Slowly, Nicky removed the tape from the bottom. His nervousness made his hands to shake. He knew that, if this gift were a glove of some kind, the untruths he told about his treasured missing glove would never disappear.

Finally, the last piece of paper fell from the box and Nicky breathed a sigh of momentary relief. The box was not the recognizable, open-ended one with the huge Rawlings "R" on it where the glove is neatly displayed.

"That's good," Nicky thought. "But what could these two guys put in this box that I will need for tomorrow. Oh, oh." He realized that this plain old brown, cardboard box still contained some interesting contents, and this worried Nicky the most.

"Nicky, are you going to open it, or do you want to guess what's in it first?" Big John said. Nicky opened the box, and it was, indeed, a glove. However, it seemed a shade darker brown than a new Heart of the Hide. Upon further review, Nicky saw Big John look at Mr. Palmieri, and he quickly jumped to give Big John as big a hug as he could, along with a chorus of "thank-yous."

"Big John, you're the best," Nicky exclaimed. "You knew my glove was stolen and you bought me another one."

"No, I didn't buy you another one."

"You didn't, but how did you get this glove?" Nicky asked.

"Before you ask all these questions, why don't you take the glove out of the box and see what it is?" Big John replied with a question.

"I don't have to, Big John," Nicky said. "I can't wait to use this glove in the game tomorrow."

"But you didn't even look at it closely, Nicky."

Big John grabbed the box and tossed the glove to Nicky.

"Try it on. Make sure it's not too big."

Mr. Palmieri walked over and recognized the glove instantly. There it was as clear as the most brilliant, cloudless blue sky day for baseball—Nicky's treasured Heart of the Hide. Everything was the way he left it in Jerry's casket. The number "22" etched just inches on the top of the traditional "R" outside the glove just above the thumb. The initials "NP" were clearly labeled inside the glove where the hand fits. The pocket remained well-oiled and smooth. The "T" web still so tight that once the baseball found its rightful place, it would never fall out.

This was Nicky's pride and joy. He always took great pleasure in playing excellent defense, and this glove meant the world to him. But now there were many equally important people who, Nicky knew full well, were prepared with many questions.

"Well, well, Nicky. It's looks like Big John and Mr. DiNapola found your glove."

"Yeah, Dad, miracles never cease in West Haven, do they?"

"Well, Big John," Mr. Palmieri began what was soon to be a great inquisition. "How did you find Nicky's glove? He's been looking for this glove for days."

"Joe, why don't you have Nicky tell you? I'm sure he knows how Mr. DiNapola and I found the glove."

After Nicky scanned the room for a place to hide, his father asked the obvious question.

"Well, Nicky, why is Big John so sure you know how he found your 'stolen' glove?" Mr. Palmieri began.

"Gee, Dad, I don't know. I'm sure that Rusty stole my glove, but I can't worry about that now. I'm just glad I have it back for tomorrow's game," Nicky said.

"We're going to talk about tomorrow's game later, sonny boy," an incensed Mr. Palmieri said. "Come on in the kitchen, everybody. There's plenty more pastry and coffee."

Every one of the Kelsey Avenue Crew sensed that the sudden change of subject matter meant two things.

First, it was time to go home.

Second, Nicky Palmieri was in trouble—deep trouble.

Chapter 27
Always Trust a Pretty Face

One by one and without much fan fare, the children left Nicky's party.

"See, ya, tomorrow, Nicky," John Ferrante said.

"Yeah, see ya, Nicky. Make sure you thank your mom and dad for inviting us over," Mark K. added.

Most of the Kelsey Avenue Crew offered their good-byes to the adults and left Nicky's house buzzing.

"Seems like Nicky's going to be in a lot of trouble," Mark K. started.

"Whenever parents change the subject that fast, it can't be good news," John Ferrante added.

"I didn't know Rusty stole the glove," a stunned Bob K. said to Gennaro.

"Nicky told me that he lost the glove in his house, and he was having trouble finding it," Gennaro responded.

"Something's up," Mark K. said. "He practically used that glove as a pillow. There's no way it was lost."

"Mr. P. doesn't look too happy," Gennaro said. "I don't know what Nicky told his father about the mitt, but it's awful weird that it wound up wrapped in a box for his birthday."

After debating Nicky's self-made dilemma, the boys muddled along Kelsey Avenue to their homes. The adults who remained at the Palmieri house strode into the kitchen while only Ann remained in the living room with Nicky.

"This is great that they found your glove," said Ann, easing and feeling her way into what was sure to be a tough conversation.

"Can I ask you something personal, Nicky?"

"Sure, Ann, go ahead."

"Why didn't you tell the truth to your dad about school today?" Ann inquired.

"Sh, I can't tell my father I got into a fight at school, or else I'll be punished from now until the end of the summer."

"But I heard it wasn't your fault," replied Ann as Nicky felt more and more comfortable with telling her a truth.

"Rusty and his friends are incredibly evil, and they need to be taught a lesson," she added. "I don't know why they pick on you. I hope we can beat them in the baseball game tomorrow."

Finally, something struck Nicky to tell Ann the truth. Ann seemed so genuine. She always looked you in the eyes when she spoke to you. She listened to every word you said. It was easy to tell that she cared.

She smiled at Nicky. Her blue-green eyes were soothing and so trusting, but even with this, Nicky's biggest question remained.

Why?

"Ann, if I tell you something, do you promise not to laugh at me?" Nicky started.

"Sure, Nicky. But why would I laugh at you?"

"It just seems that most of the girls I know point at me and giggle," Nicky continued. "I know they are laughing at the way I look and that bothers me."

"What are you talking about, Nicky?" Ann said. "The way you look? Your clothes look normal to me."

"It's not my clothes or my hair or anything I can fix," Nicky started. "It's my lip. I don't look like the other kids."

"That's ridiculous Nicky. It looks fine to me," Ann said.

"You are way too nice, Ann. Rusty and the rest of the kids have been picking on me since third grade," Nicky replied. "I held back for the longest time, but now I have had it. I'm fighting back. But if my father ever finds out that I had in-school suspension, I'm going to redefine 'big trouble.'"

"Did you ever think that lying about everything makes things worse?" Ann questioned her friend as she saw tears well in Nicky's eyes.

"I know that I should tell the truth whenever I can," Nicky said as he wiped his face with a shirtsleeve. "But when it comes to this stupid lip and cleft palate, lies are what I hear."

"The doctors, the nurses, and the secretaries," Nicky rolled onward. "They say the same thing over and over after every miserable operation."

"Wow, Nicky. You look wonderful," he added. "The operation was a big success."

"Success, my rear end, Ann. Look at my lip. All the bumps and scars. This is never going to go away."

"Nicky, it will go away if you let it," Ann replied.

"What?"

"If you can learn to just be yourself, your lip will be the last thing people will look at," Ann advised.

"I never noticed your lip until you brought it up. When I asked you to play catch today, do you think I was worried about the way you look?"

"No, of course, not, Ann. You're different. You're nice."

"You are nice, too, Nicky. You have to learn to worry about spending more time with the people that like you rather than the ones who choose to make fun of you."

"I know. You're right, Ann. It's just that, it's just that sometimes I never want to disappoint my mom and dad," Nicky answered. "The lies are so much easier."

"Your parents seem really nice," Ann said. "Why would they get mad when you tell the truth?"

"I tell them the truth about a lot of things," Nicky snapped. "It's just that they don't understand my lip. Nobody does."

"I don't think that is totally true, Nicky," Ann interrupted. "You would be extremely surprised who does."

Nicky's tears grew larger and more frequent as he turned away from her and turned the television back on.

"Good idea. Let's forget about this nonsense and watch the game," Ann said, changing the subject with adult precision. "You can tell me about the glove later."

"Oh, yeah, the glove," Nicky answered as he fiddled with his recovered treasure. "Now, that's a long story that's really way more interesting."

Ann shrugged her shoulders, sat down across from Nicky, and smiled. Nicky wiped more tears from his face and started to think that maybe, just maybe, he should investigate this truth business.

Especially when it involved Ann.

Chapter 28
Crime vs. Punishment

A solo home run by Bernie Williams into the upper deck at Tigers' Stadium, a double by Willie Randolph followed by a ribbie single from Don Mattingly clearly eased Nicky's living room mood as the Yankees grabbed a 3–1 lead in the top of the sixth inning.

Little did Nicky realize that in the kitchen, trouble was brewing faster than the second pot of espresso Mrs. Palmieri started.

Mr. Palmieri wanted answers.

The glove was the least of his concerns. He wanted to know about the in-school suspension report. Nicky heard the unmistakable sound of Mr. Palmieri's fist smashing the wooden kitchen table upon receiving the news. The tone of fist hitting wood in the Palmieri house was as easily recognizable as the sweet sound of the baseball hitting a bat.

Instantaneously, Ralph and Mary exchanged glances and pointed in the general direction of Nicky Palmieri.

"I think Daddy found out about the suspension," Mary started.

"You're right again, little sister," Ralph chimed. "Nicky's going to be in big trouble."

"Sh, be quiet. You're going to wake up baby Irene in the crib," Nicky warned. "Besides, shut up so maybe we can hear what they are talking about."

In most Italian homes, the conversation at the kitchen table was lively and entertaining, but this particular exchange of thoughts and ideas was detrimental to Nicky's baseball plans. Nicky's newfound appreciation for eavesdropping intensified.

The talk now centered on Nicky's constant battle with Rusty Alves, the dreaded neighborhood bully. Big John reminded Mr. Palmieri of the numerous times he brought Nicky to the Morse Park Little League fields. He refreshed his memory about the countless times Rusty mauled Nicky while they ran the bases.

"Giuseppe, this kid has got to learn to fight back," Uncle Nick interjected. "He can't let people continually push him around. This punk is a bully, and he needs a beating."

Mr. Palmieri heard everything, but he refused to accept his son's negative behavior in school.

"I understand most of this," Mr. Palmieri began, "but school is not the place."

"You know what we went through in Italy during the war," he reminded his brother of their treacherous treks through the mountains of Naples. "We didn't have the chance to go to school. We were too busy dodging bombs and moving from church to church."

Uncle Nick took several deep breaths, but before he answered, Mrs. Palmieri parachuted into the fray.

"Joe, you're not in Italy anymore," she firmly stated. "This is America, and I've seen the abuse this kid takes. Nobody's happy about this suspension business, but you must let Nicky learn to deal with this kid's wise cracks."

Mr. Palmieri continued to simmer as Big John rose from his seat ready to defend his favorite employee.

"What's the big deal?" Big John started. "The kid didn't get kicked out of school. He just has to sit in front of the principal's office and do his work there instead of the classroom for a few days."

"How come everybody in West Haven knows what happens to my son except me?" Mr. Palmieri exclaimed.

"Because everybody's afraid of how mad you're going to get, Joe," Mrs. Palmieri asserted. "This battle with Rusty is nothing. There are much bigger issues we need to discuss than his school behavior."

"What? Is there something else I don't know about, Netta?"

After a couple of seconds, Mr. Palmieri realized exactly what she was talking about. He had not forgotten Nicky's constant battle with truth. He easily recalled Nicky's fibs, ranging from missing pencils to dust under his bed. He remembered the countless times Nicky changed his story. He stopped to think how his son feared truth. He failed to arrive at the answers, but he knew there were problems. Recognizing this, Mr. Palmieri's anger over the school subsided, but the subject matter quickly turned to Big John.

"Now, what's the story with this kid's glove?" he asked.

"Joe, this is something you need to talk to the boy about," Big John replied. "All I will tell you is that you shouldn't be mad at him. He tried to do a nice thing, but for some reason he couldn't tell anybody the truth about it."

Uncle Nick yawned, sensed the upcoming wrath of his older brother's old-school values, and got ready to leave.

"I'd better get going, Giuseppe," Uncle Nick started. "Take it easy on my godson. I'll see you on Sunday."

"We'll talk later," Mr. Palmieri said. "I'll stop by the shop tomorrow."

Mrs. Marriotti also joined the departing crowd. She politely offered her good-byes while Nicky happily volunteered to walk Ann and her mom to their car.

"Thanks for coming to my party and talking with me, Ann," Nicky stated. "A lot of the things you said made sense. I'm going to try to do what you said.

"Thank you, thank you so much."

"You're so welcome, Nicky," Ann said. "See you tomorrow at the game."

Mrs. Marriotti smiled, looked at Ann, waved to Mrs. Palmieri, and drove away.

There was something soothing about Ann that Nicky couldn't put his finger on. Suddenly, he didn't worry about the upcoming dilemma pending the departure of the remaining guests. This, of course, didn't count Big John. He was part of the family. Nicky knew that, with Big John's presence, his father's temper could reach manageable levels. Only now Big John was leaving. Nicky knew it was time to face the music, and it wasn't one of his father's favorite Mario Lanza arias about Sorrento.

"Thanks for finding my glove, Big John," Nicky said. "How did you find it anyway?"

"Oh, I had a little help from Mr. DiNapola at the funeral parlor," Big John admitted as he walked the front steps and meandered to his house across the street.

"Good night, everyone. See you tomorrow, Nicky."

"What is Big John talking about, Nicky?" Mr. Palmieri inquired.

Nicky remembered his talk with Ann. He knew what needed to be said. He just doesn't know how to start. Lying was so simple, and one just says what pops into one's head and moves forward.

It's like writing realistic fiction without pencil and paper.

No typing required.

Just whistle while you work.

"Well, Dad, do you remember the night I snuck out of the house and came home late," Nicky began. "I told you I went to visit Jerry at the funeral home."

"Yeah, I remember."

"I went there to put a few things in the casket, Dad," Nicky continued. "I remembered how the ancient Egyptians placed things in their caskets because they believed they were going to the afterlife. I know there has to be baseball in Heaven, so I put some Yankee baseball cards, my Mickey Mantle autographed hat. And for some reason, I put my favorite glove in there, too."

"Why would you do that?" Mr. Palmieri said.

"I felt bad for Jerry. I figured that he would need the glove more than I would. He always stood up to those punks that bother me at the baseball fields. When he was around, they left me alone. This is going to be a long summer without Jerry working at the fields."

As tears steam rolled down Nicky's face, Mrs. Palmieri walked over and grabbed her son in her arms. The once raucous room was silent. Even Ralph and Mary remained quiet throughout the discussion.

Mr. Palmieri stared at the ceiling for a few moments and finally disrupted the silence.

"But why did you lie to these people about the glove?" he demanded. "Why can't you tell the truth?"

"I was afraid that people would be mad at me for putting the glove in the casket," Nicky said. "I thought it was a good idea at the time. But once I realized that I should have put another glove in there, it was too late."

Luckily for Nicky, Mr. DiNapola always checked the casket before funerals and he noticed Nicky's glove. He called the deli and Big John gave him another glove to put in the casket.

"You owe Big John an apology," Mr. Palmieri said. "He gave that glove to you to use in your baseball games. That glove cost him a lot of money. You have to learn to appreciate gifts and the value of a dollar."

"It's okay, Joe," Mrs. Palmieri said. "The kid was trying to do something nice. It's just a glove."

"It's not just a glove," Mr. Palmieri added. "I'm upset about the way he lies about everything. This is the problem, and he is going to be punished for it. He needs to learn the value of a dollar and, more importantly, the value of telling the truth."

"Do you have anything to say, Nicola?"

"I'm very, very sorry. I didn't mean to lie about the glove. It really is my favorite thing in the whole world."

Mr. and Mrs. Palmieri huddled together, and Nicky knew they were concocting a punishment of capital proportions. Nicky thought the worst—his chores doubled, cutting the grass twice a week, raking and bagging every clipping, trimming the hedges of the bushes twice a month, washing the car every other day, dusting the house without Pledge, daily window cleaning responsibilities, washing the dishes until he was in college.

But that didn't faze him until he heard whispers involving the magic word he dreaded most—baseball.

Since complications from the cleft palate included the troublesome hearing loss in his left ear, Nicky struggled in his valiant attempt to gather information. He witnessed heads bobbing and weaving.

His mother could occasionally be seen shaking her head no. This didn't do Nicky any good. Now that baseball was involved in this attempt to rehabilitate a lying twelve-year-old, pain was sure to follow. No baseball for the rest of the summer crossed Nicky's mind. Surely, even for old-school Mr. Palmieri, that was cruel but not totally unusual.

Nicky now braced himself for the ruling. This was worse than all the poor souls who lost to Perry Mason. He envisioned the highest court of the land was ready to announce their ruling.

In the back of Nicky's mind, he heard, "Will the defendant please rise?"

"Okay, Nicola," Mr. Palmieri said. "Here's the deal."

"First, you have to tell Big John the truth. Then there will be no baseball for one week, and you have to work one hundred hours at Big John's store for nothing. You need to learn the value of money and hard work.

"People buy you gifts because they care about you," he added. "I'm still upset you sold those proof coin sets that Uncle Ed and Aunt Mary bought you. People work hard to make money, and you need to learn not to lie your way out of decisions you make."

Holy cow, Nicky thought, how did he find about the proof sets, too? He sold them a couple of weeks ago to Mr. Finer at the Stamp and Coin store, so he could buy a couple of new bats for the season.

"Can you learn to start telling the truth, sonny boy?"

"Yes, Dad. I'll try my best," Nicky started. "I'm sorry for not telling you and Mom the truth about the glove. I'm really sorry. I will never, ever, lose this glove, ever."

"One week with no baseball. Do you understand?"

"Yes, sir."

"Dad?"

"Yes."

"Since Sunday starts the week and since we have a big game with Rusty tomorrow, can we start the punishment on Sunday?"

"No, sir, sonny boy. Punishments must be painful. You will start working at Big John's tomorrow at 6 A.M. You can go watch the game. But if I find out you touch one bat or one ball, you'll spend the rest of the summer in this house or working with me at the shop."

"Now go to your room and get some sleep," Mrs. Palmieri said. "You'll need to be up by five, so you can walk to work."

"Can't Big John give me a ride?"

"No way, Nicky. This is a punishment, not one of those lame work-release programs the liberals in Congress try to push through," Mrs. Palmieri joked.

Nicky walked to his room only to find his brother, Ralph, wide awake and waiting to hear the verdict.

"What did you get, Nicky?"

"One week with no baseball and one hundred hours of work at Big John's."

"Whoa, this stinks. You are going to miss the game tomorrow?"

"Yeah, Ralph. There's nothing I can do about it."

"This is serious," Ralph said. "Not even Big John could bail you out of this one, huh?"

No sir, not even, Big John.

Chapter 29
Let the Games Begin

Somehow, someway, every one deserves a "Big John" in their life. A "Big John" could be many things to many people—a mentor, a coach, an uncle, an aunt, a teacher, or a neighbor. "Big John" could be just about anybody who was special enough.

He lived across the way on Richmond Avenue where the street curves a little before straightening the rest of the way. That curve was symbolic because Big John tended to convince Mr. Palmieri to bend a little whenever punishment was concerned. This time, however, Nicky stacked lies much too high even for Big John's arbitration skills.

"Well, One Cell," Big John started with the coming attraction. "Looks like you're going to miss a few games this week."

"My dad's pretty upset," Nicky admits. "But you know, Big John, I don't think that I did anything too bad."

"What are you talking about?" Big John replied sharply. "Do you realize that West Haven is such a small town, and everybody knows every move you make."

Nicky started to think.

Small town?

This idea took his mind off missing the game with Rusty for a little while.

West Haven was huge in his little eyes. There were more than one hundred places to play baseball, basketball, and football. The best part was that they were within a bike ride. This municipality was the only place he really knew. Nicky's only other "big city" experiences came from when the Palmieri's visited his mom's family in Colchester, Connecticut. Now that was a small town.

Well, how small was Colchester?

Mrs. Palmieri's graduating class was fifty-two students strong.

The library, which was on the main road, was so tiny Nicky often joked if it had room to hold complete encyclopedia sets.

The town featured one police officer.

One traffic light.

One volunteer fire fighter.

One letter carrier.

One mail box.

One teacher for each grade in one school.

One park which centered around one baseball field.

One swing on the swing set.

One gas station.

Mrs. Palmieri often told the kids stories about how her mother had to travel twenty-five miles to shop for the not so routine groceries. The farm she grew up on mostly serviced a great portion of the family's needs. The cows took care of the milk, beef, and other necessities.

The chickens took care of the eggs, which grandpa and grandma Altamura sold to make money. Mr. and Mrs. Altamura's egg business was so strong it helped the family survive the Great Depression. The Altamura farm was one of only two in Connecticut to survive the worst financial crisis in America's history.

The entire family worked the land. Since Mr. Altamura didn't speak too much English, he never worried what the newspapers or the radio said about America's economic strife. He thought it was a scam perpetrated by the rich upon innocent Italians. The Altamuras made the farm work for the family. Their will along with lots of determination helped them overcame great odds to enjoy the American way of life.

Nicky remembered his mother's stories. He visited this small town almost monthly. Compared to Colchester, West Haven was an overpopulated city in China.

On a tour of the town, Mrs. Palmieri showed Nicky where she went to high school, Bacon Academy. There were ten rooms in the entire building. Every kid attended this one school. There was no kindergarten—only first grade through twelfth grade.

"Everyone knows everyone in Colchester," Mrs. Palmieri said. "It is a close-knit town."

Nicky registered all this. He always wondered how everyone could know everything about everybody in West Haven. Little signs always hit Nicky upside the head, but he never realized the total impact.

On one autumn day a couple of years ago, a most miserable nosy neighbor, Ray Ramada, overheard Nicky argue with his mother. Hours before Mr. Palmieri arrived home from work he knew the entire story. Mr. Palmieri sentenced Nicky to two weeks without outdoor activities after school. Luckily it occurred during the late fall, so Nicky didn't miss too much.

"Big John," Nicky started. "Why don't people just mind their own business in this town?"

"Why do they have to worry about what some little twelve-year-old kid is doing? Don't they have anything better to do?"

"I know what you mean," Big John began. "These people have no lives. They involve themselves in everybody's business, but their own. But sometimes it works out in your favor."

"What are you talking about, Big John?" Nicky asked.

"How do the busybodies in West Haven work out in my favor?"

"Never mind, One Cell," Big John said. "If you can't figure it out by now, there's no point in me telling you. By the way, you are here to work today not to worry about how the rest of this world works. Now you start by cleaning the meat coolers. When you're finished, I've got plenty of other things for you to do."

Nicky never argued with Big John. It didn't matter how ugly or disgusting the chores were. He knew Big John always helped him when the work became too strenuous for his twelve-year-old mind.

The meat coolers were sometimes difficult to clean because of the rotten smell of little bits of meat and cheese that fell underneath the wooden grating. A bucket of hot water and a set of old dingy dish towels and soap kept Nicky busy for a couple of hours.

"Not bad, One Cell," Big John said, as he carefully inspected the meat case, lifting and moving the wooden pieces along with the big roast beefs and hams.

"You took your time, too. You didn't rush to get out of here like you usually do."

Big John knew Nicky's Saturday pregame rituals. When a baseball game was on his mind, Nicky lost his concentration at work. Nicky rushed through his responsibilities. Sweeping the parking lot would turn into a moving-the-dirt sprint with a push broom.

Emptying the brown plastic garbage pails into the dumpster would result in many paper and plastic remnants around the square green container. Nicky's trail was clearly noticeable and characteristic. But on this day, he was hesitant to attend the game. He so badly wanted to impress Ann with his baseball skills, and he was humiliated that his lies about his baseball glove finally caught up to him.

"Earth to Nicky," Big John started again. "Now, listen carefully, I'm going to give you a few more things to do. If they are done properly, you can get out and watch the game."

"But you better not tell your father I let you out early," Big John continued. "You're supposed to learn what a hard day's work feels like."

"I don't know if I want to go to the game," Nicky replied. "I think I need to learn my lesson."

"What lesson might that be?"

"You know, I met this great girl, Ann," Nicky said. "She talked to me about facing the truth instead of avoiding it so much. You know, Big John, she never once asked me about my lip. There is something so nice about her. She talks to you, and she never judges anything you say. The best part is that you have got to see Ann throw and catch. She's really good."

"What's her name again?"

"Ann. Ann Marriotti. Why, do you know her?"

"That's the new girl that moved into town, isn't it?" Big John said.

"If I remember correctly, her father played in the Minor Leagues with the Yankees."

"That's right. How did you know that?"

"You would be surprised what I know, Nicky."

Nicky told Big John the whole story about how she owned two Heart of the Hides. They talked about how one could tell if a person played simply by the way he or she wore the glove.

"You never wear the glove tight to the wrist," Big John said. "It's a baseball glove, not a mitten. More than half the palm should be sticking out, so it's like an extension of your hand."

Nicky listened intently during any conversation about baseball. Big John was the one that showed him how infielders need to keep the fingers flat. He showed him how to shape a glove for every position.

"Her gloves were so cool," Nicky explained. "She had the 'T' web with number 20 on one of them. The leather was so soft you couldn't feel the ball hit the...."

"It's just like yours, huh, Nicky?"

Few things stopped Nicky in mid-sentence. The glove was clearly one of them.

After a moment of silence, Big John started to laugh. "When are you going to ask me how I found your glove, One Cell?"

"I was wondering how you found it, but I don't like talking about Rusty. I'm sure he stole it from me."

No sooner than the words hit Big John's ears did his face turn redder than a Fuji apple.

Nicky realized Big John's mood switched instantly, and he braced himself for trouble, big trouble. Bigger trouble than a week without baseball.

Disappointing Big John never hit Nicky so hard as it did now.

"Why can't you tell people the truth?" Big John screamed. "Where did you learn to lie? You know darn well that Rusty has nothing to do with how I found the glove. I deserve some answers."

The worst fears etched across Nicky's face. This was almost as bad as another failed operation. The truth cut worse than surgical equipment. Shame engulfed Nicky. In the back of Nicky's mind he heard Ann's voice. He desperately reached and wrestled with the beginning of his response.

"I'm sure Rusty stole it. He's always out to get me," Nicky mumbled in total fear as a well known but surprising customer walked into the store and saved the day.

"Hello, Mrs. Anderson. It's me Nicky. It's so nice to see you."

"Hey, Big John, look who's here, my favorite principal in the whole world," Nicky continued in classic suck-up fashion.

"Oh, yes, hello, Ida. And how are you today?" Big John asked.

"By the sound of the screaming I heard from the parking lot and the redness in your face, it looks like I'm doing a lot better than you," Mrs. Anderson said.

"My blood pressure is a little high lately, and I was talking to Nicky about a couple things," Big John admitted. "I may have gotten a little too excited."

"I'm not surprised, John. This young man is developing a penchant in exciting adults as I'm sure you know full well, my friend."

"My friend," Nicky whispered under his breath. He was sure this bearded beast of a principal had no friends—never mind a person whom he worshiped.

"You two know each other?" Nicky interrupted.

"Sure, we used to date in high school," Mrs. Anderson replied. "You know John was one heck of a baseball player. A lot of the girls used to be after him."

Nicky wanted to ask her if Big John suffered a temporary blind spell back then, but hearing Ann's voice in his head stopped him in his tracks.

"You were once Big John's girlfriend?"

"Yes, I was Nicky. He even took me to the junior prom."

"Did people actually see you two together?"

"Oh, yes, we were the talk of the town back then, right, John?"

Nicky was still stunned by the latest revelation and awaited Big John's response.

"Everybody wanted to date you," Big John started. "But I won the grand prize."

Grand prize? She must have been the booby prize. There's no way someone as cool as Big John dated the hairy principal from *The Planet of the Apes*.

Nicky's mind started to spin in high gear waiting for Big John's reply.

He must have lost a bet. Maybe Big John drank too many beers when he asked her out. Surely, their parents were friends, and Big John had to bite the bullet and take out the lonely girl next door.

In the meantime, Big John pulled out his high school yearbook and showed a giggling Mrs. Anderson a picture.

"You looked great that night," Big John said. "I was the luckiest guy in the house."

The beast started blushing, red cheeks through the gray and white beard as well.

"You were always kind, John."

"You were the best, Ida."

"You guys are making me sick," Nicky interjected.

The most unlikely odd couple continued gushing on about the old days while Nicky tried to finish his work.

"Don't forget to empty the water out of the pot after you're done peeling the potatoes, Nicky," Big John bellowed toward the kitchen.

"I got it. Don't worry."

Peeling potatoes for Big John's famous German potato salad was Nicky's last duty of the day. Any food item with vinegar was Nicky's favorite. Big John's recipe always added that little extra set of spice that made Nicky look forward to his first taste.

With knife in hand, Nicky rapidly rifled through the pot in anticipation of not missing the first pitch at Painter's Park.

After Big John and Mrs. Anderson completed their journey down memory lane, Mrs. Anderson peered into the kitchen on her way out and barked.

"Good to see you doing something constructive, Nicky. I'm on my way to watch my goddaughter play a game."

Nicky continued to mindlessly peel potatoes until it hit him like a bolt of lightening.

Game.

Goddaughter.

Watch.

"Hey, Big John, what time is it?"

Almost a quarter to two, but you aren't going anywhere until you finish this work, and I have something else for you to do."

"But Big John, I really want to go watch the game against Crusty Rusty."

"Nonsense, Nicky. You will not be watching any game until your work is done."

Quickly, Nicky ran through this pot, slicing and dicing the fastest way he could.

Big John entered the backroom and inspected the work.

"This doesn't look like it's enough for the rest of the weekend, but I'm going to make you a deal," Big John said, knowingly putting aside the glove issue and Nicky's real problem.

"You finish cleaning up this mess and rearrange the brooms and boxes, so I don't trip every time I walk in here. Then you can go watch the game."

"Sounds great, Big John. Thanks a lot."

"Oh, one more thing, One Cell. Do me a favor and fill up the pot with some more water and turn the stove on. I'll boil some more potatoes."

Nicky cleaned up the skins, washed the pot, filled it with more water, lit the gas stove, and started to leave.

"Everything's done, Big John. I'll see you tomorrow."

"Great job today, Nicky. You took care of those boxes in the back too, right?."

Before Nicky answered, he noticed that the clock showed ten minutes after two. He knew to see the game he had to do two things he knew best—run fast and fib a little.

"Those boxes and broom handles won't be in the way, Big John. I took care of everything. See ya tomorrow."

Chapter 30
The Truth Hurts

On the sprint to the park, Nicky's mind raced much more quickly than his legs. He debated going back to the store to check the boxes, but then he thought about the game.

Boxes.

Game.

Brooms.

The truth.

It's just a little lie. No one suffered any pain.

He heard Ann's voice in the back of his head.

"Just be yourself and don't worry what people are going to think," she said. "People who care about you will be able to look past your lip and know who you really are. You don't have to lie about everything because you think it is what they want to hear."

These words resonated in his mind, but he continued to run toward the baseball game. Nicky felt his punishment owed him a little fib this day.

His run led him through the West Haven High School parking lot, past the hockey rink, through the pit, across what would soon be named Jerry Gambardella Jr. Field, and to the ballgame.

Nicky arrived in the bottom of the third inning. Rusty just clubbed a two-run homer to center field, and the Kelsey Avenue Crew trailed 2–0.

"How's the game going?" Nicky asked.

"Rusty's a jerk," Ann jumped in.

"Hey, there you are, Pig Face," howled a voice even uglier than the face to which it was attached. "Look the Lip is here. I thought you'd never show up."

"Shut up, Rusty. Just go back to your position, and let's keep this game going," Ann yelled.

"What's the matter, Elephant Man? You can't speak for yourself anymore? You need girls to stick up for you."

Without hesitation, Nicky rushed toward Rusty, but Gennaro and Mark Kessler stopped him.

"It's not worth it, Nicky," Mark said. "Hang out here with us, and we are going to finally beat him and his loser friends."

"In your dreams, shrimp," Rusty shouted.

"Come on Rusty, let's play baseball," urged Rusty's pitcher, Jimmy Martin. "Forget about those retards. We came here to get some swings and play a game."

After a few more players chimed in with similar requests, Rusty finally returned to his position.

"What an idiot!" Ann exclaimed. "I don't even think his own teammates like him. They just put up with him because they think he can play a little bit."

"Ann's right, except for one thing" Gennaro added. "Rusty still stinks, and his breath smells worse than old sewer water. Let's finally kick his butt."

The Kelsey Avenue Crew burst from a small huddle and came out of the box swinging.

Lou Kessler started a rally, lacing a 2–2 fastball into the gap in left center for a triple.

Brother Mark roped a single to center, and the Kelsey Avenue Crew trailed, 2–1.

Two outs later with runners on second and third, Ann lined a bullet to left field to give the home team a 3–2 lead.

"Yeah, Annie M.," Nicky hollered. "We're going beat these bums today."

"Hey, Nicky," Gennaro leaned over to talk to his friend. "Can you play a few innings? Nobody here will tell your father."

"I'd better not, Gennaro. You never know who's watching. But you guys don't need me anyway. With Ann playing now, Rusty's finally going down. I just want to be here to see it."

The Kelsey Avenue club held the lead into the seventh inning. Ann played brilliantly at shortstop. Twice with runners in scoring position, she robbed Rusty of RBI hits with diving stops. Her baseball clothes were dirty, and she scraped her knees and elbows on the rocky field. By the fifth inning, you could see blood coming through her dirt soiled uniform.

Even though this was Ann's first game against the hated Crusty Rusty All-Stars, she wanted to win more than anything.

After robbing Rusty the second time, his big mouth started again.

"She's just getting lucky," Rusty complained. "No girl is ever going to beat me in a baseball game."

Gennaro, who pitched a great game with an assortment of curve balls and two-seam fastballs, overheard Rusty.

"Great job, Rusty, a complete sentence. Wow. You must really be proud of yourself. You now speak English."

"And by the way, carrot top. There's a first time for everything."

"Not today, loser."

"Great comeback, Rusty," Nicky contributed. "You must have worked on that one for weeks."

The Kelsey Avenue Crew felt quite comfortable, watching Gennaro dazzle the older opponents with his pitching performance.

"Don't worry, Nicky," Ann said. "They aren't touching Gerry today. We just need to pick up a couple of insurance runs, and we'll wrap this game up quite nicely."

In the bottom of the eighth, Ralph and John Ferrante roped back to back singles. John Sullivan dropped a picture-perfect sacrifice bunt down the third base-line, moving runners to second and third.

After Rusty moved the infield in to cut the run down at the plate, Bobby Kessler lined out hard to second base.

"Time out, time out," Rusty screamed from center field. "I'm coming in to pitch."

"Get out of here, Rusty. Stay in center field," his teammates cried.

"I'm going to strike this little girl out and end this mess."

"Bring it on, Rusty," Ann called from the top step of the dugout. "Bring it on."

Excitement swirled about the top diamond. People taking afternoon strolls stopped to watch this battle.

Rusty tossed his eight warm-ups and challenged Ann to step into the batters' box.

"Don't go home crying to mama if I throw too fast," Rusty shouted.

"And don't be mad if I happen to shoot one up the box and knock the stupid red hair off your head, tough guy."

Rusty threw the first pitch at Ann's head and knocked down the Kelsey Avenue shortstop.

Gennaro and Nicky started to leave the dugout.

"Guys, don't worry. Take it easy," Ann began. "Rusty's afraid to throw his fastball. He knows I'm going to crush it."

The second pitch knocked Ann down again. Now the crowd grew increasingly concerned, including Marie Kessler.

"You're real tough, Rusty," Mrs. Kessler yelled from the front lawn. "Throw the ball over the plate unless you're too afraid."

Rusty reached back and fired a four-seamer right down the middle. Ann swung violently and missed.

Strike one.

Rusty laughed. "Here it comes again, cutie pie. Don't hurt yourself swinging too hard."

The arrogant Alves painted the corner on the outer half of home plate with a blazing fastball that Ann missed again for strike two.

"Am I throwing too fast for you, little girl?" Rusty jeered. "Do you want me to throw it underhand so it's like softball and you can hit a little grounder back to me."

"Stop acting like an idiot, if that's possible," Mrs. Kessler screamed from her new vantage point next to home plate. "Ann's already three for three."

Ann called time out. She knocked some dirt from her sneakers with her favorite wooden bat, a classy thirty-two-inch, flame-tempered Louisville Slugger signed by her dad and Don Mattingly.

"Let's see what you got, Rusty."

Rusty turned to his teammates and laughed.

He set and threw another fastball, but this time Ann rocketed a comebacker to the mound that bounced off Rusty's shin and into the first base dugout.

The Kelsey Avenue Crew went bonkers laughing at Rusty Alves, who was screaming in pain. The red-headed big mouth rolled around in the dust, saying "foul ball, foul ball. The ball hit the mound."

"Nice try, Rusty," Gennaro replied. "But that ball hit your leg and we score two runs. Annie, great shot. Go to second base."

Things looked great. Two runs scored, and Rusty owned a baseball-seam mark on his left leg. The Kelsey Avenue Crew now held a commanding 5–2 lead.

"Oh, my God. I can't believe it," Mark K. said. "We're finally going to beat these bums."

"Sh. Don't jinx us, Mark," Nicky said. "We still have to get three outs."

The Crusty Rusty All-Stars retired the next hitter to strand Ann at second base and prepared for the top of the ninth.

Rusty angrily limped off the field and gathered his team around for a quick talk.

"If we lose this game, I'm going to beat the daylights out of every one of you," Rusty started. "Now whoever's leading off you have got to do something and get Gennaro out of the game. You know what to do."

This was one of Rusty's greatest and most notorious ploys. Just when a pitcher tossed a good game, he instructed one of his players to bunt down the first baseline and run over the pitcher to shake him or, worse, knock him out of the game.

"Gerry, just pour it in there, throw strikes and we got these morons," Ann instructed. "Keep the ball low, and make 'em hit ground balls."

Mark Sarno led off for the Crusty Rusty All-Stars and followed Rusty's orders. He bunted the ball along the first baseline and waited for Gennaro to field the ball.

When Gennaro caught the ball, Sarno maliciously spiked Gennaro in the leg and ran him over.

"Yeah, great bunt, Sarno," Rusty yelled. "Runner on first, no outs."

Nicky flew from the dugout and jumped on Rusty with Billy and Johnny G. right behind him. They tackled the evil red-head, but Archie Sagnella, Mrs. Kessler, and others broke up the melee.

"Gennaro, are you hurt?" Nicky asked. "Rusty told Sarno to do that on purpose. What a cheater."

"I knew it was coming, Nicky," Gennaro replied. "I wanted to run him over, but I didn't time it right. Don't worry, I can still pitch."

"Okay, Gennaro, let's go."

Gennaro dusted himself off, pulled his sock upwards to soak a little blood, and gingerly waited on the mound for the next batter.

After watching two pitches, the club knew that this was not the same Gennaro who dealt strike after strike for the first eight innings, but they knew he would not leave the mound and give the ball to a reliever.

After another single, the next two Crusty Rusty hitters popped up weakly to Mark K. in center field.

"Let's go Gerry. One more batter," Ann said.

"My arm and my leg hurt," Gennaro complained.

"Don't worry, Gerry, just suck it up and get the last out," Ann added. "You're pitching a great game."

"You're going down, Rusty," Mrs. Kessler warned with a smile.

Two fastballs later resulted in a seemingly innocent grounder to second base, but the ball hit a stone, took a wild hop, and bounced off George Carbon's chest. The bases were loaded for none other than Crusty Rusty—once again.

Surprisingly, though, Rusty was not talking. He seemed nervous. This was a first for the mouth that always roared.

This was going to be the day, Nicky thought.

Rusty was finally going to make the last out.

He's going to choke.

"I hope you can still speak, Rusty. I don't hear your big mouth," Gennaro started.

"Shut up and pitch, loser."

The crowd swelled to more than fifty people. Archie Sagnella and Frank Camp held court, informing everyone about the forty-four-game history of the Kelsey Avenue Crew and Crusty Rusty.

As the tension grew, Gennaro hurled strike one to Rusty.

"You just got lucky, loser. Try to throw that to me again."

Gennaro reached back and tossed a brilliant change up that spun Rusty into the ground for strike two.

As Rusty gripped the bat tighter and tighter, Gennaro smoothly bounced the next couple of pitches in the dirt, hoping Rusty will chase them, but he didn't.

The next pitch was low and outside. Miraculously, Rusty dropped the bat head on an amazing swing and lifted a long fly ball down the left field line.

"Oh, no," Nicky screamed. "Not again."

The ball, high and far, was unquestionably out of the park. All that remained now was to see if it were fair or foul.

"Stay fair; stay fair," Rusty roared, waving his arm running along the first baseline in his best Carlton Fisk imitation from the 1975 World Series between the Boston Red Sox and the Cincinnati Reds.

The ball finally landed well beyond the fence and over the yellow foul pole.

Eight Kelsey Avenue players screamed, "Foul."

Nine Crusty Rusty's squealed, "Fair."

Most of the onlookers had a look of apprehension while Archie Sagnella walked onto the field to stop the anticipated argument.

"Okay, boys. This is not going to be easy," Archie said.

"Don't forget me, Mr. Sagnella," Ann interrupted.

"That ball's fair, grandpa," Rusty shouted.

"That's not even close, dirt ball," Nicky followed.

Archie noticed Ann standing by third base with her hands on her hips not saying a single word.

"What did you see?" Archie asked.

"I'm sorry to say that's a fair ball," Ann admitted.

A smiling Rusty clapped his hands, circled the bases and while rounding third mocked Nicky by pulling at his upper lip.

6–5, Crusty Rusty.

So stunned was Nicky over the turn of events that he didn't react to a gesture that usually sent him into a rage.

Gennaro retired the side as they ran into the dugout for the precarious bottom of the ninth.

"That was fair?" Nicky asked as Ann charged in from shortstop.

"As much I hate to admit it, the ball cleared the fence just before it turned left," Ann said.

"Wow. You're honest," Nicky started. "I would stay here until I was fifty years old before I 'd admit to that jerk that the ball was fair."

"Hey, Nicky. Do you love baseball?"

"Of course I do."

"Well let me tell you something my Mom taught me," Ann began sharply. "She always said that if you love this game you must always do what's right because baseball always has a way of taking care of business."

"What the heck are you taking about?"

"Nicky, if you are fair to baseball, it will be fair to you," Ann continued. "My Mom always said that the cheaters and liars never win in the long run. You always have to be fair and truthful. Outs always should be outs. Strikes should be strikes. And fair should always be fair."

"That ball was fair?"

"That ball was tattooed.

"Come on, Nicky, we can't do anything now about the home run," Ann said. "Let's talk to these guys and try to rally and leave these jerks on the field."

Nicky and Ann round the players into the huddle.

"Guys, listen to Ann. Her dad played in the minor leagues with the Yankees."

Ann informed the club about how her dad said that the last three outs in the bottom of the ninth were the toughest.

"Be patient at the plate and wait for your pitch," Ann added. "We can win this game. We're only down by a run."

Chuck Stack led off with an infield single. One out later, John Ferrante and Lou Kessler singled to load the bases.

With Mark Kessler on deck and George Carbon at the plate, the Kelsey Avenue Crew tasted victory. Even if George made an out, everyone knew that Mark could win the game. He was probably the most athletically inclined of the Kelsey Avenue Crew.

In the fall, he could score three goals in a soccer game on Saturday, and then on Sunday tally three touchdowns in a football game.

During the winter, Mark could score thirty points in any basketball game. Spring and summer featured more of the same.

On a whim, Mark picked up a tennis racket, entered a tournament, and won first place, crushing people who took lessons and played everyday.

"Come on, George, just hit a fly ball into the outfield and stay out of a double play," Gennaro instructed.

George took a nervous swing and missed the first pitch by two feet. Rusty's next offering was a little high in the strike zone, and George swung and hit a towering pop up to third base.

No problem, two outs. Mark will still win the game.

But suddenly after the Crusty Rusty third baseman makes the catch, Chuck Stack tags up and breaks for home.

"Throw it home quickly," Rusty yelled. "We got him at the plate."

The Kelsey Avenue Crew was stunned.

Why was Chuck running home?

Had he lost his mind?

Was he trying to draw a bad throw and at least tie the game?

Doesn't he realize that Mark was on deck and he will certainly put a good swing on one of Rusty's fastballs?

But before these questions could be answered, Rusty ran toward home plate. He caught the ensuing throw from third base and tagged Chuck. The losing streak continued.

"Ha, ha," Rusty began. "You losers lose again. But I guess you guys are used to it by now. Don't you realize that you will never beat me and my boys, ever? Just give up, Lip Boy, and the rest of your loser friends."

Surprisingly, Nicky was silent. Usually, he coached third, and he was so focused on the fact that his punishment cost his team the game that Rusty's insults didn't bother him. Even though he didn't play, the loss was much more painful.

The Kelsey Avenue Crew watched Rusty celebrate again. Nicky walked over to Chuck, helped him to his feet, and asked him the big question.

"What were you thinking trying to tag up on that fly ball?"

"Well, just before the play, Mark K told me not to run until they caught the ball, and that's just what I did," Chuck explained.

"Moron, I meant when they caught the ball in the outfield," Mark K. screamed.

"Don't yell at him, Mark," Nicky interjected over the loud sound of an ambulance roaring down Kelsey Avenue. "This game is my fault. If I didn't lie to Big John, my parents, and everybody else about my glove, I could have played today and we would have won. This is so my fault."

"It certainly is your fault," Ann added, hitting Nicky on the head with her glove. "Maybe now you'll understand what I've been telling you for the past few days about the truth."

For the first time in history, the Kelsey Avenue Crew witnessed a world record. Nicky Palmieri was speechless.

Chapter 31
Pain and Suffering

While Nicky's silence was certainly deafening, the remainder of the Kelsey Avenue Crew said their good-byes.

There was not a word uttered about "good game."

No "nice jobs" and "atta boys."

Silence reigned.

Two years of losing to Crusty Rusty started to wear on them. This club was not happy with close games and moral victories. One by one, the club gathered their belongings and commenced what was going to be a long walk home. To no one's surprise, Ann seemed to be the most animated and furious.

"When are we going to play those idiots again?" Ann asked. "We have to beat the pants off them and wipe those stupid smiles off their faces."

"I'll set up another game in two weeks," Nicky said, breaking a record silent streak. "But everyone will have to practice without me. I'm hoping I can play next Saturday, but my punishment is no baseball for one week."

"Nicky, can't you sneak out and practice with us? You used to do it every time." Gennaro said. "None of us will tell on you."

Before Ann could give Nicky one of those you-better-not glares, he said, "I would love to play, but I can't lie to my parents anymore. I have to wait until my punishment is over."

With this, Ann located her ride home and said, "See ya, guys." The boys headed down Kelsey Avenue.

The game—loss number forty-five—bothered Nicky, but now his focus changed to the sound of an ambulance again.

"Gennaro, Ralph, do you hear that siren?" Nicky asked. "Almost everyday I hear one screaming down the street to the Oak Street Senior Citizen center."

"Yeah, I noticed that's there been quite a few racing past my house in the past few weeks," Gennaro replied. "I hope it's not anyone we know."

"I'm sure it's not. We've had enough misery this past week to last us a lifetime."

"You're right, Nicky. Let's hope for the best."

The trio walked home, and they dissected every play from the battle with Crusty Rusty. Nicky and Gennaro analyzed every situation. Ralph always listened and laughed because every game to them was bigger than life or death. But Ralph took the games in stride.

"We have to work on teaching the other players to hit the ball to the opposite field more, especially with runners on base," Nicky started.

"We don't move runners into scoring position too well," Gennaro added. "We could definitely practice that with some self-hit games."

These two were destined to be coaches. They always tried to make themselves better. They sat on the front porch of Gennaro's house for hours, talking baseball with anyone who listened. When Jerry was alive, he entertained them and taught them the finer points of baseball.

"It stinks not having Jerry around," Nicky said. "Do you remember the times we could talk to him about hitting?"

"Those days were so much fun," Gennaro said. "He wound hang out with us forever and talk baseball."

"We're lucky we still have Big John."

"Yeah, we sure are, Gennaro. We sure are."

Chapter 32
Bad News Travels Really Fast

Nicky and Ralph arrived home to the sweet smell of hot dogs and hamburgers grilling on the barbecue.

"How was the game, Ralph?" Mrs. Palmieri started. "Did you get any hits?"

"I had one of the best days ever, Ma," Ralph replied. "I hit two doubles and I drove in a couple of runs, too.

"But we lost to Rusty again," he added. "How many is it in a row, Nicky?"

Despondently, Nicky said, "Forty-five, Ralph. Forty-five."

"Hey, Nicky."

"What do want now?"

"Knock, knock."

"I'm not in the mood for one of your stupid 'knock, knock' jokes, Ralph."

"Come on. Knock, knock."

"Okay, okay, who's there?"

"Owen."

"Owen, who," Nicky said with a bit more sadness in his voice.

"Oh and forty-five, loser."

Mrs. Palmieri burst out laughing, and even Nicky chuckled as well. Deep down inside, Nicky knew that Rusty's team was better. It was just that Rusty was such a jerk and Nicky hated losing, especially to him.

Jerry always pointed out to Nicky and the other boys that Rusty's club never committed huge two-out errors. They constantly rallied when they trailed by a couple of runs, and they never rattled under pressure. Jerry also told them that good players learn to find ways to win.

He always made Nicky understand that championship baseball teams aren't usually filled with the best players. They simply have the best team.

"Ma, you should have seen Ann play today," Nicky said. "She's some player. She didn't make an error, and she got a hit every time up. She even bounced a rocket off Rusty's shins."

"Well, then how did you lose the game?" Mrs. Palmieri asked.

"We just didn't get those clutch two-out hits with runners in scoring position," Nicky said. "And by the way aren't you going to ask me if I played in the game or not?"

"No, I don't have to."

"What do you mean you don't have to?" Nicky responded. "Why did you and Daddy send some spies to the game?"

"No, I got a phone call from your favorite person."

"I didn't know Big John was at the game."

"It wasn't Big John. It was your favorite principal."

"What? Mrs. Anderson called you?"

"Yes, she went to watch the game," Mrs. Palmieri announced. "Isn't that nice?"

"Wait a minute, Ma. She was at Painter's Park watching a baseball game."

"Yes, that's what I said, Nicky. Why is there a problem?" There were not many things that confused Nicky, but trying to comprehend Principal Beast's attendance at a baseball game shot his thinking swirling into the stratosphere.

"Nah, not a problem at all, Ma. What did she say?"

"Well, Nicky, she had a lot to say," Mrs. Palmieri answered. "We had an interesting conversation."

Mrs. Anderson surely told Nicky's mother most of the facts of the Great Chocolate Milk Conflict among other things. But what concerned Nicky the most was a lingering comment from his day's work at Big John's Deli.

"Hey, Ma, I'm going to go wash my hands before dinner," Nicky said while pulling Ralph by the shirt into the house.

"Make sure your brother washes his hands, too, sometimes you kids bring half the baseball field into my house with those dirty clothes and fingernails."

As they walk the stairs toward the bathroom, Nicky interrogated his younger brother in rapid-fire machine-gun fashion.

"Did you see the bearded beast at the game?"

"No."

"Did you see what kind of car Ann jumped into after the game?"

"No."

"Is it possible that Ann's related to Mrs. Anderson?"

This one doubled Ralph's response.

"No way."

"Yes way, Ralph."

Nicky then repeated the conversation the principal had with Big John earlier in the afternoon. Ralph was stunned but still offered some words of wisdom.

"You're in big trouble with your new girlfriend."

"First, she's not my girlfriend, and secondly, how can I be in big trouble?"

Ralph then reminded Nicky of the bearded lady comments, the Irish punk cracks, and his brother's general attitude toward principals.

"You don't think she will tell Ann about how bad I am in school, do you, Ralph?"

"Nah, why would she do that, Nicky?" Ralph laughed. "You're a perfect angel."

Before Nicky started to wash his hands, he thought if anyone that old could remember his mean-spirited comments and headed back down the cement steps to the simmering charcoals on the barbecue.

"Hey, Ma, I know you didn't grow up in West Haven, but how do you know Mrs. Marriotti?" Nicky inquired.

"You mean, Ann's mother?"

"Yes, Ma," Nicky said bordering the fine line of sarcasm that usually led to an old-fashioned parental scolding and lecture on behavior.

Mrs. Palmieri told Nicky that when he was born, Mrs. Marriotti lived in West Haven. Ann's family moved to Florida when her father was demoted from the West Haven Yankees in Double AA to the Single A Fort Lauderdale Yankees.

"Ann's father was one heck of baseball player," Mrs. Palmieri said. "He should have made it to the Big Leagues, but he had some anger management problems."

It seemed that Carl Marriotti, a power-hitting outfielder, used his fist too many times on too many objects—water coolers after some strikeouts, dugout walls after strike-three calls by home plate umpires, bat racks after outs at first base, and managers after not playing after those strikeouts and outs. Finally, he took his frustration out on two wives after being released because of his .176 batting average.

While he played in West Haven, the Marriottis rented a house on Spring Street next door to a house where every Palmieri once lived with Grandpa Palmieri.

"We lived there to save money to buy this house, and your grandfather thought he was the best," Mrs. Palmieri added. "You don't remember because you were only two years old."

"But let me tell you a little story, Nicholas," she continued. "One Sunday night Grandpa Palmieri and your father went over and found Mrs. Marriotti slumped over the front steps with a four-inch gash over her left eye."

The next day the demotion came along with the West Haven Police and the Marriottis moved to Florida. The whole family was never seen together again.

"We tried to help her, but we didn't know what to say or do," Mrs. Palmieri said. "When he wasn't hitting or playing, he was mean to everyone. You should have seen how he used to yell around the house, especially after Ann's brother was born. The Yankees released him after the season. Then, months after the birth of Carl Jr., Mr. Marriotti left the family never to be seen or heard from again."

"You mean that Ann hasn't seen her father in eight or nine years?" Nicky said. "Then how did she become so good in baseball, Ma."

"Her mother helped her along with some skills and determination, Nicky," Mrs. Palmieri stated.

After Mr. Marriotti left, the owner of the New York Yankees, George Steinbrenner, hired Mrs. Marriotti for a marketing job in the Tampa Bay headquarters. For seven years, Ann's playpen was a pristine baseball diamond. Her babysitters were soon to be Major Leaguers for the Yankees that included Al Leiter, Buck Showalter, Ron Guidry, Dave Righetti, and Don Mattingly. Every day after school Ann crazily rushed to complete her homework in her mother's office and immediately raced to the batting cages or outfield for extra help.

"No wonder, she's so good at baseball," Ralph said. "And Ma, the best part is that she never gets mad—well, except for Crusty Rusty today. She really learned from the best. She learned to play like a pro."

Mrs. Palmieri informed the boys and her two daughters about Ann's talent in basketball and volleyball as well.

"She's going to be an All-American someday," Mrs. Palmieri predicted. "Her mother told me about her dedication and passion to learn."

"But Ma," Nicky interrupted. "She's probably got the gift. You can't teach that. It only comes around to special people."

"No, that's not totally true, kids," Mrs. Palmieri began. "She listened from the best. The best players are always the best listeners."

"What are you trying to say, Ma?" Nicky asked.

"Don't you two remember what I told you to do? Look at you and your brother's filthy hands and clothes," Mrs. Palmieri cracked. "That should say it all. And try to use some soap while you're at it, Nicholas."

The boys retraced their steps to running water to try to achieve some sense of cleanliness.

"Ralph, do you think Mom and Dad will allow me to run to Big John's after dinner?" Nicky asked. "I've got to check something in the back room at Big John's. Do you want to come with me?"

"Nah, you go. I'm going to sit in my room and read," Ralph replied.

"You are such a suck-up."

"Yeah, but I'll be smarter than you."

The boys' repartee continued until the sound every Palmieri recognized signaled the end of any tomfoolery—the creaking of the garage door and Mr. Palmieri's footsteps.

"Good job today, sonny boy," Mr. Palmieri started. "I heard you worked your eight hours at Big John's, and you didn't play in the game."

"No game for me, Dad," Nicky said. "I've learned my lesson. Hard work pays the bills—not the fooling around I do."

"Shut up, Nicky. You're an idiot," Mary joked. "You'll never stop playing in the sand. As long as there's baseball fields, you will always be fooling around."

"Yeah, and I'll remember that when I'm in the Big Leagues and you call me for World Series tickets."

The playful jabs continued but quickly subsided when Mrs. Palmieri announced, "Dinner's ready. Let's go."

Dinner conversation at the Palmieri table changed daily. Nicky never knew what was on Mr. Palmieri's mind. It could be a complaint about who wasn't working hard during Saturday overtime or a series of comments on America's lenient and liberal society.

Obviously, Nicky's mind was preoccupied with Mrs. Anderson's appearance at the ballgame, along with her connection to Ann.

"Ma, as soon as I'm done with the dishes, you don't mind if I go down to Big John's?"

"You better ask your father, Nicky."

"I'll be back in less than an hour. He'll never know I'm gone."

"What are you going there for at this time?" Mrs. Palmieri questioned.

"I think I forgot to do one thing today at work," Nicky lied as he remembered that Big John's West Haven High School yearbook was in the back room. Surely, it had to contain clues about Principal Beast's past.

Most likely he could also learn why she never ran Rusty into her office for even one of his mean stunts. There were so many questions that Nicky only ate one hot dog and one burger before heading off to Big John's.

"I'll be back in an hour," he said. "I promise."

Since Nicky didn't have to deliver the morning paper on Saturday, he figured it was a good time to run another sprint.

He always remembered Jerry telling him that playing baseball at the higher levels was about speed. The game became quicker, and the field became smaller because speedy fielders cut down the angles and made the tough plays look routine.

Speed, Nicky thought, "I have to work on my speed." He shot through the high school parking lot and onto Ocean Avenue. Then much to his surprise he noticed that the lights were not on at Big John's.

This was extremely peculiar because it was only 7 P.M. and Big John's was almost never closed early on Saturday, especially when he could sell thousands of lottery tickets.

Somehow Nicky sensed that something was wrong. Recalling the loud ambulance sirens after the baseball game, Nicky shook the front door violently. Nicky then ran next door to the Ocean Spirits Package Store.

"Mr. Keenan, Mr. Keenan, where's Big John?" Nicky said, trying to catch his breath. "Why is the store closed? What's going on?"

Before Mr. Keenan could answer Nicky, Mr. Palmieri arrived.

"Come with me, Nicky. We have to go see Big John at Yale-New Haven."

Chapter 33

Welcome to the Friendly Confines of Yale-New Haven Hospital

Nicky's life taught him a lot about pain.

He knew how words hurt. He knew how names hurt.

The sneers and snickers from strangers hurt.

A doctor's prognoses hurt, too.

But on this day, Nicky learned a different kind of pain—he learned about someone else's hurt.

"Big John's in the hospital," Mr. Palmieri started. "He had an accident in the back room, right in the kitchen."

Nicky's heart sank. He knew that the only good things that came out of hospitals were the visitors. His disdain for these colossal medical buildings filled with liars reached far beyond the MDs. Nicky distrusted everyone from the head nurse to the last custodian.

"Everything's going to be fine, Nicky," every nurse he ever knew lied. "Dr. Campari is an excellent doctor. He's the best."

This prompted Nicky's usual talking-to-himself response.

"Well, if he's the best, what's he doing in Connecticut?"

During the first seven surgeries, Nicky simply nodded his little noggin and accepted every word he heard. Then before the operations reached double digits, his belief in doctors deteriorated.

Promises, promises, promises.

"Your lip will be as good as new," one nurse said. "Dr. Campari always performs this work extremely well."

"Was it the surgery or the lies?" Nicky started to tell himself at ten years old. These questions constantly tried to leave his mind through his mouth, but they never did because only hope for a change in his situation kept Nicky quiet.

Hope that the bumps and scars disappeared.

Belief that the names stopped one day.

Dreams that girls in his school talked to him instead of using the old point and laugh routine. And while these words roared through Nicky's mind, something stopped him and changed his focus.

"Accident, back room, kitchen—oh, no, those broom sticks," Nicky recollected about his haste to leave Big John's for the baseball game during the afternoon.

"What happened, Dad? Is Big John okay?"

"Right after you left, Jimmy Constantino from next door came over and told me that Big John tripped and spilled a pot of boiling water on his right foot," Mr. Palmieri explained. "The water was so hot it burned his foot right through his orthopedic shoes."

"Is that bad, Dad?" Nicky asked. "Do you have to stay in the hospital for that?"

"Let's go see Big John and we can find out more."

With the change of subject, Nicky knew that there was more to the story. They ventured to Room 222. Big John was resting comfortably with his right foot in a sling above the bed.

"Joe, great to see ya," Big John said. "Bring those crutches over here and we're leaving."

"I don't think so Mr. Wizenski," Dr. Milici warned. "We would like to run some more tests."

"Tests? There's going to be no tests on me unless they are free?"

"John, you need these tests," Dr. Milici replied as Big John started to rise angrily from the hospital bed.

The head nurse entered the room and asked Mr. Palmieri to keep Nicky outside, so the doctor could speak with Big John alone.

"Nicky, here's some money. Go downstairs and grab a candy bar and wait in the hallway until Big John's ready to leave."

"I'm not hungry, Dad. I'll stay and find out what happened to Big John."

"No, sir, you won't. Go downstairs, buy a Coke or whatever you want and wait. We'll be right there."

This was not a good sign, Nicky thought. He took a few steps down the hall and hid behind the stinky hospital dinner tray cart. He heard Big John raise his voice. Dr. Milici and Mr. Palmieri tried to calm the big man down.

"Joe, tell this doctor that I'm going home because I have to go to work tomorrow," Big John said. "I've just got some second-degree burns on my foot. I still have one foot left."

Out of the corner of the doorway, they heard Nicky, "And a lot of Polish stubbornness power, too."

"Nicola, what did I tell you? The next time I hear that voice, it better be downstairs like I told you."

"Yes, Dad."

Big John was laughing hysterically, but Dr. Milici did not crack a smile at all.

"John this is serious," he stated. "This accident might affect your heart. When we took your blood pressure, the numbers were dangerously high."

"Let me tell you something, Doc, the only numbers I'm worried about are the ones next to those dollar signs that I'm going to lose if I don't get to work tomorrow."

"Joe, give me those crutches, and let's get out of here."

Big John pulled both wooden walking aids under his arms and quickly moved toward the elevator.

"John, I'm advising you to stay. You are leaving against doctor's orders."

"Just leave me alone and send me the bill."

Mr. Palmieri and Big John exited the elevator laughing uncontrollably.

"What did I miss?" Nicky asked. "I always miss the good jokes."

"Never mind, just tell me who won the game today, One Cell?"

"Crusty Rusty won again, Big John. We made a stupid base-running mistake in the ninth and we lost. We're going to play him again next week."

"Good. Joe, the kid did a good job at the store today. Let him play next week."

"We'll see how the week goes in school and at home," Mr. Palmieri responded. "This boy's gotta lot to learn."

While Mr. Palmieri walked to the parking garage to bring the car around to the hospital's front sidewalk, Nicky's curiosity grabbed center stage.

"Are you okay, Big John?"

"Yeah, I'll be fine, just wait until we get in the car, so I don't have to tell the story twice tonight."

Big John took the front seat and immediately started talking about how the boiling water hit his foot. Nicky cringed in the back seat. He wished he were a turtle so he could pull his head between his shoulders and hide.

"Sometimes I think I'm still twenty-one years old," Big John began. "I don't realize how dark the back room is, and I must have tripped over something while I carried the potato pot of boiling water to the sink.

"The water spilled onto my foot, and luckily for me, Harry Huber was around to call an ambulance and close the store," Big John continued. "I couldn't even move. The burning pain in my foot was crippling."

"How does it feel now?" Mr. Palmieri asked.

"These pain killers really do the trick. I don't feel anything but tired."

Big John explained how the emergency room doctors thought his heart was an issue after telling them his chest hurt.

"I told those idiots that my chest was bothering me, but before I could tell them it was because I got hit by brooms, boxes, and pots, they are running me all over the place and testing me."

Greater silence. Nicky's head was buried like an ostrich.

"Hey, Nicky, you awake?" Mr. Palmieri asked. "Big John's taking a cheap shot at doctors, and you don't have anything to say?"

Nicky shot up and started in with his pointed views that many of these doctors want to test, test, and test to steal money from the working people. Big John and Mr. Palmieri howled at the twelve-year-old's perspective as they approach Richmond Avenue.

Seeing Mrs. Wizenski waiting on the front porch for her injured giant, Big John offered his thanks to the Palmieris.

"Big John, I'll be at the store at 6 A.M. to help you open," Nicky started. "And if you're nice to me, I'll stay with you all day, too, from open to close. Don't worry."

"Hey, Joe, tell the little wise guy in the back seat that I didn't commit murder. I just hurt my foot. I need sympathy, not capital punishment."

"Don't blame me, John. You're the one that gave him the job," Mr. Palmieri added to the Richmond Avenue comedy hour.

As Nicky took in the jokes, he realized that there was more to the lie to explain the amazing and exhausting day.

Chapter 34

Let's Hear Three Cheers for the Truth

Just as Nicky was about to head for bed, Ann called after she learned that the sirens she heard came from an ambulance that carried Big John to Yale-New Haven.

She knew how much Nicky loved and respected Big John, and Ann always sensed others' hurt. She went to great lengths to help them.

Nicky told her about the scene with the doctors and the parting jokes at Big John's house. But now a strange feeling struck him harder than a hit-by-pitch or a punch from Crusty Rusty in the rib cage.

"Ann, this whole accident is my fault."

"Why do you say that, Nicky?"

"Well, I was in a hurry to go to the game, and I told Big John I finished with my work, but I didn't do one thing.

"I didn't move the brooms and shovels and boxes in the back," Nicky stammered. "But, but...."

"But what, Nicky?"

"But I told him I did and then later in the afternoon he tripped on those broom sticks and spilled the boiling water on his foot. It's my fault. I feel terrible." Nicky heard Ann's gasp on the other end of the phone. Even though he'd only known her for a few weeks, he felt a trusting feeling about Ann.

There wasn't any peer pressure.

She never judged him or anyone else.

His fears dissipated about his appearance with her.

Ann's attitude toward him was consistently genuine.

Turning this information over and over in his mind, Nicky knew what he had to do.

"Ann, I'm going to take care of this tomorrow morning," Nicky said. "I'm going to tell Big John the truth. I should have moved those brooms and boxes. He never would have hurt himself if I told the truth."

"Good job, Nicky," Ann replied. "I'm sure that if you tell him tomorrow, he won't be mad at you."

"You know, Ann, I've got a lot to tell him."

Nicky ran through so many lies, giving Ann numerous details. Everything was covered. The phone conversation was just like confession, without the traditional kneeling in a mildly dilapidated wooden box. The topics were endless, ranging from doctors' visits to the Great Chocolate Milk Conflict to the missing Heart of the Hide.

"Wow," Ann said. "How are you able to keep track of everything?"

"I can't remember everything, but I know how afraid I am of disappointing people," Nicky answered.

"Are you afraid of me?"

"No, never. You are so nice and you never judge me."

"Are you afraid of anything, Ann?" Nicky asked.

"Sure, I'm afraid my father's going to come home."

"What, your father, the baseball player?"

Ann poured her heart out to Nicky. She told him about her father's constant lies and the beatings she watched her mother take. Amazed, Nicky remained speechless. She also told Nicky about how her father left after her brother was born.

"He's a jerk," Ann began. "He always complained about how he wanted a son, and then after he sees my brother's birth defect, he decides to leave. You don't know how lucky you are, Nicky."

"What's wrong with your brother?"

"It's not something I want to talk about right now," Ann answered.

"I'm so sorry, Ann. I thought your father was a great baseball player. But I never realized that just because you are good at sports, it doesn't mean that you automatically become a good person, too."

"Don't worry about it, Nicky. It's not your fault," Ann added.

"Hey, Ann, do you think that one day I could come over and visit you and your brother when I'm not delivering the papers?"

"Sure, Nicky. That would be cool, but I have to ask my mother first."

"That's okay. Whenever it's good for everybody."

"Hey, Ann," Nicky added after an amazingly long silent pause. "Thanks. I really appreciate you listening to me. I got to go to bed, so I can get up early tomorrow."

"Do the right thing, Nicky," Ann responded. "You'll see it won't be that bad."

"Thanks, Ann. See ya'."

On his way to his room, Nicky spotted Mr. and Mrs. Palmieri looking suspiciously and pointing at a ceiling light fixture.

"Good night, son," Mr. Palmieri started while poking his elbow in Mrs. Palmieri's ribs.

"You better get some rest. You've got to carry the big man tomorrow."

"Thanks for the tip, Dad."

Nicky's plan included many items for discussion, many of which he mulled over in his mind.

First, he wanted to ease into the broom and boxes issue. He expected Big John's temper to hit a roof higher than the old Houston Astrodome.

Second, he figured the Great Chocolate Milk Conflict was seemingly almost meaningless, except for the mistruths. And now he finally realized that Principal Anderson knew everyone in town. And last but certainly never the least, Nicky knew the infamous glove set the stage for a tough showdown with truth.

Having regained possession of his treasured Heart of the Hide, Nicky figured this glove would help make this play as well. The only problem for him was that this truth thing featured more pressure than any baseball game or practice.

*   *   *

"Good morning, Big John."

"How's it going, One Cell?"

"Forget about me. How is your foot?"

"The pain is under control, but the second-degree burns are going to take a long time to heal," Big John replied.

"I hope it heals quickly. You know I can't stand going to the doctor, no matter what," Nicky admitted.

"Big John, there's something I have to tell you. It's my fault that you tripped yesterday and burned your foot. I'm really sorry."

Nicky's admission of guilt moved forward into an unknown truthful stratosphere. He told Big John the entire story about how he was in a hurry to go to the game, so he lied about moving the boxes. He offered his apologies, but Big John didn't bat an eyelash.

"Is there anything else, Nicky?"

"I'm really sorry about those boxes and brooms."

"Don't worry about my accident. I have to learn to be more careful in that back room, but you, however, have to learn to be honest with people," Big John stated.

"Sometimes, I mean, most of the time, I'm afraid of what people think. I'm afraid of their reactions."

"You can't live your life that way, Nicky. You have to trust people, especially those that love you."

"So, is there anything else you want to talk about?" Big John asked in high hopes that Nicky might finally confess to some, if not all, of the lies about the recovered baseball glove.

Nicky stared aimlessly for a moment. He tried to tell Big John, but he couldn't pull the trigger on clearing the baseball glove mess.

One bout of truth was enough for him. It's like having two operations in the same day.

One was clearly enough.

Chapter 35

Eight Days and Out

Nicky went to sleep that day accepting this truth business a little more. When his head hit the cozy down pillow, he realized that, when Mrs. Palmieri entered his room, there would only be eight more wake-ups until summer vacation—eight more days of Rusty's taunting, eight more chances to figure out something about Principal Anderson that was bringing her dangerously closer to him than ever before, and eight more walks to Stiles Elementary School.

This last thought saddened Nicky. He loved most of the people he met in the seven years he spent in the building.

His recollections included many fond memories from kindergarten through second grade. The kids didn't bother him then, and he did extremely well in school during the early grades.

In third grade after the seventh operation, he became the brunt of many people's jokes, and he never understood why. He wished he could put the name-calling aside. Nicky badly wanted acceptance from everyone. Many times the lunch monitors and custodians talked to him when he ran to a corner of the building during recess to hide or cry. They tried to lift his spirits, but Nicky's responses were far from a morsel of truth.

"What's the matter, son?" Mr. Zullo, Stiles' lead custodian asked when he found Nicky hiding in the basement next to the boiler room.

"It's too cold outside to play, and the lunch monitors won't let me back in the room," Nicky explained during one sunny June afternoon. "I left my jacket at home, so I figured I could hang out here with you for a little while."

Mr. Zullo told Nicky to wait there and brought back a delicious chocolate chip cookie, one of those soft treats where the warm chocolate was still melting on the top. The cookies always made Nicky smile.

"Do I owe you any money for this cookie?" Nicky asked. "I have money at home, and I could bring it tomorrow."

"It's on the house, kid," Mr. Zullo replied. "But if I see you in here tomorrow, you have to pay me double."

"And one more thing, if I see you playing with the kids outside on the playground, I'll buy you two cookies a day until school ends. Deal?"

"Deal."

The next day, Nicky ventured to the playground and joined a kickball game, booted a homer in the last inning before the whistle sounded, and made eight instant friends.

The moment, seemingly insignificant, served as a crucial turnaround point that summer. He went to work on his baseball skills. He practiced every day in his back yard for hours and hours.

He bounced ground balls off a cement wall that separated the Palmieri's house from the Constantino's. Nicky squatted like a catcher and threw pop ups to himself for hours. He took his bat and practiced his swing until his arms burned.

Then one Sunday night late in August, Mr. Palmieri took Nicky and Ralph to Painter's Park where they met the Kesslers and Gennaro. The Palmieri brothers played in the game, and Nicky made friendships that would last a lifetime. From this point on, Nicky felt so much better about school, knowing he had his own posse to combat the wise cracks and snide remarks from Crusty Rusty.

These thoughts stirred in Nicky's mind until, finally, his evening/early morning snooze was interrupted by Mrs. Palmieri's call to awake and deliver the newspapers.

"Nicky, it's time for you and your brother to work the paper route."

"Okay, Ma, we'll be ready in a minute."

The boys started the route, and Nicky completed his section in warp speed. He barreled down Kelsey Avenue until reaching the Marriotti house. Ann was there sitting on the front stairs.

"How did it go yesterday at Big John's?" she began. "I know you told him the truth about the boxes."

"Yeah, Ann, it was hard, but I feel really bad about the accident. So, I sort of told him some of the truth," Nicky fibbed. "It wasn't as hard as I thought it would be. Big John really didn't get mad. He was probably more upset about the glove lies than anything else."

Ann pressed Nicky further about the glove, and Nicky told her the whole story as he promised her at the birthday party. He started with Jerry and the wonderful way in which he graced West Haven.

Tears filled Nicky's eyes when he explained how Jerry died and what he meant to Nicky. Then he changed the subject to avoid pain. Nicky talked about what he had learned about ancient Egyptians. He was so proud of his ABC book he wrote on mummification and the afterlife. His comfort level with his friend was so different—he felt safe. He finally let go.

"Ann, I know that there is baseball in Heaven. So, that's why in the middle of the night, I ran to the funeral home and put my glove in Jerry's casket."

"You put your Heart of the Hide in there?"

"I wanted Jerry to have it in the next world. I wish you could have known what a great person he was to me. I had to do something."

The story continued and Ann learned how her friend put baseball cards, hats, and other items in the casket, too.

"Something's bothering me, Nicky," Ann remarked. "You talk about how great Jerry was, but then you lied about doing something nice for him."

"I couldn't tell people I put a $200 glove in a casket," Nicky exclaimed. "Big John and my parents would have killed me." Nicky admitted to Ann that maybe now was an excellent time to confess about this glove mess, but he wasn't sure how to start.

"Just let the truth flow, Nicky," Ann instructed before her mother came down the stairs for the morning paper along with a warning for Nicky that it was almost 7:30 A. M. with school time closing in soon.

"It will be easy when you explain why you did it. You tried to do a good thing. People can't be mad about that."

"You are so right, Ann, but I just never realized the crazy amounts of damage I created with these fibs."

"Lies, Nicky—lies, lies, lies," Ann informed him also referring to the fact that fibs escalate to the next level in which lies are born.

"When I admitted to Big John about the boxes, I know I should have told him about the glove, but I couldn't do it," he said. "By this time, I started to actually believe that Rusty stole my glove. It's time to put an end to this."

"You know what to do, so now it's up to you to just do it," Ann said without the hoopla of a Nike commercial.

Nicky hung his head like a criminal who had been sentenced to life in prison without baseball. He despondently issued his customary farewell and headed for home—slowly.

He realized that summer would only be fun if he could dump the burden he placed on himself. Every time Nicky touched or handled the mitt, he felt the sadness he knew his lies inflicted upon innocent people that he cared about.

Nicky's job was much easier than the times before most of his "elective" surgeries. He knew that the next eight days could move smoothly if he could withstand the misery and anguish of the painful truth.

Chapter 36

Education, Education, Education.

Upon Nicky's arrival at school, Rusty's greetings never changed. It was like an old rerun. You watched the show intently even though you know what was coming.

"Hey, Elephant Face." Rusty's innovative genius shined through once more. "I'm surprised to see your fat lip walk into school after we beat your butt again this weekend.

"I figured you and your team would be too tired because you girls are practicing running home from third on pop-ups to shortstop," the villain taunted Nicky, with a reference to Chuck Stack's bonehead play. He followed his comments with a creative tug on his lip.

Nicky barely batted an eyelash. He simply yawned and moved forward on his way to visit Principal Anderson for the second day of his three-day sentence for the Great Chocolate Milk Conflict.

"Look at the loser," Rusty continued. "He can't even talk. Maybe your fat lip is getting in the way. I can't wait until a week or two from now when we play you again. I'm going to stomp on you until you bleed, Lip, and one more thing...."

Rusty stopped mid-sentence while a big paw landed squarely on his shoulder.

"Mr. Alves, you are best advised to be heading to class and to leave Nicky alone," the principal commanded. "Mr. Palmieri, I will see you in my office immediately."

Rusty quickly moved to Miss Hansen's room while Nicky, stunned after hearing her use a name other than "Nicholas," sat in Mrs. Anderson's office to await another behavior lecture.

While the Beast glared at Rusty from her doorway, Nicky noticed that her room was filled with books he recognized from his passion for reading.

"Mrs. Anderson, you read sports books?" Nicky's inquiring mind wanted to know.

"Why yes. Nicky, are you surprised that a woman like me loves baseball as much as you do?" Mrs. Anderson said.

"No, ma'am," Nicky fibbed, realizing the fine choice he made between fibbing and lying. "As a matter of fact, there are lots of women out there who love sports."

"When I was younger, I played baseball every day with my little stepbrother," Mrs. Anderson offered, sending Nicky for a wild spin around the cranium.

"My stepbrother was drafted in the tenth round by the New York Yankees, and he played in the Minor Leagues. He even used to play in West Haven."

A silent Nicky pinched himself in the right arm while asking, "You had a relative who played for the West Haven Yankees?"

"Yes."

"And you have a goddaughter?'

"Yes."

"Did your stepbrother play for the Fort Lauderdale Yankees, too?"

"Yes."

"Do you still live on Spring Street?"

"Yes."

"Oh, oh," Nicky said. "I think I'm going to pass out."

"What's the matter, Nicky?" a smiling Mrs. Anderson replied. "Do you want any autographs or something else? I have plenty."

"No, but may I ask you one more question?"

"Yes."

"You were watching a game on Saturday on the top field at Painter's Park, weren't you?"

"Yes."

"I'm in big trouble with Ann, aren't I?"

"Absolutely."

"But I must say that for some strange reason my goddaughter speaks quite highly of you," Mrs. Anderson added. "She told me that you were the first person in this town to be nice to her, and she is so happy that you invited her to play on your team. That was a nice gesture, Nicky. Sometimes you are thoughtful even though you call me Principal Beast."

Nicky slumped further in his chair. The town really was shrinking.

"It's no gesture. Ann is some player. We need her to beat Rusty.

"Ann's a competitor," Nicky continued. "You can tell that she enjoys baseball—more than any girl I ever met."

Mrs. Anderson invited Nicky behind her desk. She pulled open a drawer from an old, beige metal file cabinet. She carefully withdrew a musty yellow folder filled with pictures.

"Do you recognize anyone in these photos?" Mrs. Anderson asked.

The second picture Nicky pulled from the folder was from a championship University of Connecticut softball team.

"Can you find me?"

"No, I can't. Which one is you, Mrs. Anderson?"

"Read the names on back and let me know if any of them ring a bell, Nicky."

Nicky was totally shocked. He rubbed his eyes three or four times, took two or three huge swallows, and finally blurted, "Your last name was Marriotti? You are Italian and you played sports, too."

"Why does that surprise you? You think that just because I'm a principal it means that I couldn't play baseball?"

At this moment, Mrs. Anderson's athletic talents were not what worried Nicky.

"You are related to Ann, too?"

"Yes, not only is she my goddaughter, but she's also my niece," Mrs. Anderson stated happily.

She continued telling Nicky how her stepbrother was a failure for a father. Mrs. Anderson railed him for promises he broke and for the countless times he terrorized Ann and her sister-in-law with fists, constant badgering, and negative and abusive language.

"Ann's mother is a brave person for putting up with Carl's antics," Mrs. Anderson explained. "He would never stop. He would instigate arguments with snide remarks and never leave his wife alone. He is such a loser of a person. As much as I may love him, even I had to write him out of my life forever."

She further explained how he was never appreciative of the innumerable things her mom and dad did for him. Mrs. Anderson informed Nicky about how he stole money from the entire family. She also told him of Mr. Marriotti's string of lies and stories he used to appease those around him.

"He was even a loser of a man before he ran out on his family after seeing his son's birth defect," Mrs. Anderson continued as Nicky noticed a tear roll down her left cheek.

"His drug and alcohol problems should have forced him into rehabilitation, but he doesn't care. He continued to drink and do what he wanted without any regard for anyone else's feelings. I'm so ashamed of the liar I don't even answer his phone calls anymore."

This last line pounded Nicky the hardest.

Nicky realized that this great baseball player was not so great. He was not only a mean and nasty person, but a liar and a thief as well. There were few redeeming qualities that even Nicky, the biggest of baseball fans, could find in this person.

The liar part hammered Nicky between the eyes. He knew that he didn't want to go down the same road as Carl Marriotti. Nicky wanted to live the dream. He wanted to play baseball in the Major Leagues, but he started to comprehend how his lies caught up with him. Nicky knew he must transform and quickly even if his dreams only had a remote chance of coming true.

While Mrs. Anderson grabbed a tissue to wipe away more tears, Nicky did what he knew best.

He changed the subject.

"What kind of birth defect does Ann's brother have?"

"You know, Nicky, that is something that you will have to learn on your own. Why don't you ask Ann and see for yourself?"

"Mrs. Anderson, can I ask you a couple of questions?"

"Go ahead, Nicky."

"If you are Italian just like me, why don't you stop those other kids from picking on me and saying those mean things?"

"Because it doesn't matter what nationality I am. I have to teach you to control who you are and not worry about what other people say."

"That's funny. Ann said the same thing," Nicky admitted as he politely excused himself and started to leave to start his schoolwork at the desk outside the office, but not before Mrs. Anderson stopped him dead in his tracks.

"Oh, by the way, make sure when you go home this afternoon that you tell your father and mother to send my regards to Italy and Grandpa Palmieri for me."

"How well did you know my grandfather?" Nicky asked.

"Let's put it this way, Nicola," as Mrs. Anderson pronounced Nicky's proper name with a fluent Italian accent. "If I ever told Grandpa Palmieri or your father about the names that you called me along with your disrespectful little mouth, you would be in big trouble and probably looking for a new set of teeth. That's why I always tell your mother first."

Of course. Of course. This was how Mr. Palmieri knew everything that happened in school. Mrs. Anderson, otherwise known as Ms. Ida Marriotti, lived next door to Grandpa Palmieri.

Many times after elementary classes ended and the buses departed, Mrs. Anderson drove to Mr. Palmieri's woodworking shop and delivered many personal messages. On some occasions, she spoke to Mr. Palmieri in Italian for hours, but she saved the bad stuff for Mrs. Palmieri. She told him everything that happened in Miss Hansen's class or any other room Nicky was in. She definitely informed him about the Great Chocolate Milk Conflict before Nicky arrived home from school.

This went on for seven years, and these were the things one needs to learn from teachers, Nicky thought to himself.

This was necessary knowledge.

This was social studies.

This was education.

This was miserable.

"If you know my family so well, Mrs. Anderson," Nicky started, "then why are you so hard on me? Why do you let those kids call me names and make fun of me every day?"

"Close the door, Nicola."

Mrs. Anderson told Nicky the whole truth and nothing but the truth. The stunned twelve-year-old was further shocked by more revelations of how close Mrs. Anderson was to the entire Palmieri clan.

"I was the one who used to drop off your grandfather on the way to work," Mrs. Anderson began. "I was the one who brought your mother home from the hospital after you were born, so your father could deal with the doctors."

"You knew me when I was a little baby?" Nicky interjected.

"Yes, I did, young man. Until you moved to Richmond Avenue when you were two years old, Grandpa Palmieri and I used to baby-sit. When your father, mother, and grandmother went grocery shopping, we watched baseball games together and drank espresso with a little shot of anisette once in a while."

"My grandfather did that with me all the time," Nicky blurted. "I miss my grandfather."

"I miss him, too, since he went back to Italy," Mrs. Anderson conceded. "He is a great person. Your grandfather and father always worked extremely hard to make sure you had the best doctors and education."

"But I don't have the best doctors," Nicky snapped. "Look at my lip. The kids make fun of me and these operations are never going to end. The teasing is never going to end."

"The teasing will end, Nicola, when you let it end."

"But since you obviously knew me since I was a little baby and you know my family so well, why don't you help me and make them stop?" Nicky angrily questioned, his eyes tearing up.

"Jerry would."

"And Jerry's not around anymore, is he, Nicky?"

Nicky's tears rolled faster and faster.

"And what does that have to do with anything?"

"Well, young man, when Jerry wasn't around, did the teasing stop?"

"No. Rusty and his stupid friends would wait until he left, and they would start again. But they knew that when Jerry found out, they would be in big trouble."

"But did it stop?"

"No."

"So, now you want me to stop it?"

"You can. You're the principal."

"Yes, I am the principal, but do you want me following you around everywhere you go? I can do that if you want, or I can help you learn to deal with your situation. I promised your grandfather I would look out for you and I did. I always placed you with the kindest and best teachers in this school."

At first, he half-heartedly nodded his head in approval.

However, Nicky remembered everything.

The seven years he spent in this elementary school really were a lot of fun. The teasing he could certainly live without, but the friends he made and the wonderful teachers he met stayed with him forever.

Nicky just never realized Mrs. Anderson's impact.

Every summer the school mailed letters informing the children of their upcoming teacher.

Every summer Nicky correctly predicted his teachers.

Every summer.

With just eight days remaining, he knew Mrs. Anderson was right.

Again.

In kindergarten, Mrs. Nyberg read thousands of wonderful stories while always giving him extra help with the blocks and letters.

In first grade, Mrs. Murphy took extra time with Nicky's reading skills.

In second grade, Ms. Gallagher's hugs and warm heart explained why his name was always pulled out of the hat to be line leader—Nicky's favorite job.

In third grade, Ms. Tarpinian's soft, kind voice helped him learn to write in script.

In fourth grade, Mrs. Blair constantly slipped a baseball card or two into Nicky's desk when he scored one hundred on a test.

In fifth grade, Mr. Wilgenkamp made sure pieces of Nicky's favorite Hershey's dark chocolate candy mystically appeared in his desk after a great week of school-work or if he wrote the W.O.W. (Word of the Week) in a sentence.

And now in sixth grade, Nicky knew how Miss Hansen kept the kids from openly teasing him. He recognized the nice way in which she helped him with his essay writing skills.

"You picked the kids for the classes, Mrs. Anderson? I thought the teachers had meetings and picked the kids."

"No, I pick the classes. I'm the boss. One day you will understand what I did to help you. Next year, you are going to Giannotti Middle School, and I know that principal is not going to care about you like I do.

"You have to learn to deal with these kids or else you are letting them get the best of you," Mrs. Anderson instructed. "You are too smart for that."

"But Rusty never gets in trouble, and he's always picking on me."

"I care about you. You have a chance to do something special if you want to. I don't want you to go to middle school and fight every day with kids from other elementary schools. Rusty's nothing compared to some of the eighth and ninth graders you are going to run into."

"Do you think they are going to pick on me worse than Rusty?" Nicky wondered.

"Only if you let them bother you. You have to focus on what you have to do and not worry about what the wise guys are trying to entertain themselves with. The teasing will end when you learn how to deal with it, Nicky. It's up to you."

"I hope you're right, Mrs. Anderson. I hope you're right."

Nicky wiped away the last of the tears and trudged back to the suspension desk to begin his work.

"Oh, Mrs. Anderson."

"Yes, Nicky."

"Thanks. Thanks for everything."

Chapter 37

Fire up the Barbecue. School's Almost Out for Summer

The school day ended without incident and a Crusty Rusty sighting. The usual crowd gathered for the walk home along Kelsey Avenue.

"Did Principal Beast yell at you today?" Gennaro asked.

"No, she talked to me about a lot of things," Nicky started. "She knows my grandfather and my father pretty well."

"What? The Beast knows your father?" Mark K. chimed.

"Yep. Pretty amazing, huh, Kess?"

"This stinks. You found this out today with seven days of school left."

"Whoa. Think about the trouble she could have bailed you out of if you knew this sooner," John Ferrante added.

"She's not like that," Nicky informed. "She promised my grandfather she would look after me, and now that I think about it, she did."

"But, Nicky, she never stopped those kids from picking on you in class. What's that about?" Gennaro questioned.

"She said she was teaching me about the way I have to live my life. She's probably right. I have to learn to deal with things better. I can't expect people to bail me out all the time. I learned a lot today."

Nicky explained the entire Mrs. Anderson–Palmieri connection. The Kelsey Avenue Crew's jaws dropped in disbelief.

The boys fired questions at Nicky at machine-gun speed.

"Principal Beast is Ann's Aunt?"

"Mrs. Anderson played baseball?"

"Carl Marriotti is her stepbrother?"

"She's Italian?"

"She smiled?"

"She used to have blond hair like Pam Anderson?"

"It's really unbelievable, but it's true," Nicky informed the crew. "This world is much too small for me. The only thing that would surprise me more is if I woke up the first day of summer vacation and my mother adopted Crusty Rusty."

"If that happens, Nicky," Ralph interjected as the Kelsey Avenue Crew walked home. "He's sleeping in your bed and sharing your clothes." The boys laughed hysterically as they divided to enter their own homes.

The days grew longer. The daily garb featured shorts and T-shirts, and the warm sun and the sweet smell of freshly mowed grass signaled that summer rapidly approached.

Barbecues fired up throughout the neighborhood during dinnertime. The mouth-watering smells of chicken, hot dogs, hamburgers, ribs, and steaks cooking on propane-fueled grills filled the air. Summer baseball seasons operated in high gear, and the best part was that in seven days, as rock star Alice Cooper so aptly sang, "School's out for summer."

For Nicky, the end of school held greater meaning to him than to the rest of the boys. They never realized how nerve-racking the glares from younger children bothered him. Nicky never complained how the first and second graders turned their heads for another look when he walked the hallways.

Besides not seeing Rusty and his evil friends every day, Nicky found day-to-day life less stressful. He could spend seven more hours a day with his family and friends for two consecutive months. Nicky enjoyed the learning school fostered, but he always felt that it was so much more fun if he looked like the other children.

These thoughts weighed heavily upon Nicky's mind. He anticipated that this summer was extra special. This was the first summer in four years without surgery.

No doctor's office visits in the middle of the day.

No needles stuck in his arms to draw blood samples.

No poking around by surgical teams showing interns the numerous surgeries that fixed his cleft palate.

No hospitals.

No cuts.

No healing and the best of all…

No disappointments.

Sure, there was a Little League baseball game here or there where Nicky's team lost in the bottom of the sixth, but there was a team of players and coaches who shared his misery. No matter where Nicky turned, no one experienced the pain his lip brought him. This was something he endured alone.

Baseball was the perfect sport for Nicky and his cleft palate. It provided Nicky with the sense of being alone and being on a team at the same time.

One person batted at a time—alone.

The pitcher stood alone on the mound.

Each player ran the bases by himself.

Each player was responsible for a position.

Relief pitchers sat in the bullpen away from everybody. Even catchers, infielders, and outfielders own separate responsibilities.

When a hot grounder smashed toward shortstop, there was no help and even less sympathy.

It was ball versus player. The player makes the play or doesn't.

Baseball was black and white.

It was safe or out.

It was a ball or a strike.

It was a win or a loss.

There were no ties in baseball.

They play extra innings.

Nicky always hoped that doctors finished their nine innings at bat and that his operations were in extra frames. Then there was a chance for a winning procedure. He patiently waited for the surgery to end all surgeries where he stared into that mirror to see a perfect, regular lip.

A lip without bumps and scars.

A lip similar to those of movie stars.

This dream never came true for Nicky. He never witnessed another person with a cleft palate. Not one of his many doctors ever showed him a progression of pictures displaying a perfectly fixed lip Nicky so desperately sought.

Nicky thought that if he hit the lottery he could buy the best doctors, and then someone told him that winning it was one of life's greatest long shots. Big John said that he had a better shot of being struck by lightning twice than hitting a Connecticut Lotto jackpot.

With this understanding of life's difficulties, Nicky placed being a Major League baseball player to the top slot on his dream chart. During a cold winter day the previous December, he attended a professional baseball scouts' Hot Stove League clinic at West Haven High School. He heard a scout from the Seattle Mariners express that being drafted by a Major League team was a million-to-one shot.

Nicky's mathematics' skills told him that these odds were much better than being struck by lightning twice or collecting the millions in lottery dollars. Baseball was Nicky's main artery. It was his heart. This was the road he focused upon that made his life easier.

Baseball served Nicky as a common ground with other kids. He knew he could never look, talk or act the same, but baseball transcended the differences he worried about. Nicky felt alive and wanted to be on the fields.

Sure there were incidents with children of Crusty Rusty's ilk who tried to ridicule him, but Nicky could stop them with a base hit, a stolen base, a curve ball on the outside corner for strike three, or a bases-clearing double in the gap.

This was what bothered Nicky so much about the games with Rusty. No matter how hard he practiced and played, Rusty's team always won. Rusty always enjoyed the last laugh.

These factors motivated Nicky the most. He felt that now his team, with the addition of Ann, was finally talented enough to end Rusty's winning streak. A win could give Nicky a sense of accomplishment along with the possibility of shutting down Rusty's loud mouth for one day.

As Nicky and Ralph entered the house, knowing Mrs. Anderson's too close for comfort connection, he sensed a barrage of questions waiting for a barrage of truthful answers.

"How was school today, Nicky?" Mrs. Palmieri said as the innocent interrogation process seemingly started with an easy question.

"Fine, Ma. Me and Mrs. Anderson had an interesting talk," Nicky responded. "Why didn't anyone ever tell me she lived next door to grandpa? That was valuable information that could have saved me a lot of trouble."

"Your father and I wanted it this way."

"It's not the way I wanted it," Nicky shouted. "Every time something happened in school you guys practically knew about it before I did. What a joke!"

Nicky's mother stopped preparing the evening's meal, grabbed her son by the arm, and seated him at the oblong Formica kitchen table.

"Listen here, young man," Mrs. Palmieri sternly advised. "You have a lot to learn about life. There are certain things that you don't need to know.

"Mrs. Anderson promised your father and grandfather to look after you in that school. And furthermore, your constant lying and phony stories are what put you in trouble, not Mrs. Anderson's job," Mrs. Palmieri exploded.

The inner pain Nicky suffered during the onslaught ripped through his guts in seconds. His mother rarely raised her voice. The high decibels meant Nicky moved trouble to a new level. He knew about the lies, but he never thought he would be caught. Telling the truth scared him much more than the prospect of punishment. Then for one of the few times in history, Nicky thought for a few seconds before speaking.

"Ma, you want to hear about truth," Nicky began. "I'll tell you about truth. Every time I go to those doctors all I hear are lies—lies and more lies."

Nicky ran down the list faster than Jackie Robinson stealing home plate.

"Nicky, your lip looks fine."

"Perfect job, Dr. Campari, the lip looks wonderful."

"Isn't he a handsome young boy, Nurse Pombino?"

"Oh, doctors look. The lip is healing nicely, better than we expected."

"This is the last operation. Don't worry."

After Nicky rattled off ten or twelve more versions of the same story, Mrs. Palmieri simply stared at her son.

"You and Dad heard these lies too, Ma," Nicky continued. "But nobody wanted to say anything about it. Every day I go to school and I know kids are laughing behind my back. But nobody wants to do anything about it."

"I can't change what happened to you, Nicky," Mrs. Palmieri confessed. "But as long as I'm your mother, I will help you learn to deal with this cleft palate." Mrs. Palmieri explained to her son that they couldn't tell him how close Mrs. Anderson was to the situation. They feared Nicky would run for cover in the principal's office every time a problem arose.

"People are probably going to turn their heads and stare at you for the rest of your life," Mrs. Palmieri predicted. "You have to learn to accept that you will always be different. When the day comes that you don't worry about other people, you'll be able to succeed in anything you choose. But if you don't, you'll be too busy crying, lying, and feeling sorry for yourself."

Surgical knives created less pain than this truth serum, Nicky thought, fighting back the last of the tears.

"Nobody knows what it is like," Nicky exclaimed. "Nobody knows about the bull....'

"You better stop feeling sorry for yourself," Mrs. Palmieri interrupted. "Do you remember Vincent and Fabrizio? Those two kids would trade places with you in a heartbeat."

"Nice try, Ma. They can't change places with me. They're dead. Remember, they're in a better place, just like Jerry," Nicky said as he charged to his room and slammed the door. Nicky stared at the ceiling, pondering what the next seven days of school would bring. He heard his mother's words and speculated how impossible it was to ignore the names and the laughing. Nicky hoped to find the strength to ignore Rusty's contorted faces and bullying. He accepted his mother's commitments and intentions, but understanding them was another story. He prayed that these last seven days of school were the fastest ever.

The sulking continued until a sweet smell billowed through Nicky's screen window and shook him from his deep thoughts—hot dogs and hamburgers were cooking on the grill.

Dinnertime.

Summertime.

Chapter 38

Time Flies When You're Having More Than Fun.

After ending his wallowing self-pity, Nicky moved to the kitchen and wolfed down dinner in his usual expedient manner. In four minutes, two neatly split Hummel's hot dogs with Gulden's Spicy Brown mustard, a hamburger topped with Heinz ketchup, a half-plate full of tossed salad topped with balsamic vinegar, and a glass of iced tea quickly disappeared.

Two napkin wipes later, Nicky announced his after-dinner plans.

"Ma, see you later, I'm off to Big John's."

"You better come right home after the store closes," Mrs. Palmieri warned. "Don't stop at the park for a quick game or anything else. I'm sure your father is going to want to speak to you when he gets home from work."

"No problem. See you later, Ma."

After any day's craziness, especially this one, Big John's Deli served Nicky's mind well. The questions, if any, would surely be minimal. Two hours of sweeping, dusting, cleaning, and laughing at Big John taunting incoming customers quickly erased the day's negatives.

"Hey, Harry, look who's here. It's our own One Cell," as Big John initiated the evening's banter.

"I heard your team lost another tough one to Rusty again," Harry Huber stated. "When are you going to beat those punks?"

"We're going to play them the next Saturday afternoon they're available," Nicky started. "You know we got a new shortstop, and she's really good. I know we're going to win soon—at least before the summer's over."

"Hey, One Cell, the summer didn't even start yet," Big John said. "You have seven days of school left."

"Yep, seven more wake-ups, Big John, and I know they are going to go by quickly. By the way, how's your foot doing?"

"It's not so bad, I'm still in a lot of pain because I walk around too much, but who else is going to do the majority of the work around here?" Big John told the deli's frequenters that people on death row were treated better than he was in the hospital.

Nicky reminded Big John of his promise to work five hours every day or more as soon as school ended.

Big John refocused his conversation on Nicky alone, telling him that he had been visited by his favorite principal.

"She stopped by today to rat out on me about school. Didn't she?" Nicky started.

"As a matter of fact, she absolutely did not. She told me about a long talk you and she had," Big John admitted while he and Harry Huber are howling in hysterical laughter.

"I can't believe you never realized that she was Italian and that she lives on Spring Street. You must have been shocked to no end."

"Why didn't anybody ever tell me? That is huge information. If I knew that, I would have never called her those names."

"Let me tell you something, Nicky. You have to learn how to treat people with respect," Big John's lecture started. "I always hear you complaining how kids are calling you names and now you think it's okay to do the same thing to someone else, especially a principal—my friend."

"Yeah, but I never knew she hung out with my mother and father," Nicky noted. "This world can't be that small."

"It's smaller than you think, One Cell. It's smaller than you think."

Nicky busily moved through his work but overheard Big John telling Harry Huber that he hadn't felt that well since the foot injury.

Eavesdropping was another of Nicky's favorite pastimes. Those numerous visits to doctors helped him hone his craft. Nicky swore to his friends that he could press a drinking glass against an office wall and hear exactly what the surgeons were talking about. He told the Kelsey Avenue Crew it worked for Frank Sinatra in the movies.

"The doctor said my blood pressure's a little high," Nicky overheard Big John say while changing the garbage bags in the baskets. "I know I'm more tired than usual, but these high priced buffoons don't know what they are talking about. Half the time they guess and send you out for tests." Nicky almost blew his cover with a cough but held it and inched closer for more information.

"It is probably the stress from having to walk around with that bandaged foot," Harry Huber diagnosed. "The doctors checked your heart last month, and everything's fine, right John?"

"Sure, sure. My heart's fine. I just have to watch what I eat. That's all."

"Seeing the food you eat and watching what you eat are two different things," Harry Huber joked. "You've been on a see-food diet your whole life."

Big John hurled a sleeve full of cups at his buddy while Nicky bust out laughing.

"Hey, Harry, Big John's got 20/20 vision when it comes to see-food diets," Nicky declared. "If Big John ever told people about his diet, they would forget about any other silly plan you saw on television.."

"But he does have his own weight plan. It's a competitor of Weight Watchers. It's called Weight Gainers."

Even though they enjoyed a few moments of friendly banter with the big man, Nicky knew that Big John would even the score.

"You guys just wait until this foot heals, and I'm going to bang your two heads together like the Three Stooges," Big John promised. "You guys are really funny."

Hiding behind the donut counter, Nicky waved a white towel in surrender because he knew Big John was authorized by Mr. Palmieri to inflict any appropriate disciplinary measures. He was allowed to use hands, feet, or any items not nailed to a wall.

"You can come out from behind there," Big John informed Nicky. "I'm too worn out to start throwing things at you. Just help me out with the meat case and sweep the parking lot."

"No problem, Big John. Consider it done."

The two hours always passed quickly. Not once did Nicky think about Rusty's mean-spirited comments. Big John's was the place where his problems disappeared. No one dared pick on him under Big John's watch. Big John's protection was better than President Jimmy Carter's with the FBI, CIA, and Secret Service combined.

Eight o'clock arrived quickly, and Big John locked the store. He offered Nicky a ride home. This particular evening had been great for Nicky, with lots of laughs and without tough questions about a glove or his school behavior.

"My grounding is over next Saturday, so I set up another game with Crusty Rusty," Nicky opened the baseball can of worms on the ride home. "I'm looking forward to playing after this week's suspension. I feel like a Big Leaguer."

"But sometimes you act like a T-ball player," Big John cracked. "I hope I can come to the game, but it depends on how busy the store gets."

"This game is going to be the one, Big John. I want you to be there when we finally beat Crusty Rusty and his punk friends. We keep coming so close the last couple of times. I know we will catch the big break soon."

Nicky rambled on about the upcoming game. He ran through the lineup with Big John. He knew that if he continued talking long enough, eventually they would arrive at his house and the Heart of the Hide topic wouldn't reach Big John's mind.

Mission accomplished.

In fewer than five minutes, they reached the Palmieri house. Nicky breathed a huge sigh of relief. The day ended much better than he ever thought. Nicky was completely overjoyed that the glove issue was postponed for another day.

Chapter 39

Surprises Always Come
in Big Packages

During the next morning's paper route delivery run, Nicky recognized that he must come clean with Big John about the whole truth as to why he put the Heart of the Hide in Jerry's casket.

He figured that, with summer near, he would work at least five or six hours each day at Big John's Deli. That was plenty of time to work up the nerve to tell him.

Every day he learned more and more of how tightly intertwined the great city of West Haven stood. Everyone knew about the glove.

Big John certainly knew.

Nicky's parents knew.

Bigmouthed Mr. DiNapola knew.

The entire Kelsey Avenue Crew knew.

Even Mrs. Anderson knew.

Despite this common knowledge, Nicky lived every day with the inability to tell the truth to his mentor and friend, Big John. Ann was the only one fully enlightened by Nicky's story. Big John, his great protector and surrogate daytime father, should know as well, Nicky thought.

Somehow, somewhere, Nicky lost trust in people. It probably happened in one of his many doctors' offices. But where it occurred was not important now.

Nicky realized that the truth needs to be unlocked and set free. The problem is that he couldn't find the keys.

As he completed his morning paper route, several scary thoughts galloped through Nicky's mind. He wondered what might happen after he told Big John the truth.

He thought about Big John firing him. Another daydream transported Nicky to an angry Big John screaming, "You're a loser. You are never going to beat Rusty in baseball. Losers like you don't appreciate anything people try to do for you. You're a waste. I don't know why I bother." Nicky also considered Big John's disappointed face with its long stretch of silence—Nicky's least favorite form of communication.

Suddenly, Nicky snapped from his reverie as he delivered the final paper of the crisp early summer morning. A sweet familiar voice descended on Nicky's ears.

"Nicky, Nicky, Nicky—wake up, moron. I've been calling your name for the past twenty seconds."

"Oh, Ann, it's you. I was just thinking about a whole lot of stuff. What's going on?"

"Nothing much. Did you tell Big John about the glove yesterday?"

"No, it just didn't seem like the right time to do it. I'm going to do it soon, though, I promise."

"Well, when you do, I guarantee you'll feel better about it."

"I hope so, Ann. I hope so."

Ann tossed Nicky a glove and a game of catch ensued.

"I heard you met my Aunt Ida yesterday. She's my godmother, too," Ann laughed.

"I never knew she was your father's sister. That's amazing."

"My mom told me that, when I was little, we lived with her to make ends meet," Ann added. "Minor league baseball players only make about $700 a month, so Aunt Ida gave us a room in her Spring Street house."

"I lived there too you know. Right next door in my grandfather's house for two years," Nicky added of his Spring Street experience.

"Your mom and my mom are best friends," Ann reported. "They used to hang out with Aunt Ida all the time."

"Yep, I found that out the hard way, Ann. It just took seven years to put two and two together. I felt really bad yesterday."

"Why is that, Nicky?"

"On account of the names I used to call her."

"Like Principal Beast?"

"You heard about that?"

"Every word."

"And you still want to be my friend?"

"Sure, Nicky. You didn't know me then. But if I ever hear you call my godmother another name, I will kick your butt so hard you will wish Rusty gave you the beating and not me."

"Not a problem, Ann. Not a problem."

"When my mom didn't have any money, Aunt Ida sent us thousands. She's one of the nicest people around. She really cares even though my father is a total jerk."

"Yeah, she really is nice. I realized that yesterday," Nicky confessed. "I am going to write her an apology letter and thank-you note for the countless times she tried to help me."

"My Aunt really cares about you. She told my mom that she was so hard on you because you remind her of her stepbrother and she didn't want you to turn out like him."

"She said that?"

"She sure did, Nicky."

"Boy, do I feel like an idiot. I have to tell her I'm sorry for the grief I caused," Nicky concluded as the game of catch ended. Mrs. Marriotti called Ann into the house.

"Nicky, I have to go take care of my brother. I'll talk to you later."

"Thanks for playing catch, Ann."

Nicky's enthusiasm for school lifted to a new level. The Great Chocolate Milk Conflict was behind him. He was also returning to class.

His first plan included going directly to Mrs. Anderson's office to apologize. He prepared to follow that personal visit with a letter as well.

It was the right thing to do.

Nicky's biggest problem in his warped little mind was that he lumped principals and priests together.

After all they both were in charge of their buildings.

You never saw them until there was an assembly or a mass.

They told everybody what to do.

They dressed funny.

And you rarely saw them out in the real world.

Ann's talk opened Nicky's brain to the thought that there are people outside one's immediate circle that could care about you. Nicky thought that God created priests and the principals to boss people around.

"Mrs. Anderson, may I see you for a moment?"

"Sure, Nicky. How can I help you today?"

"I want to apologize to you for the many mean names I called you."

"Don't worry. You're forgiven."

"Also, I want to thank you for helping me understand how to handle my lip situation better and for the nice teachers you put me with. Until yesterday, I was too stupid to realize how much you tried to help me. I'm sorry for the times I talked back to you."

"Your apology is accepted, Nicky. Now move along to your classroom. I heard that Miss Hansen is having some great lessons on the Korean and Vietnam conflicts today."

"My grandfather told me those were wars, Mrs. Anderson. He said that conflicts were whether he decided to invite me over to eat cavatelli or angel hair pasta. Now, that's a conflict."

"I'm sure he did," Mrs. Anderson responded laughing. "I'm sure he did."

The school day rolled by quickly. In Writers' Workshop, Nicky wrote for forty-five minutes. He wanted his letter to Mrs. Anderson to be perfect. No spelling or grammatical errors were to be discovered.

"Where's my thank-you letter, Nicky?" Miss Hansen asked after closely observing the surprisingly quiet student busy at work.

"You'll get yours. Don't worry," Nicky assured her. "I have six days left. I'll get it done."

Nicky then dedicated every remaining school day to his teachers. Graduation day was huge at Stiles Elementary. Elementary school was the one building where Nicky spent the longest amount of time.

Seven years.

Most people only need three years to complete Junior High School.

The average student can graduate high school in three more.

College should take four years or less. This leaves elementary school as the one structure where the majority of learning takes place.

Nicky's principal was extremely well aware of this information as well. Mrs. Anderson went to great lengths to make graduations special

She closed the school at 11 A.M. for everyone. The PTA decorated the cafeteria, and she threw a tremendous bash for the graduates. Hot dogs and hamburgers were cooked and served by the cafeteria staff while several flavors of bubbling soda flowed freely.

This great graduation day signified the end of an era for Nicky. He was entering a world of lockers, changing classes, and wider hallways with cathedral ceilings.

No longer will he be the big man on campus. He's on a two-year hiatus. For 360 days, he would also have new bullies to contend with, but with summer vacation just moments away, this was far from Nicky's greatest concern.

"Nicky, grab a couple of hot dogs for the road," Mark Kessler said. "We're out of here. Your suspension's over. Let's go to the park and practice for Saturday's game with Crusty Rusty. We've waited two weeks to finally beat this punk."

"I can't play too long this afternoon," Nicky replied. "I've got a game tonight at Bailey Field. We're playing for first place in the American Division."

Each one of the Kelsey Avenue Crew played on an organized team in the West Haven Little League. These games were important, but compared to the battles with Rusty Alves, these games were pre-season exhibitions for the summer schedule.

"Oh, yeah, I remember. Mrs. Ferrante is picking up some of us at Gennaro's house and we're going to watch the game," Mark recalled.

On any given night, there were twenty to thirty parents and kids from the Kelsey Avenue Crew at any Little League game. These kids loved going to the field and supporting each other until their clubs locked horns.

"I'll be in center field tonight," Nicky informed. "West Shore Cleaners is in for a tough game. Hopefully, Chuck Stack will pitch. We'll rip him to shreds."

"What time are you getting to the field, Nicky?"

"My father is leaving work early to take me to the field an hour before game time. I want to take some extra batting practice."

"Take some BP with us," Mark said. "We don't mind shagging the balls."

"That's great, but I'll wait until I go to the game. See you tonight," Nicky concluded while starting his walk home to drop off his graduation certificate and head to work at Big John's.

"Hey, One Cell, you made it," Big John said while he started the congratulatory clapping of hands from customers. "Good old Mrs. Anderson couldn't hold you back."

"The kid made it through clean unlike you, John," Harry Huber interrupted. "It took you two years to get out of kindergarten because you never put the blocks away in the right bins."

"Okay, okay, wise guy, so I got a little confused once in a while," Big John admitted. "But, Nicky tell me about the spread. How was the food?"

"The party was awesome," Nicky reported. "Hey, Harry, they cooked so many hot dogs and hamburgers they could have fed some small third world country and Big John at the same time. All the food they had there was crazy."

"Good one, wise guy. Now come here, Nicky, I have your graduation present."

"Big John, I came here to work not look for any gifts. You give me too much already."

"Take this, Nicky, and congratulations," Big John said while handing Nicky one of his famous envelopes. "I heard you got straight As on the final report card."

Before Nicky could even spit out the first syllable of "How did you find out?" he quickly figured out the source.

"Mrs. Anderson was here already?"

"You catch on quickly, One Cell."

"Open the envelope, Nicky," Harry prodded. "Let's see what kind of boss you've got."

"I've don't even have to open it, Harry," Nicky announced. "Everybody in town knows how generous Big John is. This is embarrassing. I'm not deserving of this gift, especially after my lies caused Big John's accident."

"Forget about the foot, One Cell. Let's hope you learned your lesson after that along with the one-week suspension from baseball your father handed to you," Big John commanded in the typical baseball lingo that Nicky surely understood.

"By the way, how's the foot anyway?" Nicky asked, postponing the tough Heart of the Hide question.

"The foot is healing at a pretty good pace the doctor told me. I still have a little tightness in my chest, though, but I think it is still hurting me from the fall."

Harry Huber waited two seconds and then unleashed a loud roar.

"Ha, fall, you mean earthquake. Your fat butt is so big the whole city of West Haven shook when you hit the deck. I think the people on Channel 8 News reported that the Richter Scale hit seven."

Big John, always in the mood for friendly banter and a few chuckles, fired back at his 400-pound friend in true competitive spirit.

"At least when I get on the scale, I don't have to do any math."

"What the heck are you talking about, John?"

"Well, since most scales only go up to 300, you're so fat you need two of them to weigh yourself, one for the left foot and one for the right. Then it takes you another ten minutes to add the two numbers together, Tubby."

"Hey, Harry, you better quit while you're ahead," Nicky interjected. "You can't stop Big John when he's on a roll."

"Okay, wise guy, now open the present and see what's inside," Big John insisted.

"I can wait until I get home. Mom and Dad will want to see what you gave me."

"Open it now before I have to get up out of this chair and bang you on the head with my cane."

Nicky rapidly ripped the envelope and pulled two crisp $50 bills and a note.

Congratulations on a great report card. Take the day off and good luck in tonight's game.

Best of luck,

Big John.

P.S. I'm coming to the game on Saturday to watch you beat Rusty. Bring your glove.

"What did ya' get, Nicky?" Harry Huber asked.

Before Nicky spoke, the angel of truth pushed him toward Big John to give him a huge warm hug.

"There's something I have to tell you, Big John."

An awkward pause followed as Big John and Harry Huber exchanged glances. They looked as though the note prompted Nicky's confession about the glove.

No one but Nicky Palmieri knew about his obsession with perfection and disappointment. The tug-of-war between right and wrong started many years ago, and Nicky could never seem to end this battle.

Nicky's mind drifted to the origin of this struggle. In the last month or so, his mind constantly flashed to another time. He tried valiantly to understand why he does what he does.

It started after Nicky's fifth operation when he was five years old. He looked in the mirror and saw a mangled face. The reflection showed a lip with many bumps along with a flattened nose that leaned to the left. He started staring at other people's features after the operation and dreamed that he could trade something for their lips. This was a blockbuster of a deal, something not even George Steinbrenner could agree to.

He would have offered his entire collection of New York Yankees' baseball cards to look like everyone else, no card excluded in the deal.

Joe DiMaggio, Mickey Mantle, Billy Martin, Phil Rizzuto, Yogi Berra, Jim "Catfish" Hunter, Graig Nettles, Joe Pepitone, Elston Howard, Roger Maris, Ron Guidry, Dave Righetti, Thurman Munson, Sparky Lyle, Reginald Martinez Jackson, Don Mattingly, and Goose Gossage were in the pack. Nicky treasured his favorite players the most. He loved the history of the Yankees so he kept these cards separate, but this deal for the perfect lip required major resources.

"So, Nicky, look, the operation came out fine. The lip looks wonderful," Dr. Campari lied, holding the mirror in front of his patient.

Over the top of the mirror, Nicky could see Mr. Palmieri in the background. He never wanted to upset his father so his reply became simple.

"Yes, Dr. Campari, it does look better."

This routine occurred seven more times, and Nicky's answer barely changed. Nicky always steered away from disappointing his father. He wanted his parents not to think that the tremendous amounts of money and time they spent went unappreciated.

Many nights, Nicky lay awake in his room and overheard his parents loudly discussing money issues. He felt solely responsible for their dismay.

He also heard the stories of how his mom and dad would wake in the middle of the night to spoon-feed him because he couldn't use traditional baby bottles and pacifiers. Small details filtered into his thoughts—Mr. Palmieri's side jobs to pay for his operations to Mrs. Anderson's unknown help.

But the doctors' lies set something in motion in Nicky that made him a lying machine to compensate for the pain and misery of his lip. But given his parents' sacrifice and the operations' failures, Nicky chose not to add his concerns and worries to his parents' list of troubles. He chose lying. Lying always became the better option.

"Nicky, did you go to religion after school today?" Mrs. Palmieri often asked.

"Certainly, Ma. Nothing's more important than a couple of hours with the Lord."

The truth was that Nicky spent two hours in the DiNapola's Laundromat eating Three Musketeers and Snickers bars playing video poker with the neighborhood hoodlums.

Sometimes when those cardboard dons weren't hanging out, then Nicky made a guest appearance or two at religious instruction.

"Mr. Nicholas Palmieri, where's your religion homework for the past two weeks?" Father John J. Ladamus said sternly.

"Oh, Father Ladamus, I want to tell you that my dad was so proud of my excellent work and love for Jesus he brought my homework papers to his woodworking shop to show his friends. He's really surprised I knew the Ten Commandments so well."

"Especially. The ones regarding truth, correct Nicholas?"

This was just a small spattering of how Nicky delayed disappointment. Now that he faced a gargantuan task of truth with the man who gave him his most prized possession, Nicky's options simplified. He could tell Big John a lie or skirt the truth. Or Nicky's favorite—avoid the truth and change the subject. The tug-of-war never ended unless Nicky decided to end it.

"Well, One Cell, spit it out," Big John demanded. "What do you want to tell me?"

"Thanks. Thanks for everything. The glove you gave me that I really don't deserve and now this money and the day off. You are the best. I'm sorry I lied to you so many times. I'm sorry I lied about the...."

"Hey, Big John, telephone," Harry Huber announced. "It's Better Eatin' Donuts. They want to know if you called in tomorrow's order."

"I called in the order two hours ago. Those morons in the office don't know what they're doing over there, but they know how to take my money," Big John hollered loud enough, so the person on the phone could hear him clearly.

"One of these days, I'm going to start making my own donuts and put them out of business."

"It wouldn't work, John," Harry Huber said. "You would be too busy eating 'em."

"Give me the phone and tell Nicky to get out of here and enjoy his day off."

Before Harry Huber could turn around, Nicky sprinted out the front door and off he went.

With the battle of truth averted once more, Nicky realized that he must one day soon stare reality straight in the kisser.

Big John deserves to hear the whole story about the glove and why it took so long for Nicky to tell him.

But today, Nicky Palmieri was far too happy. Graduation day arrived, and the real start of summer was here. There was a baseball game a few hours away.

The truth was without feelings.

It could surely wait one more day.

Chapter 40

One Day Never Comes

On game days, the clock ticked slowly for Nicky Palmieri, a young boy of many routines. His list of dos and don'ts before games was quite impressive.

<u>Dos</u>

Brush teeth.

Floss.

Use mouthwash.

Make sure the game uniform was clean.

Check the bat bag and look over equipment.

Tug the shoe laces on both spikes. Broken laces may cost an extra base or, worse, a run.

Pack an extra belt and baseball socks.

Swing the bat one hundred times in the back yard. Preparation was always the key to success.

During a hitting streak, wear the same T-shirt. However, it can be washed if the pungent smell deems it necessary. (Mother's option)

During hitting slumps, find new T-shirts and change socks repeatedly. (Mother's happiness)

After a win, eat the same pregame meal in same seat.

After a loss, change the pregame meal and seat.

Only change socks during losing streaks of two or more.

Never wash socks during winning streaks of three or more.

Never, absolutely never, wash socks or T-shirts during playoff runs to the championship. Never. (Mother's nightmare)

And last but certainly not least, always arrive at the ballpark one hour before game time.

Don'ts

Swim in a pool before a game.

Take a pregame shower or bath.

Eat Mexican food on game day.

Figure out your batting average.

Change uniform numbers with anyone.

Change spikes mid-season.

Change bats during hot streaks.

Change route to the game during winning streaks.

Show up to the game late.

Nicky's lists evolved over time. Losses could change anything on the do or don't list, but dramatic changes didn't happen overnight. Nicky believed that a consistent list was the key to baseball success. He rarely made game-time changes in fear of a bad game or a loss.

Nicky's club, the Ferrie Asphalt and Paving Cardinals, were on a hot streak, steam-rolling through their first fourteen games without a loss. Chuck Stack's team, West Shore Cleaners, stood in second place with a 13–1 record. That night's game decided the regular season championship.

The playoffs were scheduled to begin the following week. The winner of the American Division played the National Division champ. Rusty's team, DiNapola's Card Shop, led their division by two games with three games remaining.

Nicky wanted Rusty's team to win, so they could face each other in the West Haven Little League championship. Even blockhead Rusty admitted that Nicky's Little League team was far better. A win in the title game would give Nicky some justice over his foe, but it would never be enough.

Nicky always took greater pride in his neighborhood sandlot team, however. The Kelsey Avenue Crew's games with Crusty Rusty meant much more to him. The kids in the neighborhood were Nicky's closest friends. These sandlot games were the only way the entire Kelsey Avenue Crew could play on one team. The players were much too talented to be on one Little League team.

Big John constantly said that, if someone in the West Haven Little League hierarchy was smart enough, they would put the entire Kelsey Avenue Crew on the All-Star team. Big John was sure that this group of kids would win the games to make it to Williamsport, Pennsylvania, for the Little League World Series. Everybody in town knew that the Kelsey Avenue Crew could play, but parents who ran the All-Star team and politics interfered with selecting such a roster.

Big John asked how a certain player made the team, and Nicky's reply was simple, "His father has Myson disease."

"What's that?"

"You know, Big John. My–son disease. It starts when the kid stinks. My son batted .450. My son has a twenty-two-game hitting streak in a seventeen-game season. My son never struck out. My son should be on the All-Star team. That's why the All-Star team can't win outside the region. Too many parents have Myson disease."

When Nicky hung around the fields, he often bragged how another great well-known liar, Danny Almonte, couldn't throw a fastball by John Ferrante, Bill G., Ann, his brother Ralph, Gennaro, the Kesslers, or any one else on his squad.

The Kelsey Avenue Crew was Nicky's team, and his friends could really play. In the summertime, it was Major League baseball played in a little kid's world.

They ate breakfast, lunch, and dinner together just like the pros did on the road. They practiced baseball every day for at least four hours, rain or shine.

Just like the pros.

They shared the same equipment. If one kid owned a catcher's mitt, everyone used the glove. It didn't matter whose house it wound up in at night. They knew it was at the field the next day.

Just like the pros.

They held meetings to discuss strategy against Crusty Rusty, with scouting reports and hitting charts.

Just like the pros.

The Kelsey Avenue Crew wasn't handpicked by parents. Friendship built the team and baseball cemented their love and respect for one another. This was why Nicky took those losses to Crusty Rusty so hard.

He knew Rusty's club was a couple of years older and more talented, but he always believed that his friends could beat anyone.

After loss thirty-five last summer, many kids questioned Nicky as to why he wanted to keep playing Rusty's team.

"These games are making us better," Nicky would say. "I can't stand losing to that jerk, either, but his older buddies are helping us improve."

"We can't get that much better playing against ourselves every day," he continued. "They throw harder and run faster. You guys see how much better we're getting. Don't worry. One day we will beat him and wipe that stupid smile off his freckled face."

Ten games later, the smile would remain, but it never deterred Nicky or anyone else on the Kelsey Avenue Crew. They still wanted to beat Rusty now more than ever. They wanted to prove to themselves that underdogs could win. David could beat Goliath—it wasn't just a legend.

These thoughts occupied Nicky's mind this glorious day as he prepared for an easy game. He was seldom nervous for Little League games. However, Rusty's encounters had shaken him. The never-ending name-calling from the bully ate at Nicky's insides. He wanted to beat his team of wise guys in the worst way. The Little League games were great, but they were not Nicky's games with Nicky's team.

"Hey, Nicky, you're back from Big John's already. That was fast," Ralph observed, as he walked into the Palmieri house after a little baseball practice with the Crew.

"Big John gave me $100 bucks and the day off."

"Get out of here. Lemme see the money."

Ralph examined the crisp $50 dollar bills while Nicky explained to him how his good grades earned him this money.

"Nicky, you have a game tonight. I heard Mark K. say that if your team wins tonight, you're in the championship," Ralph added.

"Yeah, we should wrap it up with an easy win. Their best pitcher already threw this week. Chuck Stack is going get pummeled."

"Then you play Rusty's team for the title next week," Ralph continued while holding up Nicky's new treasures to the light.

"That's going to be a good game, but I want to beat his freckle-faced butt on Saturday. Those games mean more to me than anything."

"But, Nicky, this is the Little League championship. Doesn't that game mean more than the games we play with him down at the park?"

"Ralph, you don't understand. Most of the kids in the neighborhood are a lot younger. I'm never going to be on the same team with most of you. This is the only chance we get to play together."

"I don't get it. You always say how a win is a win no matter what, and now you're telling me that it's no big deal if your Little League team beats Rusty. I still don't get it," Ralph responded.

"I want to beat Crusty Rusty with you guys around—my brother, my friends, the neighborhood kids. This is what baseball is about. Remember how much fun we had during the times we practiced together all these years."

"Yeah, it's been great. We had a lot of laughs and fun."

"That's the whole point, knucklehead. None of these parents who run these organized teams will let us be on the same team. This is the only chance we have to play together.

"Plus, Rusty is the only one who can get players way older than us. The rest of the kids around town won't dare come here. And when they do, they stink," Nicky continued. "Remember when we played Big Jim Kennedy's team? We pounded them 24–2, and they quit in the fourth inning. That game was a big joke."

"I remember now," Ralph admitted. "You got mad at Mike Horonus because he missed a fly ball in right field when he slipped on dog poop in the first inning, and they grabbed a 2–0 lead."

"I didn't get that mad, but that's not the problem. Baseball is my favorite sport, and it's the most fun when I'm playing with my brother and our friends."

"Don't forget Ann, lover boy."

"Shut up, Ralph. You know what I mean."

"Okay, I'm starting to get it. Hey, Nicky, I want to tell you that at the field today Ann was talking with most of the guys, and they are getting sick and tired of Rusty's names, too."

"Really. What did they say?"

"Nothin' much. It's just that nobody likes it when he tugs his lip and calls you those mean names."

"Now, do you see what's going on?" Nicky asked his younger brother. "I want to beat Rusty with you guys. I want you guys to be there when he walks away from the field with nothing to say."

Nicky railed further, explaining how Rusty won't act up at the Little League fields in fear of losing his spot on the All-Star team for acting with unsportsman-like conduct.

"I noticed that too," Ralph admitted. "Rusty's a whole different person. I'm always waiting for him to pop off and do something stupid, but he never does. I don't know why he thinks he can be such a wise guy everywhere else?"

"This is what two-faced jerks do. Rusty acts one way in front of people he needs something from, and then he acts another way to be the big tough guy in front of his friends."

"We are going to beat him on Saturday, Nicky. Don't worry," Ralph assured Nicky, as Mr. Palmieri arrived from another day of buzzing electric saws. "We're not going to be 0 and forty-six. The whole team can't wait. It's going to be a great summer."

The happy brothers strolled into the kitchen for dinner, catching Mr. Palmieri's watchful eye.

"What are you guys so happy about?" Mr. Palmieri started. "You look like you are up to no good."

"It's summertime, Dad," Ralph replied. "No more school for two months. No more homework and no more teachers, too. This is the life."

"Good. Then you boys will have plenty of time to read books this summer," Mr. Palmieri instructed. "And I have plenty of jobs for you to do around the house, too."

"Way to go, Ralph," Nicky sarcastically cheered, as the boys helped Mrs. Palmieri set the table.

"Let's eat," Mrs. Palmieri ordered. "Nicky's got to be at the park by five o'clock. This is a big game tonight."

Mrs. Palmieri knew that every game was a "big game" to her son. She knew how well baseball kept him occupied. It wasn't just the games and the winning. Baseball was so much more than that to Nicky Palmieri. Not only did he keep his own statistics, Nicky compiled the numbers for the entire league.

At the end of the week the Little League President, Mike Siwek, gave Nicky the scorebooks. Nicky spent hours compiling hitting and pitching statistics for the entire league. Nicky loved the mathematics of baseball—earned run averages, on base percentages, batting averages, strikeouts, walks per six innings, and hits with runners in scoring position. If the Elias Sports Bureau had a statistic for the Big Leagues, Nicky tried to figure it out for the Little League.

The time Nicky spent with the many facets of baseball proved to be the greatest treatment program for his cleft palate. It wasn't just a distraction; it was a passion. Without question, the Palmieri's knew everyone of Nicky's pregame rituals, and they accommodated each precise move. The knife and fork rest on separate sides of the plate with the spoon next to the knife on even days. The napkin was folded into a rectangle, never a triangle. It reminded Nicky of the Bermuda triangle. That was bad luck. His drinking glass was always half full with Lipton's Iced Tea.

When everything was set, the meal could be served. The pregame meal followed a specific regiment. Nicky ate a special salad first. Romaine lettuce, tomatoes, cucumbers, and red peppers neatly tossed in balsamic vinegar and olive oil from Sicily.

In honor of his father and Grandpa Palmieri, Nicky ate one form of pasta before every game. If Wade Boggs could eat chicken before every game, Nicky decided that an Italian who thrived on similar baseball superstitions should eat pasta. The shape didn't matter. Rigatonis were his favorite followed closely by ziti, cavatelli, and angel hair pasta. Nicky was amazed when he learned that his father never went a day without eating pasta.

Ever.

That was perfection, and Nicky admired that conviction and wanted to create his own version of perfection.

"All right, Nicky, you finished your pasta. You wiped your face five times with both sides of the napkin and drank the iced tea. Now grab your stuff and let's go to the game," Mr. Palmieri directed.

Nicky grabbed his baseball equipment bag, raced to the car, buckled his seat belt, and rolled the passenger window up and down twice. Off to the game they went.

Mr. Palmieri always drove, and Nicky proudly sat in the front seat. Mrs. Palmieri and the rest of the family arrived later. Nicky appreciated this time with his father.

It was a seven-minute ride to the field. They often talked about school or doctors but never about baseball before the game. Nicky believed this jinxed the game. The ride moved routinely as they navigated through West Haven High School and onto Platt Avenue. Nicky couldn't wait to attend this high school. Every time he rode his bike, walked, or drove through the property, there were so many sports activities taking place.

People were everywhere. Kids played football on the state-of-the-art artificial turf field. The state of Connecticut held most of the state football championship games at this field. During late fall, Nicky led the Kelsey Avenue Crew to climb the fence and they sneaked in to watch every game. It didn't matter if West Haven played in the game or not, Nicky often grabbed accomplices Gennaro and John Ferrante to break into the event.

Pristine tennis courts were constantly filled with singles and doubles action while others sat on the benches and waited for their turn to play.

The school had its own year-round private hockey arena. Even during the spring and summer, the rink bustled with travel hockey activity or skating lessons. The building opened every day at 6 A.M. and rarely closed. One time Big John arranged with Mr. Conlan, the rink director, to let Nicky ride the Zamboni ice machine.

The city of West Haven loved sports. Through the Board of Education and Athletic Director Tom Hunt, the city made sure West Haven owned the best facilities for every sport. But what Nicky looked forward to the most was the construction of a new baseball field that would open the following spring. The city spent millions of dollars on a baseball and softball complex to be found no other place in New England.

Tremendous light towers hovered over a field with the same type of turf they used for those fancy fields in Florida. Nicky marveled at how a scientist, who was obviously a baseball fanatic, developed artificial grass blades for baseball diamonds. A ten-foot tall page fence symmetrically enclosed the park. Three batting tunnels filled the spacious land in foul territory. This was great for the Kelsey Avenue Crew.

Nicky's plans were endless. When this field was ready, the Crew had a new place to play either way. They would either find a way to sneak onto this field or they intended to use the top diamond at Painter's Park.

"Dad, did you see that field? That field's going to be beautiful. Look at those huge lights, and they put that new turf on the field. When it rains, the field soaks up the water. And there's never a rain-out," Nicky exclaimed.

"It is a nice field, but my taxes on the house are going to go sky high," Mr. Palmieri explained.

"It'll be worth every penny. Don't worry, Dad. Ralph and I are going to be playing on that field a whole lot. The Palmieris will get their money's worth."

The car quickly made the right turn onto Platt Avenue. The ensuing sight one hundred yards in front of Nicky turned a bubbling enthusiastic young boy into a reserved one.

Mysteriously, the store lights were out at a closed Big John's Deli. The remaining car in the lot was the big man's easily recognizable brown Chevrolet. Harry Huber's maroon Cadillac was not there.

Mr. Palmieri glanced over to the deserted Deli as well, but neither of them spoke. They simply continued to the baseball field.

Nicky arrived first, laced his spikes, and started stretching. Within minutes, the rest of his club joined him. Their coach, the heralded Mr. Umbriago, stumbled out of his dented Ford Escort shortly before game time.

"That was nice of coach Umbriago to leave happy hour a few minutes early," Mr. Palmieri acknowledged. "I hope he realized that this game is for first place."

"Don't feel bad for him, Joe," Mr. Luciano Coletta joked. "Feel bad for the poor bartender. Think of the money he lost because of this game."

"I'm sure your *paisano* will make up for it later," Mr. Palmieri concluded.

As predicted, Chuck Stack took the mound for West Shore Cleaners. Nicky started the hit parade, lacing a lead off double to left center, and the rout was on.

By the top of the fourth, the Ferrie Asphalt and Paving Cardinals flew to an 11–0 lead. Chuck Stack threw his last pitch, prompting many fans to leave, including Crusty Rusty Alves and his even more obnoxious father.

"We'll see you in the championship, Nicky," Rusty yelled from the right field fence. "Enjoy this while it lasts because I promise to throw a lot harder than your boy, Chucky, over there."

Remarkably, Nicky made no response. He was sitting in the first-base dugout.

Rusty screamed again. "I know you hear me. You must be afraid to talk to me because I know you can't hit my fastball."

"Hey, Rusty," John Ferrante popped his head out of the dugout and interrupted. "You and your father better get going and get you to bed. You're going to need your rest for summer school tomorrow, loser."

"Shut up, Ferrante. You'll get yours, too. I'm going to summer school to get a jump on seventh grade."

"Don't forget to pack your snack, Rusty. Say 'Hi' to Mrs. Anderson for me."

Nicky enjoyed learning of Rusty's extra school sessions almost as much as clinching the American Division title. With Jerry not around this summer, Rusty could probably have a field day with seven hours or more to levy his wide variety of insults.

Mrs. Anderson ran the summer school reading program at Stiles Elementary. She strongly recommended to both Rusty's parents that their son would not be promoted to Giannotti Middle School unless he enrolled in the summer reading program. His test scores were far below the national average.

For two months, Rusty attended special reading instruction classes from 10 A.M. to 1 P.M. four days a week. This kept the big mouth off Nicky's back for at least half the day yet still allowed Rusty to bring his team to the park for some afternoon baseball games.

"I didn't know Rusty had to go to summer school?" Nicky asked John Ferrante before moving to the on-deck circle. "What's that about?"

"My mom said that Mrs. Anderson caught Rusty cheating on the test back in April. She showed the proof to Mr. Alves, and now Rusty has to go to summer school."

"I didn't hear about Rusty cheating on the state test"

"I didn't know, either, but Mrs. Anderson found some pretty convincing proof because his father's a lawyer. And he didn't even argue with her for one second."

"That's great info, John F. This summer's turning out to be better than I thought it would," Nicky finished as he knocked the weight off his bat and strode to home plate. He ripped a single up the middle to drive in two more runs as the Cardinals rolled to a 15–2 victory.

Coach Umbriago, who after a couple of more beers was living up to his last name, gathered the team together.

"Great, umm, game, guys," he mumbled in Walter Matthau fashion from one of the most famous baseball movies of all-time, *The Bad News Bears*. "I want to … I want to ah, ah, treat you all to some pizza at my favorite place."

"They don't serve pizza at Randall's Bar and Grill," John F. informed Mr. Umbriago. "Take us to Lorenzo's. They have the best pizza."

President Siwek stepped in to inform the kids about next week's championship schedule. Coach Umbriago wrote the information on the scorebook and the team started to leave.

"Nicky, you want to go to Lorenzo's?" Mr. Palmieri asked.

"Nah, I ate too much today. I don't want to celebrate until we beat Rusty and win the championship. The Division title doesn't mean anything unless we win next week. Let's go home."

The entire Palmieri clan piled into the car while Nicky sat in the front seat, gently hoping that, when they pass Big John's Deli, the scene he witnessed earlier would have a change or two.

Mr. Palmieri enjoyed routines as much as, if not more than, his oldest son. As such, Nicky sat comfortably, knowing that the drive home would retrace the same route. They approached Big John's Deli, and much to Nicky's dismay, nothing changed. Absolutely nothing.

Worry about the strange lack of traffic at Big John's shot through Nicky's mind, and Nicky never uttered a sound. Upon his arrival home, he undressed, showered, slipped into his New York Yankees' boxers, grabbed a book, and jumped into bed.

He knew there could be 101 logical reasons why Big John closed the store early. Harry Huber took him to a doctor's appointment to look at the foot, and it ran late. At the last minute, somebody dropped off some box seats, so Harry took Big John to the Yankees' game in the Bronx.

These explanations topped Nicky's list. Whatever the other ninety-nine might be, Nicky planned to find out the one reason the next day.

Chapter 41

A New Arrival to a Better Place

Nicky's restless sleep was awakened by a nonroutine event, as Mr. Palmieri entered the boys' room for the 6 A. M. paper-route wake-up call. This signaled immediate trouble.

For the past three years of the boys' paper route, Mrs. Palmieri woke the boys from their slumber. Rain, snow, sleet, hail, or the crisp early morning sunshine that highlighted this June morning should not have any effect on her appearance. Not seeing her smiling face the first thing in the morning meant something was wrong.

Maybe something tragic occurred in Colchester.

Nicky knew that Grandpa and Grandma Altamura were in the best shape. Nothing could happen to them. They worked between fifty and sixty hours per week on the egg farm in Colchester. They never took a day off. Their seven-day rituals always included at least eight hours of labor per day.

With the help of Uncle Mike Altamura and his family of five, they fed the chickens and cleaned the four two-story chicken coops. They gathered, washed, sorted and sold the eggs every day. The Altamura farm provided the entire town of Colchester with eggs. It was the 7-11 of chicken embryos.

"Dad, why are you waking us up?" Nicky asked, rubbing his eyes ever so slowly. "Where's Ma? Did something happen to her? Is she okay?"

"Your mother's fine," Mr. Palmieri assured. "There's something I have to tell you."

"Is everything all right in Colchester?" Nicky asked. Before Mr. Palmieri could answer, another higher authority required his father's immediate attention.

"Joe, can you come in the kitchen for a moment? There's a telephone call for you," Mrs. Palmieri interrupted, as Nicky's mind began to buzz.

Nicky knew time zones, and now he worried that there might be a situation in Italy because who would call the Palmieri house at 6 A. M. and remain alive in West Haven to talk about it.

He remembered that his father might call Grandpa Palmieri or his brother Antonio at this early morning hour because it was a little after noon in Italy. But they never called America at this hour because Mr. Palmieri was well on his way to work already.

"What's going on, Nicky?" Ralph asked while his older brother gathered his clothes.

"I don't know yet, but you have to help me. Try to lean outside the doorway and see if you can hear what language Dad is speaking in."

Since Ralph's hearing was far stronger, Nicky figured that if he could discern whether his father was speaking in Italian or English, clues would develop about this potential problem. If Mr. Palmieri spoke in broken English that meant Uncle Nick was on the phone, so he's okay. Now, if he spoke his native Italian, that could mean trouble overseas.

The last time Grandpa Palmieri visited America his health was fine, but Nicky listened and read in school. He grasped the warning labels about tobacco and alcohol. Nicky understood the dangers, but he never heard a whisper that his grandfather abused the stuff. Nicky remembered how the jovial Grandpa Palmieri enjoyed his life to the fullest, with Winston cigarettes, Ballantine beer, and other forms of epicurean delight.

Whenever family members tried to tell him to stop smoking and drinking, Grandpa Palmieri's response silenced everyone. "The English captured me and I was a prisoner of war for many years," he sometimes said in English.

It always sounded much nicer in Italian.

"We lived with machine guns in our faces every day, and we went years between hot meals. This cigarette and this beer won't hurt me today."

Oftentimes during his visits from Italy, Grandpa Palmieri retold his tale of his Ethiopian capture with Nicky on his lap. "Who can argue with him?" Nicky thought. "This guy's tougher than anyone I know."

With Grandpa Palmieri rumbling in the background of Nicky's mind, Ralph emerged from his hallway hiding spot with vital information.

"Dad spoke in English, and he didn't sound too happy."

"That's good. That means that Grandpa's okay. Now, Ralph, did you hear any names?"

"Harry's the only name I heard."

Nicky breathed a temporary sigh of relief. This might explain last night's scene at Big John's. But before he left his room, Mr. Palmieri returned wearing a woeful, sad face.

"Ralph, I need to speak to your brother alone," Mr. Palmieri whispered. "Go to the kitchen, eat your breakfast, and start the paper route with your mother."

"What's going on, Dad? I can do my part of the route. Mom doesn't have to do it. The news can't be that bad."

Nicky lied again. He knew something terrible happened, but this was his way of dealing with disappointment. It troubled him greatly to pull the trigger on the truth instinctively.

"Sit down. I have to tell you something about Big John."

"They rushed Big John to Yale-New Haven Hospital last night. That's why the store was closed."

"Dad, is Big John okay? Can we go see him today? I'll get dressed quick."

Mr. Palmieri struggled to let the words loose. His knew his son suffered enough this past month.

"Big John had a massive stroke. He died last night. I'm sorry, Nicky."

Stunned by the news, Nicky didn't move a muscle. He sat on the edge of his bed and looked out the window toward Big John's house.

Big John's car still wasn't there.

It will never be there again.

Neither will Big John.

Big John was in a better place.

Chapter 42

What Else Can Happen Now?

The news shocked Nicky Palmieri to the point where his volatile emotions didn't even react. He did not shed a single tear. As Mr. Palmieri hugged his son, Nicky simply stared at Big John's house.

Language was a strange phenomenon.

"A massive stroke stopped that massive man," Nicky thought.

Certainly, a man of Big John's physicality at six foot seven and 300 questionable plus pounds didn't die any other way.

Massive.

Three previous heart attacks couldn't drag Big John six feet under. The good Lord needed something mammoth, something of colossal proportions.

Massive.

God knew that Big John would easily defeat any cancer.

It was the only way to take the big man out. His enormous persona and charisma were bigger than life itself.

A massive stroke, it figured.

"Dad, do you know if Ralph started his piece of the route first or mine?" Nicky inquired.

"You know your brother. He probably started his end first so he could say he beat you."

Nicky smiled. He couldn't possibly laugh. His emotions were frozen. He knew that delivering the papers helped him think, and off he went to Kelsey Avenue.

"How's Nicky taking it?" Mrs. Palmieri wanted to know.

"It's amazing, Netta. He didn't say one word. He didn't even cry. It's like he expected it to happen."

"I saw his face last night when we went past Big John's," Mrs. Palmieri noted. "He must have felt something. When Mrs. Ferrante brought me to the game early in the evening, we went past the store too, and it didn't look too good."

Mr. Palmieri nodded his head in agreement. He recorded the scene as well and just hoped for the best.

"When did Harry say they were going to have the wake?" Mrs. Palmieri asked her solemn husband.

"They will have the wake on Saturday and Sunday at DiNapola's. The funeral will be Monday morning."

Mr. and Mrs. Palmieri debated whether Nicky should finally experience this unchartered territory of death.

"Nicky's ready to handle this," Mr. Palmieri predicted. "After what went on with Jerry, he should learn to pay his respects to Big John. He'll come with me."

Mrs. Palmieri affirmed his thoughts but convinced her spouse that Nicky needed to make the decision.

"If we force him to go, Nicky's going to rebel and do the opposite," she offered. "Let him have some time, and let's see what he does."

"We should also let him play in the game against that Rusty boy," Mr. Palmieri surprisingly added. "Nicky can go to the wake at night. Besides, Harry Huber said to convince him to play because everybody knew that Big John wouldn't let him cancel a game even if I died."

"Hey, Joe. What would you do if I died?"

"Oh, honey, I'd make sure the whole towns of West Haven and Colchester shuts down. Nothing would go on. Not a thing. Not even a game of bocce. It would all stop in your honor."

"You're a real dear, Joe."

While the joking changed the mood in the Palmieri house, Nicky hurriedly caught his brother on the back end of Richmond Avenue.

"What happened Nicky?" Ralph started. "All of the sudden, Mom is throwing food down my throat and telling me I have to do your side of the paper route."

"Are you in trouble?"

"No, I'm not in any trouble. It's just that Big John died last night in the hospital."

"Oh, my God, this is terrible. I'm really sorry, Nicky. Why don't you go home, and I'll do these papers. I can do it."

"Thanks, Ralph, but I need to run around. I'll see you when I get home," Nicky uttered as he grabbed twenty-two papers and went to work.

Nicky realized that life had not been too kind to him the past few months. While he sprinted from house to house delivering papers, he wondered if the recent string of lies about the Great Chocolate Milk Conflict, the glove, school, and almost any other topic created some bad karma. Few people were quite as superstitious as Nicky Palmieri. His baseball mannerisms needed to be in order, and the only time bad luck entered his mind was during his own baseball games.

But maybe baseball wasn't that important.

Maybe his lies were creating bad luck in more significant aspects of life.

Maybe his lies were what caused Big John's accident.

Maybe his lies induced the stroke.

Maybe he should stop lying.

The last stop on the paper route led to a place where Nicky's lies never penetrated—Ann Marriotti's house.

"Hey, Nicky, how are you doing?" rang the sweet voice from the upstairs window.

"My mom just told me about Big John. I'm really sorry. Is there anything I could do?"

"How did you hear about that already, Ann?" Nicky answered while Ann gave him a friendly, caring hug. "I just found out an hour ago."

"Your mom called. She was worried about where you were—usually you are done with your route in no time."

"Yeah, Ann, you're right." Nicky replied. "Today I ran through the route, but then I was walking around and thinking about lots of things."

"I know that Big John was a good friend to you."

"Ann, he was the best. He was like a second father. He did so much for me."

"You are so lucky, Nicky."

"What do you mean?"

"You get to know what it's like to have two fathers. I wish I could know one."

Ann's statement stunned Nicky. He was sad about Big John's untimely death, but he knew by some miracle, cleft palate or no cleft palate, how fortunate he really was.

"I'm sorry, Ann. You deserve the best. It must be hard for you and your mom."

"Don't forget my brother, too."

"Oh, yes, your brother. His name is Carl, right?"

"Yeah, he's a great kid. You have to meet him some day," Ann offered.

"How old is he?"

"He's ten."

"Great, Ann. You should invite him to play baseball with us. The rest of the team would welcome him."

"Carl loves baseball, too, but he can't play. He's got some problems that I really don't want to talk about now."

Sometimes Nicky forgot to think before he spoke. This was one of those precious moments.

"I know about birth defects, Ann. Let me tell you."

Ann started to cry.

"You don't know how lucky you are," Ann sobbed as she ran into her house. "You really don't know how lucky you are."

Nicky didn't know what to think. He vaguely remembered something he heard about Ann's brother, but he was too consumed with himself and his own problems to remember.

"I have to learn to keep my big mouth shut sometimes," Nicky concluded on the way home. "And I really have to stop lying."

Mr. Palmieri spotted Nicky walking the steep Kelsey Avenue hill on his drive to work. He rolled the window down to check on his son.

"Nicola, come here. How are you doing?"

"I'm sad, but everything's okay. Big John is in a better place, right, Dad?"

"I'm sure he is, so you better not say anything bad about him. He's already got spies down here to find out who's knocking him."

Nicky laughed before asking his father, "Dad, when's the wake? I think I better go. I owe it to Big John."

"We'll go tomorrow and Sunday night," Mr. Palmieri said. "Big John will be happy."

Nicky knew how strict his father can be with punctuality, so he carefully asked his next question about baseball.

"Dad, do you think it will be possible for me to play in the game against Crusty Rusty tomorrow? I know we will be finished by four o'clock at the latest. Besides, the rest of the kids are really looking forward to beating the cocky redhead."

"I'm sure Big John would want you to play the game," Mr. Palmieri assured his son. "I won't have a problem with it as long as you are ready to go to the wake by 6 P. M. on the button."

Nicky leaned in the car window and hugged his father. "Thanks, Dad. Thanks for everything."

On his way home, Nicky stopped and told Gennaro to spread the word for a practice at the top field in one hour. He remembered how Big John would love to see Nicky and the Kelsey Avenue Crew beat Crusty Rusty.

After a phone call to Ann, Nicky rushed out of his house and met the crew at the home diamond. They were shocked after learning about Big John's death, but they didn't utter a word to Nicky.

They knew the entire story about his glove. Nicky's friends understood his special friendship with Big John, and they tried to keep everything simple—business as usual. The Kelsey Avenue Crew set up a little batting practice and went to work.

The team sensed that this was an awesome day to play baseball. The Kelsey Avenue Crew practiced as hard as ever in hope that the moment finally arrived for the defeat of the Crusty Rusty All-Stars.

This was great, Nicky thought, but losing the game with Big John in attendance was much better than any win without him.

Chapter 43
It's Just Another Game.

This Saturday started in grand West Haven summer fashion. The sun shined brightly on the miles of beaches, which awaited hundreds of cars rumbling along Kelsey Avenue and Captain Thomas Boulevard. Folks from many parts of the city often ventured to taste the summer sun and kick-start their deep, dark tans. While these people's plans headed south, Nicky's game plan moved in the opposite direction—to the north, to the baseball diamonds at Painter's Park.

When Nicky looked out his window, he felt something was in the air. "We're finally going to beat Crusty Rusty," he announced to his dozing brother, who probably loved sleeping more than Nicky loved baseball.

"I just wish Big John were here to see it."

"What time is it?" Ralph mumbled.

"It's almost half past ten."

"You're talking about baseball already. I've got to listen to some Creedence Clearwater Revival to wake me up."

"Allow me, Ralph, to blast you out of bed with a little CCR favorite, 'Born on the Bayou,' Nicky added as he turned the music on and raced from the room. "This will be a Palmieri family tradition."

Without papers to deliver, Nicky announced to Mrs. Palmieri his departure and headed to his sanctuary for an early morning prayer. At Big John's.

Normally, Nicky would be hard at work. He would be cleaning the meat and donut cases, but there was no need for that. The store was closed. It was almost darker than death itself. The pastry and donut cases were empty, and there was no sign needed on the front door.

Everyone in town knew about Big John.

Nicky simply stared into the window and wondered.

"If Big John didn't spill the boiling water on his foot, would he still be alive today?" he pondered.

"It's my fault. This is every bit my fault."

He walked to Big John's car, jiggled the back window, and unlocked the station wagon's door. He maneuvered his way around the back seat and sat in the passenger side. Nicky recalled many of Big John's pep talks.

"You have got to learn to be tough. You can't let the names bother you. Try to find something you do well and beat them at it."

As much as Big John's advice rang in his mind, the names bothered Nicky.

Losing a baseball game to Crusty Rusty was not half as bad as the post-game ridicule. Nicky just wanted it to end in front of his friends—the Kelsey Avenue Crew.

Nicky assembled this club. These players did more than play baseball together. They shared meals in each other's homes.

Mrs. Ferrante, Mrs. Gambardella, and Mrs. Kessler treated Nicky like a son. John, Gennaro, Bill and Johnny G. along with the Kessler brothers were Nicky's family. They played every sport imaginable together. Stickball on the tennis courts, street hockey in the school yard, basketball in backyards, and football anywhere there was a patch of green grass.

These were the people Nicky went to war with against Crusty Rusty.

These were the people that Nicky wanted to win with.

These were Nicky's real friends.

The 1 P. M. start with the Crusty Rusty All-Stars arrived quickly. The entire Kelsey Avenue Crew warmed up for more than an hour. They took batting practice, and Mr. Camp hit the infield and outfield routine.

"Hey, when can we take our turn for some infield/outfield?" cried Rusty.

"Take it now if you need it big mouth because today your team in going down," Ann confidently told the surprised visitor.

"I don't think so. I am not losing to some girl shortstop," Rusty retorted.

"Shut up and play ball, Rusty," Gennaro said. "You're leaving here a loser in a couple of hours."

Nicky remained quiet. Big John's wake took center stage and occupied his mind while Rusty's club prepared for the first pitch.

"Ann, what do you do at wakes?"

"Don't worry about it, Nicky. Just follow everybody else in line, kneel down in front of the casket, and say a prayer. It's easy."

"I'm going to be too sad. I don't know if I could do it."

"Nicky, you have to say good-bye to him. This is not that bad. Your surgeries hurt more than this."

"I don't know, Ann. The pain in the surgeries go away, but this hole I feel inside my heart seems like it's going to last forever."

Ann put her arm around Nicky, shook him a little bit, and started his second favorite pastime—the sweet science of changing the subject.

"What's the lineup, Nicky? Let's beat this blockhead."

The Kelsey Avenue Crew featured their most impressive lineup. Everybody was there.

Mark K.—2B
Bob K.—C
Nicky P.—LF
Ann M.—SS
Bill G.—CF
Ralph P—RF
Lou K.—3B
John F.—1B
Gennaro C.—P

Chuck Stack, George Carbon, John S., and John A. were there as well. They knew their roles. They would come off the bench if necessary. Their loyalty belonged to Nicky and the other eight members of the Kelsey Avenue Crew. This was the best team Nicky could put on the field. Rusty looked nervous.

Before the first pitch, Nicky asked both teams to stand on their respective foul lines, take off their caps, and honor Big John Wizenski with a moment of silence. Surprisingly, Rusty echoed Nicky's sentiments. Everyone in West Haven knew the powerful clout of Big John. He commanded respect in many circles of life.

An hour of silence was more appropriate even though Nicky couldn't possibly do it.

"All right. Let's play some baseball," Nicky said.

Since the game was played on Nicky's home turf, the Crusty Rusty All-Stars were always the visitors. Rusty agreed to that one, too.

Gennaro pitched on two days' rest. In his last Little League game, he tossed a one-hitter with fifteen strikeouts. His arm never bothered him. He threw between sixty and one hundred pitches every day. Gennaro was a strike machine. Every game at Painter's Park was a nine-inning affair, and Gennaro was prepared. This was real baseball.

Gennaro rolled through the Crusty Rusty lineup. Meanwhile, the Kelsey Avenue Crew only managed to scratch out a couple of singles. After three complete innings there was no score.

In the top of the fourth, Rusty tattooed a shot with two outs and runners on the corners, but Nicky saved two runs with an over-the-shoulder catch in left center field.

The Heart of the Hide Big John gave him worked its magic.

"Nice catch, Nicky," Rusty yelled dejectedly.

As mean as the evil red head could be, he really appreciated the finer points of baseball. In the past, Rusty sometimes complimented Nicky on a good swing or a defensive web gem, but Nicky was always too wound up to hear him.

"Gennaro, did the jerk say 'nice catch?'"

"Yeah, I think he did," Ann interrupted. "He's losing his edge. They're going down today. Let's go guys. Let's put some runs on the board."

Nicky led off the fourth with a double past a diving third baseman. Ann drove him home with a single to left for a 1–0 lead. The Crusty Rusty All-Stars came back in the top of the sixth with a three-run homer by Richie McCarren. Rusty came into pitch in the bottom of the sixth, and he was throwing hard.

Ralph and Lou K. crushed solo homers to tie the game at 3–3.

"How does your arm feel, Gennaro?" Mark K. asked. "If it's bothering you, tell us. We'll bring Nicky in to win this thing."

"Just give me one more inning and then bring him in."

The Kelsey Avenue Crew waited two pitches too many. Ed Hall singled and Rusty slammed a monstrous two-run homer over Nicky's head in left for a 5–3 edge.

"Good job, Gennaro. Don't worry we have three at-bats left," Nicky said as he moved to the mound to change positions. "Go play left field, and I'll try to keep it close."

Miraculously, Rusty's good sportsmanship lasted for six-plus innings. And then he started.

"Here we go. Now, you bring in the Elephant Man," Rusty said while tugging his lip and laughing. "Are you afraid to pitch to me so now you come in, Lip."

Nicky barely batted an eyelash. He simply stood on the mound and waited for the next hitter.

Archie Sagnella and Mrs. Kessler inched closer to the field just in case another classic Nicky Palmieri explosion erupted. Nicky easily retired the Crusty Rusty club, and the game moved to the bottom of the seventh. John Ferrante singled and advanced to second on Gennaro's sacrifice bunt. Mark K bunted for a hit to put runners on first and third. Then with two strikes, Bob K. lofted a soft fly ball to left.

A bang, bang play at the plate ensued with Nicky calling John safe from the on-deck circle. Rusty screamed out, but Archie Sagnella stepped in and reminded Rusty of his homer from two weeks ago. Rusty, begrudgingly, scored the run, and the Kelsey Avenue Crew sliced the lead to 5–4.

"Oh, boy, look who's up? It's the Lip."

"Throw the ball and shut your face."

Nicky grabbed the bat so tight he almost turned the wooden handle into sawdust. He violently overswung at three pitches, and Rusty laughed his way to the dugout.

"Come on let's go and put the Elephant Man away with a couple of runs."

Still there was no reply from Nicky.

The game moved into the top of the ninth with no change in the score. The Crusty Rusty club loaded the bases with two outs on a couple of Texas League singles and a bad hop past John F. Tension grew as none other than Crusty Rusty strode toward home plate, tugging his lip and mocking Nicky in hopes of stimulating a reaction from his target.

Everyone knew that a base hit here would make the bottom of the ninth especially tough for a Kelsey Avenue Crew comeback. Ann sensed a small problem, called time out, and visited the mound.

"Nicky, do you hear what he's saying? Why aren't you saying anything back?"

"I can't get mad," Nicky calmly responded, holding his treasured Heart of the Hide over his mouth so the opposition could not read his lips.

"Big John told me to keep my cool and concentrate on what I have to do. I'm going to reach back and throw this carrottop one fastball over his redhead, and the rest will be changeups."

Crusty Rusty dug in and Nicky fired a fastball behind his enemy's cranium. Rusty started to charge the mound, but Bob K. tackled him. Nicky quietly stood on the mound. This angered Rusty to no end. He swiftly dusted himself and moved back to the batter's box.

"I'm sending one up the box, and I'm going to fatten the other side of your lip. Just throw it over the plate, Elephant Man."

Again, not a syllable was heard from Nicky.

The remainder of the Kelsey Avenue Crew was extremely animated. Gennaro screamed from left field. In right field, Ralph's arms moved faster than Muhammad Ali trying to battle his way out of a corner with George Foreman.

Nicky took a deep breath and sent another fastball whizzing past Rusty's head.

"Missed me again, Chicken. Throw it over the plate, and I'll hit another homer off you, Pig Face."

Softly, Nicky rolled the ball around in his hand without a response. He wound up and his next pitch was a dazzling circle changeup.

Rusty's eyes lit up, and he swung mightily only to send a soft one-hopper back to Nicky. The trusty Heart of the Hide snared the grounder, and Nicky flipped it to first to end the inning.

"Great pitch, Nicky," Ann said. "You really fooled him. He was so far off stride he couldn't hit a bull in the behind with a banjo."

"We got 'em now. Let's win this game."

The bottom of the ninth started off well for the Kelsey Avenue Crew. Lou K. and Mark K. singled around a couple of outs. Bob K. rocketed a blistering shot to Rusty, but he lost the handle to load the bases for Nicky.

"This is perfect, loser. Now, I get to strike you out again."

Not a word from Nicky.

"Come on speak, Lip boy. Say something or are you too nervous. Let me check and see if you're going to pee your pants."

Rusty started walking toward home plate at Nicky.

"Knock off the baloney, you jerk, and pitch," Gennaro screamed. "We're winning this one. Let's go Nicky. All we need is a single."

Nicky tapped his Roy White model white-ash, tempered-flame bat on both sides of the plate. He loosened his grip a little, aligned the knocking knuckles for the perfect swing, and stared at the mound.

The first pitch was on the outside corner. Nicky recognized the pitch, kept his head down, and laced a rocket to right field.

Butch Caulfield, an outstanding player on the Giannotti Middle School club, was charging hard and made a great catch, but he obviously trapped the ball.

Lou K. easily crossed home plate to tie the game while Mark K. raced home, trying to score the winning run.

The rocket throw from right field and Mark K. arrived at the plate at the same time. Crusty Rusty covered home plate. He tagged Mark on the leg in the middle of a huge dust cloud. Rusty started to scramble to his feet and he lifted his glove triumphantly in the air.

"Come on guys. Let's hit. We're playing extra innings."

"No, we're not Rusty," Ann chuckled.

"Because we won, 6–5."

"What are you talking about? I have the ball right…."

Ann, who was the on deck hitter, proudly held the ball in her hand. The Kelsey Avenue Crew piled on Mark K. and celebrated.

Rusty dropped the ball.

"We won. We won," Gennaro yelled. "Can you believe it, Nicky? We…Where's Nicky?"

Nicky sat on second base, holding his head in his hands. Tears streamed down his face, cutting streaks into the dirt, which only moments ago fully covered his cheeks.

Butch Caulfield walked in from the outfield toward Nicky, patted him on the back, and said, "That's a real nice clutch hit. I know Big John was watching."

"You knew Big John?" Nicky inquired, lifting his head.

"I sure did. He used to call me One Cell when I worked at his store. He's the one who gave me my first glove."

"He gave me a glove and called me One Cell, too."

"Big John was the best," Butch added. "He and Jerry said you were a good player, and they're right. Make sure you keep practicing."

"You knew Jerry, too."

"Sure did. Jerry and his father coached my Babe Ruth League team. He always talked about you and Gennaro. He told me that you boys loved baseball as much as he did."

"I sure miss Jerry," Nicky said.

"So do I," Butch admitted. "Listen, kid, I've got to go, but I will tell you one more thing. I promise to make sure idiots like Rusty don't bother you again as long as you keep working hard at baseball."

"Deal."

"That's a real good deal, Butch. Thanks," Nicky replied.

Nicky brushed himself and met a happy Kelsey Avenue Crew behind the mound.

"You were talking to Butch Caulfield for a long time," Gennaro noticed. "What were you guys talking about? He's some player. Do you realize how good he is at football, too?"

"We were just talking about Big John, Jerry, and baseball," Nicky answered. "No matter what other people say about him, Butch's a pretty decent guy."

The Kelsey Avenue Crew caught Gennaro and started the celebratory punching of Nicky in the head for collecting the game-winning hit. Nicky finally started to smile until a most familiar voice interrupted his joy.

"Nicky, I got something to tell you," Rusty started. "First, I'm sorry about Big John. And second, good game. Your team deserved to win."

"That's awful nice, Rusty."

"We're going to play again next week?"

"Sure. We'll be here," Nicky assured Rusty.

"Good. See you next week."

Only disbelief could describe the looks on many of the Kelsey Avenue Crew's faces.

"Was that Rusty Alves?" Ann asked.

"Must be an imposter," Ralph added. "I think I heard him speak a couple of compound words."

As soon as the laughter started, the kids realized that the dreaded losing streak finally ended.

Now, Nicky Palmieri knew exactly what to do when he attended Big John's wake later this happy day. He had two stories to tell and he knew which one he would tell first.

Chapter 44

This wake thing wasn't really that bad.

Each one of the Kelsey Avenue Crew knew it was only a sandlot baseball win. There were no standings, no statistics, and no championship trophies for the winning teams.

For some it was just a game.

For Nicky Palmieri, it was an enormous burden lifted from him.

One and forty-five.

It was certainly better than O and forty-six.

The win against the talented Crusty Rusty All-Stars would never be forgotten. More importantly, the victory changed Nicky's perspective toward his evening responsibilities.

Big John's two viewings would surely be much easier. People at DiNapola's Funeral Home would be buzzing about the game, distracting Nicky from the misery of seeing Big John motionless. The win softened the tension. Nicky knew that the funeral would be difficult but not impossible.

Nicky understood what to tell Big John at the wake—the game, the glove, and the truth.

Nicky hoped that Big John would hear him in his better place.

"That's a huge win, guys," Nicky said while bidding farewell to his friends. "If I don't see you at the wake tonight, I'll see you guys tomorrow."

Ralph and Nicky pushed the noisy steel shopping cart home, banging and clanging at a happy pace.

"Congratulations, boys," Mrs. Palmieri exclaimed as she greeted her triumphant sons at the backdoor. "I heard it was an exciting game."

"How did you hear about the game already?"

"Don't worry about it, Ralph. You will learn soon that this is a really small town," Nicky said.

Mrs. Palmieri chuckled and instructed her boys to put their baseball equipment away and wash up for dinner.

A much more relaxed Nicky took a quick shower, ate, and waited for Mr. Palmieri to drive them to Big John's wake.

"Now, Nicky, you just follow me and do everything I do," Mr. Palmieri instructed.

Clearly, this was easy for Nicky.

One time when he was seven years old, Grandma Palmieri visited from Italy. She gave Nicky two crisp dollar bills and told him to attend mass at St. John Vianney's alone.

"I don't know what to do, Grandma" Nicky offered.

"Don't worry. Just do what everybody else does."

This also sounded much nicer in Italian.

Nicky followed the orders perfectly, except for one thing.

"Nicola, how did it go?" Grandma Palmieri asked.

"Everything went great. I kneeled and prayed. I put the money you gave me in a picnic basket, and then the best part was I got to go in line and get half a cookie and drink some yucky grape juice to wash it down."

"You took communion?" Mr. Palmieri questioned.

"No, Dad, I took a cookie and it didn't taste too sweet."

A playful tap to the head followed by *"cuccio,"* the Italian word for donkey, meant that Nicky screwed up something.

"You're not ready for communion," Grandma Palmieri announced. "You have to talk to the priest and confess your sins."

"Sins? Where do you get those, Grandma?"

While the four Palmieris in attendance laughed and smiled, Grandpa Palmieri offered genuine words of wisdom.

"Don't worry about the sins, Nicky. I'll give you some of mine to use."

"Do I have to give them back?"

"No, you can keep them."

After a two-hour lecture on sins and lies from Mrs. Palmieri, Nicky understood a little about why they were amused with the sins portion of the story.

Nicky realized he had another confession to make—this one to someone else in a different pine box. Big John, who no longer could respond.

No prayers or reading homework in the Bible would be assigned from this wooden crate. This confession should have taken place weeks ago. Upon arrival, Nicky noticed cars parked all over DiNapola's. An amazing long line of mourners waited in the street.

Nicky led his father to the same back door he slipped into that fateful night when he put the Heart of the Hide in Jerry's casket.

"How did you know about this way, Nicky?" Mr. Palmieri asked.

"Gennaro remembered this door when his grandmother died a couple of years ago. During Jerry's wake, he beat the lines by going this way."

Luckily for the boys, Mr. Casserta opened a spot in the front of the line for Mr. Palmieri and Nicky. Minutes later, they took their place, kneeling in front of Big John.

"Dad, he looks like he is just sleeping. This is amazing."

"Sh, just say your prayers and move along. You see how long the line is."

"I have a lot to tell him."

"Try to make it quick. I'll stay here with you."

"Hello, Big John, it's me Nicky. My father's here, too. I've got good news and bad news. I'll give you the bad news first.

"First, I'm sorry about the lies with the glove. I should have told you what I did. But after the first couple of lies, I didn't know how to stop it. I should have trusted you. I know you wouldn't be mad."

Mr. Palmieri placed his arm around his tearful son.

"I hope my lies didn't cause that accident," Nicky continued as his voice softened. "You're the best friend I ever had. I'll never forget you. I'll love you forever."

"Are you finished, Nicky?"

"Wait, there's one more thing," he continued. "I almost forgot the good news. Big John, we finally beat Crusty Rusty today. I hope you weren't too busy, and you made some time to watch the game. We played the best game. Thanks again."

Nicky turned to his father and asked, "Dad, do you think Big John heard me in Heaven?"

"Of course he did. You were so loud they even heard you in California," Mr. Palmieri cracked. "That was nice, Nicky. See, this wake business isn't so bad."

"No, it's not. I just wish that I told him these things a few days ago."

Mr. Palmieri nodded his head in agreement and led the two to look around the room. They were amazed by the collection of black-and-white and color photos of Big John's life on easels around the room.

"Look, a picture of Big John in high school. Wow. He was skinny."

"Sh, wise guy. I know he heard that one."

"Big John won't mind, Dad. He's in a better place."

And so was Nicky Palmieri.

Chapter 45
Moving Right Along

The wake soothed Nicky's soul. Sunday night wasn't quite as eventful, but Monday's funeral was another story. For Nicky, the funeral was hours away. He was looking forward to the Kelsey Avenue Crew's typical Sunday afternoon gathering on the top diamond at Painter's Park at one o'clock.

"Hey, Nicky, how did the wake go last night?" Gennaro asked.

"It was sad, but tomorrow's going to be the worst," Nicky admitted. "We should do something for Big John like we did for Jerry."

Gennaro pulled from his pockets a couple of containers of Wite-Out.

As the remainder of the team arrived, Ann peered over Nicky's shoulder. "What are you guys doing?"

"We're writing JW with white out on our hats," Ralph smiled.

"Big John's name is John Wizenski."

Ann noticed some other Wite-Out work on the boys' hats.

"What's twenty-two about then?" Ann wondered.

Mark K. explained how they honored Jerry Gambardella Jr. by writing his uniform number on their hats.

"Here then, put a "JW" on my hat, too," Ann said, handing her hat to Nicky and Gennaro for their handy work.

"You realize now that when we do this to your hat, you're part of the crew forever," Nicky said.

"I would like that more than anything."

"Great, Ann. That means that if we play basketball, baseball, or football, you are picked before any outsider. That's the deal," Nicky said.

Ann was part of the Kelsey Avenue Crew long before the rites of initiation. Her play at shortstop and the win over Crusty Rusty lifted her to another level.

The teams then moved to their usual Sunday routine. During summer, there was an abundant flow of baseballs popping out of the players' equipment bags. Game and practice balls from their organized teams fell into their bags over time, and this ad hoc "collection" allowed the Kelsey Avenue Crew to warm up as a team. With dozens of baseballs, they didn't have to worry about losing foul balls in the woods. The one-ball days were over for a while. They even held real batting practice just like the pros.

The kids placed a stolen milk crate on the edge of the outfield for batted balls. There was another one behind the BP pitcher, so everyone took a lot more swings. After everyone took two rounds of BP, they broke the group into two teams for a game. They played nine innings every time—real baseball but with a Kelsey Avenue twist.

The sandlot rules were different. There was no leading off the bases. No stealing. No walks. Everybody swung the bat, and everybody understood the rules. Most importantly, everybody had fun. Two hours later after the game, Gennaro approached Nicky about the funeral. "Nicky, are you going to put anything in Big John's casket like you did for Jerry?"

"I've got a few things in mind."

"Why did you do that?" Mark asked.

"When you get to sixth grade, you study ancient Egypt," Nicky started. "You'll learn about how the rich people put things in their tombs to take to the afterlife."

"They put crazy things in with the pharaohs—food, drinks, gold, money, and jewelry. Some of them even had their pets killed, so they could take them with them."

"That's crazy. But what does that have to do with anything?" Lou K. said.

Ann quickly stepped in.

"Nicky believes that there is going to be baseball in Heaven, so you have to send the baseball stuff ahead of time to have it ready for when we get there."

"Why do you think there's going to be baseball in Heaven, Nicky?" Mark asked.

Nicky told the story of his friend, Fabrizio, who suffered from severe cerebral palsy and spent his life in a wheelchair. He described how Fabrizio said that he wasn't mad about not being able to walk or do the things other kids took for granted.

"Fabrizio said that Heaven should be whatever you want it to be," Nicky said. "Heaven will be the place where he can walk and talk like everybody else. Heaven will be the place where he and I can play catch.

"Heaven is the place where, if you're not happy being short, you can be tall. Heaven is the place where, if you have a weak heart, you get a strong one," he added. "Heaven is the place where if you want to play baseball all day, nobody will stop you. Heaven should be the place where every single one of your dreams and wishes come true."

"Wow, Nicky," Mark K. said. "I hope there's baseball in Heaven, too."

Secretly Mark K. and the rest of the Kelsey Avenue Crew understood that Nicky Palmieri hopes that there was more than just baseball in Heaven.

Chapter 46

Good-bye, Big John

Mrs. Palmieri woke Nicky on a dark, dank, rainy Monday morning. The paper required a little more effort in these weather conditions. Nicky and Ralph placed the papers in plastic bags before delivery. This ensured nice tips at the end of the week and even larger ones at Christmas time. A torrential downpour soaked Nicky before he finished his route at the Marriotti's. Ann eyed her drenched friend and welcomed him inside with a clean shirt and a towel.

"Boy, Nicky, it's really raining hard out there," Ann commented while handing Nicky one of her father's Fort Lauderdale Yankees' undershirts. "You earned your money today."

Nicky carefully examined the shirt. The traditional dark Yankees' blue was faded around the collar and shoulder from the bright Florida sun. The number twenty on the back was cracked in some spots, and it was really big.

"This shirt's too big. I can't take it. I'll just dry off and run home. I have to get ready for the funeral."

"Take the shirt. I don't want it anymore," Ann offered. "You keep it, and you can wear it when you get older."

"It's like a dress on me. I'll never be big enough to wear it. Keep your father's shirt."

"You are taking the shirt, and that's it," Mrs. Marriotti interjected. "You'll get sick if you don't change shirts. Besides, Ann wants you to have it, and trust me you don't want to make Ann mad."

"Okay, okay, I get it. Thank you, Ann. Thank you, Mrs. Marriotti."

"What time are you going to the funeral, Nicky?" Ann asked.

"My father is going to be one of the pallbearers, so I'm going to funeral home in a couple of hours. Mr. DiNapola said it would be okay for me to put some stuff in Big John's casket."

"What are you going to put in there?" Ann inquired.

"I don't know yet, Ann. I've got a few things ready, but I'm debating about one more thing."

Ann nodded her head and showed Nicky to the bathroom. He dried his hair and face, changed shirts, and emerged smiling and ready for the sprint home.

"Can I give you a ride?" Mrs. Marriotti offered. "Ann can stay here with her brother. You shouldn't be walking around in this rain."

Nicky peered out the screen door and saw the rain subsiding. "The rain is slowing down. I'll be fine. Thanks, Mrs. Marriotti."

With a tug and pull on his hat, Nicky lowered his head and sprinted home to prepare for the toughest morning of his young life. Mr. Palmieri was already dressed in his neatly tailored dark blue silk suit made in Italy by his brother Antonio. Nicky owned a much smaller version of the same suit.

As they left Mr. Palmieri's car in the funeral home parking lot, Nicky's father noticed a brown shopping bag.

"What's in the bag, Nicola?"

"Oh, just a couple of things I need to put in Big John's casket."

Nicky walked into Mr. DiNapola's office and asked for permission to see Big John one more time. The gregarious funeral director agreed to open Big John's room.

A teary-eyed Nicky kneeled at the coffin and opened his bag. He gently placed the game-winning ball from the upset against Crusty Rusty near Big John's right hand. Nicky filed an envelope filled with New York Yankees' baseball cards in Big John's right pocket.

As he withdrew his prized possession out of the bag, a warm soft, hand touched his right shoulder and kneeled next to him.

"Here, Nicky, don't put that in there. Take this one. It'll be from the both of us. This one's so old anyway. You'll need yours for the rest of the season."

"I can't do that. That Heart of the Hide was one your father gave to you when you were little."

Before Nicky could reply, he caught the remainder of the Kelsey Avenue Crew behind him. Each kid carried an item to place in Big John's casket.

Gennaro brought a hat Jerry Gambardella Jr. gave him.

Mark K. grabbed his worn out Wilson A2000 glove.

John F. held onto a Johnny Bench catcher's mitt.

Lou K. fiddled with his Green Bay Packers hat.

Ralph P. pulled a Jimi Hendrix tape from his pocket.

Bob K. rolled a golf ball in his hands.

Bill G. carried his Wilson midget football.

John G. grasped a deck of Bicycle playing cards.

John S. showed Nicky a hockey puck.

John A. gently tugged the strap of his old catcher's mask.

George C. tapped his drum sticks against a chair.

Lastly, Chuck Stack flipped the pages of *Green Eggs and Ham*.

"Before we all do this, we better make sure it's okay with Big John's family." Mr. Palmieri announced.

"Let the kids do it," Mrs. Wizenski said as she entered the room with an envelope in her hand. "We've got plenty of room."

"Here, Nicky, I have something for you."

Nicky nervously peeled open the envelope. Inside there was a small picture of Big John and Nicky in front of the deli.

"I just found this an hour ago in Big John's wallet. You should have it."

Nicky took the photo, placed it in the pocket of Ann's Heart of the Hide, and delicately placed the glove next to Big John's left hand.

After giving the sign of the cross, Ann and Nicky rose. Then one by one, the Kelsey Avenue Crew located spots for their items for Big John's trip to that better place.

Chapter 47
One More Surprise

Since Mr. DiNapola needed eight pallbearers for Big John, there was no room for Nicky in one of the funeral cars. Mr. Palmieri arranged for his son to ride with Mrs. Marriotti to the church and St. Lawrence Cemetery.

"I'll pick him up at your house later," Mr. Palmieri said as they prepared to move Big John into the black Cadillac hearse.

"Are you going to be all right with the rest of the funeral?" Mr. Palmieri asked. "You can go home if you want to."

"Nope. No way. I want to see the end of this. Gennaro and Ann are here, too. I'll be fine." The service at the church was extremely emotional and everyone wept. St. Lawrence Cemetery tripled that misery.

"I'm glad that's over," Nicky said to Ann and her mother from the backseat of the Marriotti's van.

"Ma, do you think Nicky can stay and have lunch with us?" Ann asked. "And hang out and play with Carl for a while."

"Sure. I don't see any problems with it. I think Nicky's dad won't be ready to pick him up for at least a couple of hours."

They arrived at Ann's house. Mrs. Marriotti paid the babysitter twenty dollars and instructed her daughter to bring Carl into the living room.

"Nicky, do want to play a baseball game with Carl and me? I have to warn you, though, we're going to kick your butt."

Ann wheeled her brother into the hallway. Nicky busily set up a trivia baseball game.

"Nicky, I want you to meet my brother, Carl."

After he finished preparing the game cards, Nicky looked up and saw Carl's legs strapped to the wheel chair first.

Nicky's head moved a little higher. He noticed some too familiar scars right under Carl's nose.

"Hello, Nicky, I'm Carl. It's nice to meet you," as Ann's brother reached with his right hand.

Nicky was stunned. He shook Carl's hand with its strong grip. Nicky felt as though he were looking into a mirror as he saw Carl's cleft palate. He then realized what Ann meant when she said, "You don't know how lucky you are."

Nicky was ashamed and bowed his head for a moment.

"Is everything all right, Nicky."

"Yeah, come on. I was just thinking about something you said a couple days ago. Let's play."

While the rain continued outside, the baseball trivia game brightened the inside for the three energetic children. Ann and Carl tied for first place.

"We need a tiebreaker," Ann insisted.

"I've got a good one," Nicky said while Mrs. Marriotti and Mr. Palmieri spoke in the foyer.

"Name the three Italian-American baseball players that have hit more than forty homers in one season."

Carl buzzed first.

"That's easy, Nicky."

"Go for it, big shot."

"Joe DiMaggio, Rocky Colavito, and Jim Gentile."

"Wow, Carl, that's tremendous. How did you know that?"

"You've got to read a few books once in a while, Nicky."

"That's right. You see what I have been trying to tell you for all these years. Read books," Mr. Palmieri shouted from several feet away. "Come on. It's time to go home. You've bothered these nice people long enough."

"I've got to go now. Thanks for lunch, Mrs. Marriotti. The cavatelli were great."

"You're welcome, Nicky."

Carl pushed his wheelchair over to Nicky and extended his arms as far as he could. Nicky leaned forward and gave him a warm hug.

"Ma, can Nicky come over tomorrow?" Carl pleaded.

"Why don't you ask him yourself?"

Before he even started to turn his head, Nicky quickly replied, "Carl, I will come over any day you want. See you tomorrow at 7 A.M. You better be awake because this time I'm going to win."

Nicky left the house with a new and amazing perspective.

"Dad, did you see Carl? I feel terrible for him because he's worse off than anybody I know."

"I knew Carl when he was born in West Haven," Mr. Palmieri reported.

"It's a shame his father ran out on the family because he was paralyzed," Nicky commented.

"That's not true, Nicola. His father ran away when he saw the cleft palate," Mr. Palmieri added. "Two years ago, Carl was crippled by a hit-and-run drunk driver while chasing a baseball in the street in Florida."

Nicky sat in the passenger seat stunned.

"A father abandons his family because of a cleft palate," Nicky thought. "That's brutality."

Nicky recalled how Ann never once said anything about her brother's bad fortune. Not once did she complain while Nicky moaned and groaned about what now was his own meaningless cleft palate.

"Dad, I just realized something. I appreciate everything you and Mom do for me. I'm going to try to stop complaining about what I don't have and learn to enjoy everything I do have. This lip isn't really that bad."

"Boy, you learned a lot and you weren't even in school," Mr. Palmieri said. "I think you should take some of the money you saved from working at Big John's and buy Carl another Heart of the Hide."

"But Dad, it was Ann who gave me the...."

Heart of the Hide.

Epilogue

The rest of the summer went well for the Kelsey Avenue Crew. From that Saturday forward, they never lost to the Crusty Rusty All-Stars again.

Never.

It didn't matter what kind of game they played.

Football, basketball, soccer, or baseball.

Crusty Rusty left Painter's Park without tasting victory.

Nicky's new friend, Butch Caulfield, convinced Rusty to stop with the name-calling, or else he would beat him to a pulp and then, worse, not play on his team.

Since Butch played every sport he touched in championship form, Rusty curtailed his comments. He never completely stopped bullying Nicky, but Nicky's attitude eventually changed Rusty's actions. Rusty wasn't having as much fun with the teasing anymore.

Nicky's club, the Ferrie Asphalt Paving Cardinals, swept Rusty's team in the Little League championship. Nicky slammed two homers in the two games and went two-for-three with five RBIs in the title game. Rusty Alves never said one word.

Big John's son-in-law bought the deli from Mrs. Wizenski. They opened the store on Labor Day. They invited Nicky to return to work, but he politely declined. Nicky was really too busy for work now.

Every day after Nicky finished his paper route, he spent two hours a day with Carl Marriotti. They played the baseball trivia game. They talked baseball, and they watched old films. One month after Big John's funeral, Nicky purchased a brand new Heart of the Hide from Anquillare's D & N Sporting Goods. He gave the glove to Carl for his eleventh birthday. Even though Carl was paralyzed from the waist down and he lost most of the power in his throwing arm, they still played catch every day.

Nicky bought a bucket full of baseballs just for Carl. When they played catch, he placed one milk carton by Carl's chair, so he could drop them in after snaring them with the new mitt. When Nicky's bucket was empty, he switched them with Carl's. Then they did it over again. Carl loved the smell of the new glove. He just wanted to feel the thrill of a baseball softly landing into his mitt. He enjoyed the fresh air that baseball brought.

Nicky pleaded with Mrs. Marriotti to let the Kelsey Avenue Crew take Carl to the field. After hours and days of Ann and Nicky's begging, Mrs. Marriotti conceded.

The Kelsey Avenue Crew took turns playing catch with Carl. They let him sit at home plate and swing the bat, and Carl played in the games and wheeled himself around the bases.

As the first day of school approached, Mrs. Marriotti called Mrs. Palmieri one late August afternoon.

"Netta, I want to thank you for the wonderful things your son is doing for Carl. He really enjoys being a part of those kids. My son is finally happy again."

"You know that's funny," Mrs. Palmieri said. "It is I who should be thanking you. Because of your daughter and your son, my son is happy, too."

*   *   *

As a kid, the mysteries of life are countless. Kids never know how life unfolds before their very eyes. Most times, children are too busy to realize the magnitude of what is happening around them. Sometimes they think they know what has happened, but in a split second, it just seems to escape them at the wrong times. It is when people grow older that they wish that the days in life were pages in a book. Ones that grown-ups could always look back upon and relive.

This was why somebody smarter than all of us gave us stories.

This was why somebody smarter than all of us gave us memories.

This was why somebody smarter than all of us gave us memories to make into stories.

Kids always have the memories—memories that last longer than most lifetimes. Memories that affect the way children conduct their lives that honor those who are important.

This was a memorable and most remarkable story of truth and learning how wonderful telling it really was.

978-0-595-67595-1
0-595-67595-6

Printed in the United States
45529LVS00004B/121-510

9 780595 675951